KT-496-994

THE MEMORY BOX

Margaret Forster

PENGUIN BOOKS

PENGUIN BOOKS

Published by the Penguin Group
Penguin Books Ltd, 80 Strand, London WC2R 0RL, England
Penguin Putnam Inc., 375 Hudson Street, New York, New York 10014, USA
Penguin Books Australia Ltd, Ringwood, Victoria, Australia
Penguin Books Canada Ltd, 10 Alcorn Avenue, Toronto, Ontario, Canada M4V 3B2
Penguin Books India (P) Ltd, 11 Community Centre, Panchsheel Park, New Delhi – 110 017, India
Penguin Books (NZ) Ltd, Cnr Rosedale and Airborne Roads, Albany, Auckland, New Zealand
Penguin Books (South Africa) (Pty) Ltd, 24 Sturdee Avenue, Rosebank 2196 South Africa

Penguin Books Ltd, Registered Offices: 80 Strand, London WC2R 0RL, England

www.penguin.com

First published by Chatto & Windus 1999
Published in Penguin Books 2000

22

Copyright © Margaret Forster, 2000
All rights reserved

The moral right of the author has been asserted

Printed in England by Clays Ltd, St Ives plc

Except in the United States of America, this book is sold subject
to the condition that it shall not, by way of trade or otherwise, be lent,
re-sold, hired out, or otherwise circulated without the publisher's
prior consent in any form of binding or cover other than that in
which it is published and without a similar condition including this
condition being imposed on the subsequent purchaser

For Joan White, of Loweswater

Chapter One

SUSANNAH was apparently perfect, as the dead so often become. She was, it seemed, perfectly beautiful, perfectly good, and perfectly happy during her comparatively short life. It was that last bit which made me determined not to have anything to do with her. The idea of anyone being 'perfectly happy' struck me, even as a child, as absurd. How could anyone but a moron be perfectly happy? It made me picture her as someone with a fat smile on her smug face all the time. It made me squirm to imagine this happy-clappy woman, and I did not want to acknowledge her. She wouldn't have liked me. No one was ever going to describe me as a perfect anything (except maybe a perfect nuisance) and certainly not as being perfectly happy. My face more often has a frown on it than a smile – 'So serious,' people say of me, as if being serious is a crime. And my nature, far from being sunny, is woefully cynical – 'How suspicious you are,' everyone tells me. True. I am suspicious, and lack spontaneity.

Not Susannah. She was apparently a wonderfully spontaneous person. She was said to meet life with open arms, ever buoyant and optimistic. They told me she was happy right up to her death, that everyone marvelled at her serenity. I do not believe a word of this. I think it was an image made up in a misguided attempt to comfort me. How, after all, could she be happy, knowing she was likely to die soon, when she was a mere thirty-one years old and I, her baby, her only and much-longed-for child, barely six months old? Prove to

I

me such a woman was happy then, and I will prove to you she was insane. But nobody has ever spoken to me properly of the circumstances of this distinctly unhappy death. These seem forgotten in the general overview of her life, which I suppose is some kind of tribute to her. Perhaps her death was too tragic for those who loved her to dwell on. It was not, as it turned out, all that tragic for me. I had only just over a year without a mother, and even then I had a grandmother and was not without mothering. I nearly always had a woman's loving arms around me; I was kissed and cuddled and sung to by a comforting mother figure. I was never in the least deprived of maternal love.

My father was lucky. He undoubtedly grieved for his young, happy wife, but he was young himself, and attractive and kind, and he very quickly fell in love again and married. I am sure that in terms of months and weeks and days and hours he suffered dreadfully, but he did not sink into absolute despair. Susannah's mother, my devoted Scottish grandmother, looked after me, helped by her other daughter, my Aunt Isabella, and he managed to go on working and have some semblance of private life. He sold the house he and Susannah had lived in and rented a small flat in Edinburgh's New Town. Weekdays he stayed there, weekends he came to be with me at my grandmother's house. This system worked well, to everyone's satisfaction, I gather, but in any case it was short-lived. He married Charlotte shortly after the first anniversary of Susannah's death had passed and I was given another mother who adored me and whom I quickly adored. He was happy ever after and so far as anyone could tell, and I include myself, never yearned for his dead first wife.

I have a feeling that the existence of the memory box may have troubled him from the beginning. He didn't give it to me until my twenty-first birthday even though it had been in our house all that time, waiting for me to open it. Charlotte knew about it, of course, but neither she nor my father could bring themselves to mention it. I think they thought it would be morbid to do so, and they were afraid of its significance. Neither of them knew exactly what was in the box and though Susannah was so famous for being happy, and therefore could reasonably be counted upon not to have put anything in it which would be distressing, they could not be sure of how I would react to the legacy. I was a highly imaginative child, and they simply didn't know how to introduce this memory box into my life. It was too big a thing to make light of, and yet if they didn't make light of it, its importance might terrify me. Susannah had left no instructions as to when it should be given to me, at what age I should receive it. They thought it best to wait until I was grown up and give it to me on my eighteenth birthday. But I was not at home then, and so they put the presentation off.

Their apprehension strikes me now as curious. What exactly were they afraid of? Did they think I might be shocked, and if so why? It suggests to me an unexpected lack of trust on the part of my father. Charlotte never knew Susannah, so she cannot be blamed for his hesitation. The box, or rather the contents of the box, had, it seemed, been a secret. Susannah had kept them to herself, and maybe this had hurt and somehow alarmed him. She had apparently become obsessed with what she might put in it, almost feverish with a kind of awful excitement, or so my father told Charlotte, who later told me. She had pointed out that the box would have represented to Susannah the future of which she was being robbed and that therefore it was natural she should guard it fiercely, keep it entirely to herself. (Charlotte was good in that way, always trying to put herself into other people's minds.) At any rate, both of them were visibly uneasy, almost guilty, when eventually on the morning of my twenty-first birthday they told me about it. It was clear they were relieved when I showed little interest in it. I said I didn't want to open it, or even see it.

This was a lie, and yet not a lie. I always sensed what would please my parents and whereas, when I was younger, I had often deliberately used my knowledge to torment them, by then I was more anxious to please and make amends for a tempestuous adolescence. I especially wanted to please my mother. I watched her face as I said I felt spooked by the idea of receiving a present from beyond the grave. I saw the tension in her eyes fade and felt I'd passed some kind of test. I was Charlotte's and always had been and would not acknowledge Susannah's claims. Even my father seemed relieved, though afterwards it struck me as just a little feeble that he did not attempt to persuade me – after all, he alone knew what the wretched box had meant to Susannah. But he was clearly glad to have the subject over with, and perhaps he thought he had been wise to wait until I was an adult before mentioning it at all. But if that's the case, I am not sure he was right – not in the long term. The box did in fact arouse my curiosity even if I found I wanted to suppress the instinct. Aged ten, say, I don't think I would have been able to. I'm sure I would have been too excited at the thought that it might contain all sorts of treasures; and then around fifteen I'd have found it irresistibly romantic and would have been ready to weep on discovering dried roses, or some such, pressed between the pages of meaningful poems. But at twenty-one I was very self-centred; my curiosity was only slight and I could more easily deny it. I did feel a kind of nausea, in fact, at the notion of a dying woman selecting what to put in a box for me. And besides there was something sentimental about the whole idea of the box that I found repugnant.

But there was no doubt that it forced me to think of Susannah. Growing up, I could hardly have thought of her less, wanting Charlotte to be my only mother, and believing her to be so, against all the evidence. I was always furious if anyone referred to her as my stepmother, though Charlotte herself would try to calm me by pointing out that whether I liked it or not that was what she was. Luckily, this didn't happen often because hardly anyone knew Charlotte was not my biological mother. When my father married her, he had also moved from Edinburgh to Oxford, and all those who came to know him there assumed Charlotte was indeed what I called her – my mother. It rarely came out that she was not, though no deliberate evasion of the truth was practised. If anyone had cared to look, they would have seen photographs of Susannah holding me, a few weeks old, in our house. If asked, my parents wouldn't have hesitated to reply that this was Susannah, my father's first wife, who had died tragically when I was a baby. I was the one who sometimes lied. 'It's some relation,' I would say, and feel only vaguely ashamed.

I never liked the constant reminders of Susannah which I was given, especially by my grandmother, when I was young. It irritated me to be told stories about her, or hear comparisons – 'You're just like Susannah, she used to laugh just like that.' I would stop laughing immediately and consciously try to alter my laugh afterwards for as long as I remembered. The words 'It's odd, you're nothing like Susannah' were what I wanted to hear, or even better, 'It's odd, you're so like Charlotte.' What was truly odd was that for a while, when I was rather a plump child, before I grew tall and thin, there was an actual physical resemblance between Charlotte and me and none at all with Susannah. She was blonde, fair-skinned, blue-eyed and quite petite; I was dark, brown-eyed, and rather olive-skinned – just like Charlotte (though also, which I discounted, like my paternal grandmother and my father). I was quite triumphant when, shortly before she died, my grandmother was moved to say, rather sadly, 'There's nothing of Susannah in you, you're all your father's side.' I was glad. I didn't want to be like a dead woman. If I had to be 'like' someone in our family, I wanted it to be someone living.

My father and Charlotte had no children. They had wanted them, in Charlotte's case passionately, but they had none. They were sad about this, and so was I. Naturally (at least, I think it is natural) I wanted brothers and sisters, but I'd smirk with pleasure and feel proud whenever Charlotte said how lucky she was to have me. Looking back, as I am doing now, I see how brave and sensible she was about her own infertility. She didn't make an issue of it. It was hard for her, when she had so wanted a large family, such as she herself belonged to, not to have even one child. But she had me from eighteen months and I believe that I was young enough for her to come to feel, as I felt, that she really was my mother. If I had rejected her, or if she had not been able to love me, it would have been different, but we bonded, as they say, perfectly. Even her own family seemed to forget I was not actually hers. She had two sisters and two brothers who between them had eleven children and I was absorbed effortlessly into this band of cousins. They all came to stay regularly. I think my father found these visits, some of them lengthy (one of the brothers was in the RAF and we had his children to stay for long holidays when he was stationed far away), a bit of a strain, but my mother loved the house to be full of children, and not just because it gave me companionship.

It was a large house with plenty of room for everyone. My father had converted it himself, thinking of all kinds of ingenious ways to modernise it without destroying the more attractive features of its Edwardian character. From the outside, it was impossible to tell, unless you were an architect (as he was), how the dark rooms had been made light. I loved that house. Everyone else's seemed dull or cramped by comparison, claustrophobic and fussy, whereas ours was all pale wood floors, and glass skylights and doors, and white paint. It was spacious and sparsely furnished, and full of greenery. Converted in the early Seventies, it was ahead of its time, or ahead of what became the fashion, in being Scandinavian in taste. My Scottish grandmother thought it was comfortless, cold and austere, but the cousins admired it. The top floor was turned into a kind of permanent dormitory for them, complete with bathroom and kitchen, and they could hardly bear to leave at the end of the holidays. I slept up there with them, excited at first to be part of a huge gang.

I don't know what happened to that feeling. I don't even know what happened to most of those cousins. The closeness, I now realise, was all Charlotte's doing – she created the atmosphere in which those relationships flourished. Left to myself, I have not bothered to keep in touch with any of my cousins except Rory, and he was never part of that gang. Rory came to stay on his own or with his mother and had nothing to do with Charlotte's side of the family. He was my sole cousin on Susannah's side, the son of her sister, my Aunt Isabella. It was Rory who looked like Susannah, a fact our grandmother constantly remarked upon – 'Sideways genes,' she said, not that I knew what she meant. All I knew was that unlike my other cousins he didn't go in for sport and noisy games, and I wasn't in awe of him as I was of them. But it took a long time for me to feel more drawn to him than to them. By the time I was seven or eight years old, however, Rory's so-called wickedness was already becoming deeply attractive and I was fascinated by him.

It was Rory who found a way into the attics. I had never been in the least curious about what lay under the roof of our house, though I knew well enough there was something above the top floor. From time to time bits of old furniture would arrive – things left in wills to one or other of my parents – and they would groan and look at each other and ask whether they should sell whatever it was, or put it in the attics. Usually they decided to wait a decent interval before getting rid of the item, and someone would come to help my father cart it up the stairs. Rory was intrigued by what was stored up there. He thought there might be hidden treasure we could discover. I jeered at him for getting silly ideas from reading 'kids'' books (whereas I was very proud of reading practical how-to-do-this-and-that books). But he persisted in imagining what lay above our heads, and so persuasive was he that against all my strong common sense I almost came to believe there might indeed be wonderful things, long since forgotten and waiting to be discovered. Eventually I agreed it was worth looking and said I'd ask my father. But that was the last thing Rory wanted – he was all for secrecy and making an adventure of it and somehow he drew me into his plan.

He insisted we should go exploring at night. We were sleeping on the top floor. With just the two of us there it seemed quite echoey, we seemed lost among all the beds. But Rory liked that, he liked things to be a bit creepy. We slept next to each other and he said he'd wake me when it was time. But he didn't need to; I didn't sleep and longed for him to nudge me and say we should go. When eventually he did – he'd been waiting for the noises below that would indicate that my parents had gone to bed – I bounded up, excited in spite of myself. Rory exaggerated every movement, pausing dramatically to listen every few steps, and I remember I found my heart thudding ridiculously. He led the way to the end of the huge room and to the top of the stairs and then pointed upwards. There was a handle, painted white and quite distinct, in the middle of the wooden ceiling. He had earlier fetched a tall stool, and now I held it while he clambered up and pulled the handle. Smoothly, silently, a metal ladder unfolded.

We went up into two attics separated by a thin wall with a small door in it. I think this plywood wall corresponded with a valley in the roof. The wall itself was only about five feet high, and the door was tiny, so that we felt like Alice in Wonderland as we crawled through (I couldn't imagine how an adult could have managed it, but maybe they didn't; maybe the attics were always approached separately from different ends). Rory had a torch and shone it round each attic in turn. They were full of the old bits of furniture, mostly chairs, dark wooden things with velvet padded seats, and small tables with spindly legs. But there were chests and boxes too and we peered inside some of them, only to find they were packed with brocade curtains and musty old clothes. It was very disappointing and not even Rory could sustain my interest. I went back down the ladder on my own, to his annoyance, and left him to close the trapdoor, which he managed only after a great struggle.

But what we missed up there was the memory box, my box. It was in the further attic all the time, the one I hadn't had the patience to inspect thoroughly. Rory had shone his torch round and all we had seen were books, dozens of big volumes stacked up round the walls, and lots of huge rolls of what looked like paper (and I now know were maps and architectural drawings). I only found the box, hidden behind these piles, when I came to sell the house. I had to force myself then to inspect the attics, as well as every other room, to make decisions about where everything should go.

And that was only a little over a year ago, a terrible year, too terrible to dwell on, so I won't. My father, aged only sixty-five, and my mother – Charlotte, that is – only fifty-nine, both died within eight months of each other. The shock was agonising, my sense of outrage violent. This double blow seemed to me an injustice far more monstrous than the death of Susannah when I was a baby.

I don't know which death hit me hardest. My mother's, I think, because it took so long, and I had time to realise what was happening, but my father's was the more unbelievable, and in some ways more painful. He died first, of a stroke, without any warning. My mother went on living in the family house in the brief interval between my father's death and the onset of her own terminal illness. She had no desire to sell it, to leave and move somewhere smaller where there would be no reminders of him. She wanted to be reminded of him: in fact, she found every reminder a comfort, her only comfort apart from me. Perhaps eventually, as she aged, she would have been obliged to move. I might even have tried to persuade her to do so since the house was so very large for one person, but she didn't have time to grow old. She died in hospital, slowly, and it was left to me to dispose of our beloved home and its contents.

There was always the option of living in the house myself, but I never considered this. It wasn't anything to do with its size, there were other reasons. The house was in Oxford. I didn't wish to live in Oxford, desirable though many people think it is. Being in that house after she and my father died was torture to me. The memories she wrapped round herself like a warm blanket pricked me like a hair shirt. Forced to enter it, to get things occasionally for my mother when she was in hospital, I had been overwhelmed by a longing to be back in my early childhood with my parents, loved by them and loving them. All the time I was fighting my way through crowds not of ghosts but of sensations. I felt slightly faint even putting my key in the lock, and once I was through the front door and had closed it behind me, hearing that distinctive click it made, and the light rattle of the brass letter box, I felt a kind of unpleasant excitement. The power of houses has always bewildered me – that mere bricks and mortar should possess such atmosphere is uncanny.

After my mother died, the hardest thing I had to do, far harder than organising her funeral, was go into our old home.

I wept then as I had not done before. For a whole month, I was obliged to go there day after day until every bit of furniture, every object, every book and picture, every piece of clothing, every last curtain and cushion was sorted out and ready to be collected by all manner of people. Someone suggested that I should employ a house clearance company, but I saw it as my duty to Charlotte to do the job myself, and I did it. This was, of course, how I found the box, though I very nearly missed it. I left the attics until last, and almost succumbed to the temptation to let the owner of a second-hand shop nearby do this final part of the clearing out, since I knew, or thought I knew, there was only junk up there. But then I recollected that glimpse, so long ago, of what had looked like drawings or plans. They might be work of my father's and if so I felt I should at least look at them.

I was very tired that last day, when I made myself go up there. The ladder didn't glide down easily as it had done all those years ago for Rory. It was stuck through disuse, I suppose, and I had to yank it hard. I had difficulty, too, clambering up through the remarkably small gap and realised only when I'd hauled myself through that there must be a far bigger entry into the other attic or no furniture could ever have been taken up. I should have looked for another trapdoor. But once in the attics everything was as I remembered – chairs, little tables, chests of clothes. The second-hand dealer could come for them, his lucky day (because some might be of value). The rolls of paper were indeed old architectural drawings, though none was signed and I didn't know if they were my father's. I began pulling them along, covering myself with dust, ready to drop them through the trapdoor so that I could take them into the garden and make a bonfire.

My father could never throw anything away – he was a hoarder, everything had to be kept, either in case it came in useful (however unlikely), or simply because he was fond of whatever it was. He was very fond of all his old plans and drawings – the very paper seemed precious to him. When I was little, he used to let me help him roll up the huge sheets he worked on and I loved to do it. 'Slowly now, Catherine,' he'd say, and, 'Keep it even, keep it even, don't press too hard.' I'd roll up the paper at one end, struggling to do it neatly and keep pace with his rolling at the other, and together we would achieve the perfect roll he wanted. I found it hard to be slow and methodical and careful. I was all rush, and wondered why I couldn't be like my father. When I 'helped' him do such simple jobs he'd smile at me and say I'd done well. He knew, even then, when I was only five or six, that I was not like him and he made allowances for my clumsiness and impatience all the time. Later, when I used to get upset because I wasn't the person I wanted to be, wasn't like him or Charlotte, he'd comfort me and say nobody could help their nature, all they could do was try to curb what they didn't like about themselves. My grandmother, if she was around and heard him, would sigh and say, 'Some people have a lot of curbing to do,' or, more puzzlingly, 'Some people I knew never learned to curb their waywardness.'

But I couldn't keep these dusty old rolls of crackly paper. And they were too personal to give away, even if anyone had wanted them, so I had decided I would have to burn them, however upsetting this proved to be. (I didn't have time, though, in the end, and took them with me after all.) It was in moving these rolls that I found the box. What I actually saw was something that looked like a tarpaulin wrapped round a roughly cylindrical bundle and tied very securely. My attention might not have been caught if it had not been for an incongruous pink label attached to the cord knotted round this parcel. On the label, written in ink which had faded but was still decipherable, was my own name – 'For my darling Catherine Hope, in the future', it said.

I felt instantly cold. Cold, and also apprehensive. Yet there was nothing frightening in itself about this pretty pink label, which was decorated all round the edge with tiny drawings of flowers, the petals of each one carefully coloured in. It looked, this package, as if inside its wrapping there would be a present, to be uncovered and put under a Christmas tree or on a table with a birthday cake, and yet I was afraid of its innocence. I crouched down beside it in the dim light of the attic, wondering what I should do. I would have to take it with me and open it, but I was afraid not only of further grief but of pathos, which I dreaded even more. How could this not turn out to be a pathetic task? Whatever my indifference towards Susannah, I could not help but be affected by the sight of her box. I wished passionately she had not done this. Who had thought of it, or was it her own idea? And what had she imagined was the purpose of her legacy? To tell me about herself? To make some kind of statement? To try to share in my unknown future? But she must have known I would be surrounded by information about her, that I would have photographs and memorabilia, that my father and her family would talk about her. What she could not have guessed was that I hadn't wanted to know very much. My extreme contentment with Charlotte might have hurt her – and thinking that suddenly made me wonder if there was another motive behind the leaving of this box. It could be a sort of weapon, to be used from beyond the grave. A way of combating my denial. Was it screaming, '*I* was your mother! Listen to me!'?

I knew I was being melodramatic. The box wasn't screaming at all. It had been stuck quietly here, muffled by its shroud of thick material, for nearly thirty years. It had been silent all that time, exerting no influence whatsoever, except perhaps over my father. I imagine every now and again he remembered its existence and fretted about it. Fingering the label, I realised

13

he must have detached it from the box itself and tied it on to the cord when he had wrapped the box in this protective covering. Why had he done that? To alert me, to make sure it could be recognised for what it was when the time came? I struggled to remember precisely what he had said that morning of my twenty-first birthday. He'd briefly described how Susannah had kept this memory box absolutely private. She had told him she was preparing it for me, 'in case', but he had had no part in it. She didn't want to discuss it, nor did she want help in deciding what should go in it. It had occupied her when she was too weak to move much from her bedroom and he had never seen what went inside. He had urged me, unconvincingly, to try to think of it as a happy experience. Susannah wanted to be secretive, and since by then she had so little privacy left in her life he had not pried. After she died, and he went through the miserable business of clearing her things out, he had been surprised how heavy the box was. But he hadn't looked inside. He'd sealed the edges with masking tape and wrapped it in waterproof material, and put it in the basement of their Edinburgh house until it was sold. It went with the rest of the furniture into storage during the time I lived with my grandmother and he lived in his flat, and then, when he married Charlotte and moved to his new job in Oxford, it went with them. Every now and again he and Charlotte had discussed when I should be told about the box, but for years the time had not seemed right.

I could understand this. I wasn't an easy child. All sorts of things upset me, even if on the surface I seemed strong and tough. I had nightmares regularly – I can't recall what they were about, except there was a lot of blood in them – and was for years a poor sleeper, often ending up in my parents' bed. It was natural that they should fear the effect of giving to me a box full of unknown objects left by a dying woman who very possibly was not always in her right mind. And then later, as a young adolescent, I was given to violent rages alternating with spells of studied gloom – all very typical, but hardly the best background to cope with such a legacy in a balanced way. I don't blame my parents at all for their hesitation. And I was sure that for years at a time they actually forgot about this wretched box – it was literally out of sight, out of mind, up here in this attic.

Now the box would have to go with me. I shrank from having to touch it at all, but finally grabbed the cord where it was knotted at the side and dragged it to the trapdoor. I'd left a pile of cushions at the foot of the ladder so that I could throw down on to them any fragile objects I might find which were worth keeping. So far, I'd only selected one rather pretty old lamp. There was plenty of room for the box. It fell through the gap satisfactorily, and I climbed down after it. I was in a hurry by then. The estate agent who was to sell the house was coming to collect the keys and he was due any minute. I wanted the handover to be rapid so I had to be ready to zoom off. My car was already laden with stuff, the boot and back seat entirely filled, and only the passenger seat next to me was empty. The box had to go there. I shoved it in, then secured it by using the safety belt strapped through part of the cord. Doing this – hurriedly, roughly – I dislodged the pink label. It lay on the gravel beside the front wheel of the car and my stomach lurched. I stared, mesmerised, at the piece of innocuous cardboard and willed myself to pick it up. I couldn't leave it there, to flutter pathetically in the wind and be rained upon or trampled by some stray dog. I snatched it up and put it in my pocket, then slammed the door shut just as the estate agent turned into the drive.

I would never see our house again. I'd told the estate agent, untruthfully, that I was leaving the country and had given him full powers to sell the house as soon as possible to the first buyer who came up with the asking price (fixed by him). If it failed to reach that price, he was to reduce it as he thought fit – I wanted no consultations, I wanted nothing more to do with it. He would see to the final clearance. I think he was startled by my abruptness, and had been disposed to stay and chat. I left him standing on the front step looking bewildered and waving his hand slowly. I didn't wave back. I didn't look back through my mirrors either, and drove far too fast until I turned on to Woodstock Road. It was done. Our house was left abandoned and the sooner I got used to it the better. Better to think of it obliterated, with all it had meant to me in the past, than to imagine it inhabited by other people. I would destroy its power by annihilating its memory.

It wasn't a long drive back to London, and it was a route with which I was very familiar, but that day the journey seemed unending. I hated driving with that sinister box lumped beside me. I thought about bombs and the comparison seemed appropriate until I realised I couldn't have it both ways: the box could not be both explosive *and* pathetic. I was getting in a state on its account and, as Charlotte would sensibly have pointed out, making it the object of all my distress over leaving our house. I reminded myself I'd been miserable and depressed before ever I found it in the attic. I was alone, at the age of thirty-one, Susannah's age when she died. That parallel was not lost on me. She could never have anticipated that I would be so old when I finally received her gift. It suddenly struck me that the box might be full of things suitable for a young girl, or a teenager. This cheered me a little. It would be easier to deal with the contents if they turned out to be toys or even mementoes of my babyhood. Perhaps all I would find would be my first rattle, my first bonnet, and so on. My common sense told me this was unlikely, Susannah had surely been too imaginative to want to fill a box with such sentimental tokens, but I found the idea strangely comforting.

I think I'd always known that she was imaginative, that she had left behind her many clues to this, which as a child I absorbed without understanding. There was my kaleidoscope, the first toy I remember loving. I had soft toys, the usual teddy bears and pandas, and dolls, but it is the kaleidoscope which I remember carrying round with me and hugging to myself when I was only about three or four. 'She isn't old enough for it yet,' my grandmother had apparently said to my father. 'She won't be able to close one eye and look properly.' But I could, and he knew I could. In that respect, if not others, I had the necessary patience and balance. He gave it to me. 'Shake it,' he said, 'and look in the little window and you'll see something pretty.' I shook and shook, fiercely (as I did most things), and then, quite cautiously for me, I squinted through the glass opening and was dazzled by the myriad patterns which swirled before me. I shook and looked, and shook and looked, with such concentration that I developed a red ring round my right eye from pressing the kaleidoscope to it. My father took it away, but I screamed till I could have it back and finally some compromise was reached. Susannah made that kaleidoscope, actually made it, my father once told me, in a rare moment of nostalgia, when she was pregnant and well and happy. Other pregnant women knitted. Susannah made a kaleidoscope for a child who would not be old enough to use it for years.

Reaching Hanger Lane and becoming part of London's ceaseless traffic dulled my senses in more ways than one. I relaxed into the stop-start halting progress round the North Circular Road and the highly emotional frame of mind I'd been in gave way to idle speculation as to where I would choose to live when the Oxford house (already I was thinking of it like that, as 'the Oxford house', not 'our' house) was sold. I was going to be rich. In my terms, anyway. The Oxford house was certain, or so I'd been told, to fetch what I thought of as a fortune, and there was a cottage in Cornwall which now belonged to me, as well as life insurance policies and a hefty sum in the bank. The inheritance tax would, I'd been warned, be substantial, but still I would have plenty of money. The news had given me little pleasure at first, but gradually I was adjusting to it. I would be able to buy a house of my own wherever I wanted and that realisation excited me. I cared about my surroundings. My flat had never been simply a roof over my head. I had loved decorating and furnishing it, and had spent time and taken infinite trouble making it as beautiful as I could. I was aware that I'd tried to imitate my father's style, with the wooden floors I'd had laid and the use of cream and white paints and pale grey fabrics – the whole aim to give an impression of space and light. Every time I came back to my home I was soothed by the atmosphere I'd created.

But my flat was not perfect. For a start, it had no garden. It was a maisonette, two floors at the top of an ugly house in Crouch End. No garden and no views, except of other dreary houses and a long, narrow street crowded with parked cars most of the time. Now I would be able to buy a house somewhere green and leafy and set about making it truly beautiful. I would search for it thoroughly. It would give me a purpose in life and, sad to say, that is what I knew I had singularly lacked for a long time. Work had recently failed to excite me as it had once done, and my personal life was a disaster. What a contrast with Susannah's happy, purposeful life at thirty-one. She had loved my father, and he had loved her, since they were final-year students. My birth was, according to my grandmother, in what I thought of as a sickly phrase, 'the icing on the cake'. I'd never liked thinking of myself as icing, sweet and sticky. I'd had this image of myself melting slowly in someone's mouth. Anyway, my arrival completed Susannah's famous happiness. That, and the hanging of a picture she'd painted in the Royal Academy Summer Exhibition the year before.

She wasn't really an artist. Like my father, she'd qualified as an architect, which was how they met, and unusually for that time – there were not many women architects – she did well in the all-male practice she joined. In fact, she won a prize – something my father never did – designing a shopping centre. I always got the impression that she'd been much more ambitious than my father and that this had created a slight problem, or what would have become one if her poor health had not held her back. I'm not quite sure how I picked this up (though, when I think about it now, it is remarkable how much I did pick up considering I made such a thing of not asking direct questions). It must have been from Charlotte's family, which is surely odd. I remember these aunts and uncles of mine, who of course were not really my relatives at all, sitting round the dinner table, when they brought the various cousins to stay, and one of them saying they'd been to 'that shopping centre' and my father saying how he admired it and had this aunt – no, I think it was an uncle – noticed how cleverly Susannah had solved the space problem, how ingenious she'd been. I must have been quite old because I remember asking what 'ingenious' meant and saying was it the same as 'genius'. My father laughed and said that wasn't a bad guess and then someone asked, 'Was she a genius, Susannah?' and there was a kind of silence while they waited for an answer. I don't recall precisely what the answer was but I did register the praise it was full of and I was uncomfortable when my father added words to the effect that Susannah had been much more talented than he was and would have 'risen to the top'. I thought of a cake, and laughed. If Charlotte was there, and she must have been, unless she was in the kitchen, she said nothing.

But Susannah never had the chance to rise to any top. Her

health deteriorated and she had to work from home and, though the pretence was kept up that her career still flourished, it didn't. She turned to painting and everyone was glad to see her do so – less tiring, less of a strain for her. She painted watercolours, mostly landscapes. The one chosen in the Summer Exhibition was of a meadow. It hung in my father's study, though not in a prominent position. When I was a child, I could see nothing in it. It looked virtually blank to me, an expanse of flat green with a few dots in the background that might or might not have been cows. If I was told where this meadow was, I have forgotten. My father never commented on its merits, never passed any comment at all.

I sent it to be auctioned, together with all the other pictures I didn't want to keep when I cleared out the Oxford house, and was quite surprised to learn later that somebody had paid £200 for it. Part of me had felt bad about selling it, but another, stronger part defiantly insisted the painting was of no special significance just because it was Susannah's and had been hung in a Royal Academy Summer Exhibition – everyone knows that half of that is dross. There was nowhere in my flat I could have hung it and I had nowhere, no attics, in which to store it. I had done the sensible thing, but it was true I felt faintly guilty all the same, even though no one else knew what I'd done. I had salvaged too much as it was, and looked with despair at all the clutter I'd laboriously carried in from my car. My lovely rooms looked offended, strewn as they were with bags and boxes. It upset me to see this disorder and I couldn't rest until I'd dragged the lot into my spare room and closed the door on it.

Except for the memory box. This I took into my sitting-room and put down on the floor in front of the sofa. The sooner I got the opening over, the better. I would need a knife or scissors to cut the cord – the knots looked far too corroded with age to undo easily. Pausing to wash my hands, as though I were about to perform a surgical operation and had to take meticulous care with hygiene, I hacked away at the cord with the bread knife and then cut through the tough waterproof outer covering. Then I got a surprise. I'd assumed that the box itself would be a wooden or strong cardboard crate, of the packing-case variety, but what I found was an old-fashioned hatbox. It was large and round, about two feet tall and eighteen inches or so in diameter, and was covered in a vivid fuchsia grosgrain material with purple ricrac round the lid and a purple satin ribbon tied in an ornamental bow on the top. It was the most marvellously vulgar and yet glamorous box. I found myself smiling. My grandmother, Susannah's mother who had looked after me when she died, had had several boxes like this, though none quite so colourful or flamboyant. Rory and I used to play with them and try on the weird hats, all veils and feathers, carefully preserved but never worn.

For some reason, I still delayed the final act of opening, though I was feeling so much more relaxed about it. I went into the kitchen and poured myself a glass of wine, wondering as I did so why my father had never described the brash appeal of this box. It would, I was sure, have helped me feel more kindly towards Susannah's box and tempted me to want to see it. Slowly, I went back to contemplate it again. Experimentally, I pulled at the purple bow. It did not give. Carefully, I cut across the ribbon underneath the bow and when the lid still would not lift I saw that it was taped all round, and remembered my father had said he had sealed it. More delicate snipping with scissors and I felt the lid move a fraction as the pressure was released. I eased it off slowly, feeling a strange sort of breathlessness as I did so. Under the lid, flattened by years of being pressed down, were several scrunched-up layers of coloured tissue paper, white, yellow and green, all arranged to look vaguely like a flower. A pretty effect, and I sat admiring it for a moment before disturbing the paper. When I had lifted it all out, placing it inside the upturned lid, I expected somehow to find a note. Instead, there was another layer of covering, a thin disc of corrugated cardboard. It was tightly wedged and took some time to remove.

What met my, by then, eager eyes was puzzling.

Chapter Two

THERE was no letter, no note, not a word of explanation in the whole box. I kept expecting to find something written. I searched thoroughly, shaking the tissue paper out piece by piece in case some message was hidden in its folds, and I examined the linings of the box and its lid to see if anything might have been secreted there. Nothing. The contents were obviously meant to be self-explanatory. Staring at them arrayed before me, I wondered if my father was supposed to hold the key to all this. Susannah couldn't have known he would be dead, too, before I opened her box. But on the other hand if she had been as secretive about it as he had said, would she have depended on his explaining to me? I didn't think so. I was meant to understand the significance of these miscellaneous objects myself.

They were all individually wrapped in different kinds of decorative paper. Such a lot of care had gone into the wrapping, and I had a sudden vision of Susannah selecting the papers, looking for unusual patterns and combinations of colours. Some were stencilled by hand – her hand? – gold crowns on a white background, purple butterflies on pink. When everything was unwrapped and all the papers smoothed out and piled up I saw I had enough to wrap presents for years ahead, except that it might feel blasphemous almost, to use them for any lesser purpose. I told myself that was what I had to remember. Susannah was not playing, she had a purpose. Nothing in her box had been selected randomly, nothing wrapped with the first bit of paper that came to hand. She had apparently had such confidence that her gifts would mean something that she hadn't felt the need to leave any written coda. But she had left numbers. On each parcel there was a coloured circle of sticky paper with a number written in black ink in the middle. I took everything out very slowly, turning each object over before unwrapping it, and so I had time to notice that the numbers were not in order. On the very top were parcels numbered 8, 4 and 1, all lying side by side, forming a complete layer. Once I had unwrapped everything, I realised the fragile items were on the top, so the numbers were presumably to alert me to the need to examine everything in order and not as they came out of the box. But was this assumption wrong? All I could think was that the numbering was too clear and deliberate not to have a point.

I felt I had to try to do what I had always resisted, which was to imagine myself, knowing I was going to die within months, maybe weeks, assembling a memory box for my baby daughter. But, however hard I strained to do this, such a feat of empathy was beyond me. I did not have a baby daughter. I had never had a baby, girl or boy. The emotional field of maternal love was so far closed to me. But there was another obstacle. Not only could I not imagine Susannah's feelings, neither did I relate to what she had done. I couldn't imagine *wanting* to leave such a box, whatever my state of mind. Why would I want to? To tell my daughter what I was like, give her some flavour of myself? But I would know she would have that in abundance. She would have the testimony of her loving family. She would be in no doubt of what I was like, just as I was in no doubt about Susannah. My father bought a cine-camera in the Sixties and later he had his old films transferred to video so I could watch them and see Susannah walking and moving if I wanted. I think I watched one film, once, and that was enough. The movements were jerky, the focus poor, and it seemed an hour of tedium, with the odd comic moment. But I had seen the living, breathing Susannah, as she must have known I would be able to. I had even heard her voice – light, rather high – on a couple of tape recordings. And my grandmother gave me her schoolgirl diaries, which I had glanced through, cringing at how banal they were, and I had her school reports and certificates for everything from cycling proficiency to diving. I had more information than I could possibly want about her and I hadn't wanted any of it.

Now there were these objects to burden me further and bewilder me. If she had something private and special to say, I wondered why she hadn't said it in writing, in a letter easily read and unmistakable in intention. Apparently that was too simple. Or was it, on the contrary, too impossible? Did she not trust words enough? Did she prefer to place her trust in solid things? At any rate, there was her decision, bequeathed to me in the shape of these eleven objects. I contemplated them once more, starting with the one I had unwrapped first, number 4, on the top. It was a shell. A very large shell, about ten inches long and almost the same width across its broadest point. It had two big prongs, sticking out like arms without hands, and on the closed part there were eight spiral prongs in a circle, rising in a cone effect. The ear, or fan part, was fluted, with a delicate wavy edge. The colour was a dirty cream with faint black patches all over the back, and on the inside of the ear there was a faint apricot blush. The outside was very rough to the touch and there was a straw-like substance clustered round the prongs.

I had never seen such a big shell of this type and yet it looked ordinary enough, without any exquisite beauty of its own such as some shells have. What was it supposed to tell me? That Susannah liked shells? So do most people. Or was there something significant about this shell that I was missing? Was the important thing the place, the sea or shore, it came from? I knew I could always go to a library and find a book about shells in which it could be identified and its origin described. Maybe it was so rare I'd find it could only have come from one place in the world; maybe this shell would lead me to a place Susannah wanted me to visit for some secret to be revealed. And thinking along such romantic lines I smiled. How easily I was allowing myself to be carried away. A shell was only a shell. A pretty thing, something decorative for a daughter to find in a box left to her by her mother, nothing more.

Beside the shell, next to it on the top layer, and numbered 8, was another mystery. It was a silver-backed mirror, shaped like a diamond with a long handle. I turned it over to examine it, looking as ever for clues to what it signified. The silver work was elaborate and intricate, a complicated raised design of leaves and stems. The silver did not shine but was heavy and dull, and dust was caught between some of the bumps. The glass was not perfect. It was a little loose in its setting and there was a small chip out of one of the points, where the glass was kept in place by a delicate network of fine silver strands. I held it up, as it was meant to be held, and looked at myself, at arm's length. How hard I was frowning, how cross I looked, the crease between my eyes horribly evident. I tried to relax my expression. The crease stayed there. I wasn't in the habit of staring at myself in mirrors, in fact I rarely look in them, and I suppose I am proud of my lack of vanity. Was the message of this mirror to do with vanity, then? And if so, whose – mine or Susannah's? But maybe I was missing the point entirely. Was the point of the mirror its value? Was it perhaps an heirloom, left by Susannah to link me to my heritage? Funny, I liked the idea of that, and it was possible. Her family were all proud of their Scottishness, especially on her father's side, especially the Camerons. My grandmother was forever telling me tales of her dead husband's brave ancestors, going right back to great-great-great uncles and cousins who had fought at Culloden. But there was nothing obviously Scottish about this mirror. The pattern was of ivy, if anything (it was hard to be sure), and not thistles. It was old, that was all I could tell, but how old I would have to find out – more visits to a library, more looking up in books. I'd end up an expert on shells and silver mirrors, but what good would that do me?

I was becoming exasperated as I picked up the last parcel which had been on the top layer. This was a thin folder, very light and fragile-seeming to touch. It was labelled number 1 and had rested between the shell and the mirror, protected by their bulk. Inside the blue tissue paper I found a plastic, see-through bag in which there were three feathers, lying side by side. They were all white, each about eleven inches long, with dark grey markings along one edge, light grey on the other. They looked freshly plucked, the quill points sharp and very clean. I didn't take them out of their bag, but merely turned the bag over, then put it down. What was going on here? By the time I began unwrapping what had been in the middle layer, I was beginning to feel I was being made a fool of. I could hardly bear to open number 7, though when I did it was something of a relief. I recognised it. It was a necklace, and I'd seen Susannah wearing it in photographs and heard my grandmother describe it. Her own father had brought it back from India, where he served in the army, for her mother, and it had been handed down first to her, then to Susannah. It was a beautiful, ornate piece of jewellery, the setting silver and the stone pendant a large emerald. Susannah had worn it on her wedding day and I was told her unusual dress had been designed to compliment the necklace and that the fern among the roses she carried was the exact shade of the emerald. My grandmother had apparently expected my father to give it to me when I was eighteen, the age Susannah had been when it was given to her. When he didn't, she'd later asked him about it in my presence, after I came home and she was staying with us for what turned out to be the last time. Some whispering had gone on and she had seemed disturbed by whatever he had told her, but she said nothing to me and I didn't question her. I suppose my father had been telling her he couldn't find the necklace. Perhaps he even told her he suspected it was in the memory box.

My father had given me some of Susannah's other jewellery by then, though, and some of her clothes. Over the years, once I was thirteen, he'd marked each birthday with gifts of them until I asked him not to. I had never liked being given her things. I didn't want anything that had been worn by a dead woman. It made me squirm to think of putting in my ears the pearl studs that had once been in hers – I couldn't help it. I always thought of Susannah as dead, dead, dead, and the fact that she had been as alive as I was when she wore these earrings was irrelevant. They were reminders to me only of death and I didn't want them. I put the studs in once, to please him, and my ears immediately felt thick and heavy and I had to take them out. And I never did like jewellery. When other girls were into collecting silver rings and bracelets, I was more interested in old posters and sepia or black and white postcards. Being given Susannah's clothes was even worse, but at least my mother understood that and made my father realise he was mistaken in thinking I would treasure what Susannah had once worn. He was dissuaded easily enough, probably because he'd only been offering these things out of a vague sense of guilt that he hadn't worked harder to keep Susannah's memory alive. Once he'd had his efforts rejected, he gave up with relief.

The other objects from the middle layer were bulky but not heavy. There was a hat, rolled up; a small, soft rucksack; and a map. The map was the first thing that made any sense at all and I opened it out eagerly. It was an ordinary Ordnance Survey map, two and a half inches to a mile, of the north-western area of the Lake District. I love maps, all maps. My father loved them too and was delighted I grew to share his interest. He used to make maps for me and Rory, just of the immediate area around our Oxford house at first. He did them all properly, using signs that appear on Ordnance Survey maps, and gradually weaned us on to sheets 164 and 165 covering the Oxford area. He'd drive us to a certain spot, show us where we were on the map, and then say he'd pick us up at the end of a route he'd marked. No wonder we both excelled at geography, or that side of it, at school. Rory, in time, stopped enjoying these jaunts but I never did. I made my own routes and though Charlotte worried about my being on my own my father encouraged me. I joined the YHA with a friend and we went off to Wales and trekked around. We were thirteen, I think: it was just before I rejected the whole idea of youth hostelling as embarrassingly naff, so we never did it again. Maybe my father would have pointed me in the direction of the Lake District if I'd kept it up. He knew I didn't stop enjoying maps and that I spent ages in his study scrutinising them, 'reading' them like books.

So, I felt familiar with this map although I'd never been to this part of England, but I knew my father had been born in the coastal town of Whitehaven and that he had spent his youth fell-walking and climbing. He and Susannah had also spent their honeymoon somewhere in the Lake District and though she hadn't been strong enough to climb much, she had apparently enjoyed walking and loved the landscape. I suppose it was odd that my father had never taken me there, if he had such happy and significant memories, but then that in itself might explain why he never did revisit his old haunts once Susannah had died – too sad, too much part of a past he was trying to get over. And Charlotte was not a country lover, so it would have meant leaving her to go off by himself, something he never had any desire to do.

Whitehaven was not on this map, but I reckoned it could not be far off it. My eye went at once to a red cross marked at Buttermere and from there followed the pencil markings alongside a green dotted path almost parallel with the lake, then turning to go up a stream called Scale Beck. At what I could see from the contours was the top of this pass through the fells, the pencilled trail turned right and on to what was marked as the Mosedale Holly Tree. There it stopped, at another red cross. Beside this cross there was a small exclamation mark, also in red. (Rory would have loved it – X marking the spot, treasure definitely buried there, etc.) Clearly, I was meant to take this map and follow this route. I supposed I should be grateful for some positive directions at last. Doubtless the rucksack was meant to go on my back, but I had my own excellent rucksacks, of various types and sizes, and would have no use for such a flimsy version. The straps were too thin and would cut into my shoulders, it wasn't waterproof and the fastenings were inadequate. There was one main pouch, closed with a drawstring, and two small ones. I felt inside each of them but they were empty. Something had once leaked, juice of some sort by the look of the stain, and there were bits of dried tissue in one of the small pouches. I scraped them out painstakingly and gave the whole thing a good shake. No, I wouldn't use such a rucksack if ever I decided to follow the trail.

The hat was red. Was it to partner the necklace, meant to be worn with it, or was it a companion to the rucksack? It wasn't elegant enough to match the jewellery but far too frivolous and fragile to be worn fell-walking in the famous Lake District weather. Made of crushed velvet, it was of the sloppy variety, the kind of hat that can be pulled into different shapes. The wide brim was overstitched, giving it a little more substance than the crown. It was the sort of hat that had absolutely no shape until it was put on, but I was reluctant to place it on my head. I picked it up and found myself smelling it. It had a spicy, pungent smell, quite pleasant, not at all musty. I saw there was a flower sewn on one side, a dried rose, the petals partially disintegrated. Nervously, I played with it for a while, turning it round and round, and then, to get it over with, pulled it quickly on to my head. It felt immediately comfortable, but then it was the sort of hat that was so soft and pliable it would fit any head. I picked up the silver hand mirror and cautiously looked at myself. The hat suited me. I played with it again, twisting and turning the brim, pulling it first to one side and then the other until I was satisfied. I never wear a hat, except sometimes a cotton baseball cap to keep the sun out of my eyes when I am working. I knew I would never go out of the house wearing this hat. It wasn't my style, any more than the necklace was.

Did Susannah put it in my box just because she had loved it? Or more than that? Had it been worn on some momentous occasion? I would have to get the photograph albums out to check. Then it occurred to me that perhaps, if, as I suspected, she'd imagined I'd open this box when still a child, the hat was for dressing up. It would have been too large, and would have fallen over my eyes, but being pliable it could have been rolled back and, yes, I knew I would have enjoyed playing with it. So would Rory. He would probably, aged six or seven, have looked even more like Susannah than my grandmother always vowed he did. Too late. I had a glass head, the sort used to model hats, which I'd picked up in a junk shop, admiring the green of the glass and thinking it would make a pretty ornament on my sitting-room shelf, where it would catch any sunlight. I put the red hat on it. It looked perfect, the red velvet and the green glass together.

There was only one layer left. All four objects remaining

were wrapped in the same paper, plain gold with silver ribbon round, and all were roughly oblong in shape. Books? The first was indeed a book, small but thick, with a cover made of a William Morris patterned material, grey with peacock feathers of paler grey and washed-out blue. It was an address book, made for Liberty of London, and had the customary letters of the alphabet cut into the right-hand side. There was space for three addresses on each page, the words 'name', 'address' and 'telephone number' printed in purple. Flicking through, I noticed it was not overfull, but it was a while before I realised there was something strange about the entries. There were no names. None at all. There were addresses, and sometimes telephone numbers, but no names of people. This was literally an address book and nothing more, and the addresses seemed to be mainly of hotels and similar establishments. Most of them were in England and Scotland with a smattering in France. Holidays? Were these places where Susannah had enjoyed holidays? Was she attempting to send me off on one long holiday? If so, she would be disappointed. I was well travelled already and none of the destinations I registered as I turned the pages attracted me, or if they did I'd been there already. Paris, for example. She'd written down the name of an hotel on the Ile St Louis which I knew. A perfectly nice but ordinary small hotel. Perhaps to Susannah it had been exciting. The 1950s, the decade she was most likely to have gone there, as a student, was not a time when foreign travel was common.

I put the address book down, and picked up the next offering. It was a paintbox, a Winsor & Newton box of watercolour paints complete with well-used brush, sitting neatly in its slot between two rows of the paints. These were square, six either side. The greens, yellows and the white and brown were well worn down, the reds hardly touched. The box was that hard black plastic – plastic? I think so – on the outside and white on the inside. Someone had clearly mixed colours on the inner white lid. It would have been her own paintbox, of course, though only one of several she'd possessed, because I'd seen others. My grandmother had had one. She gave it to me when I was about ten and staying with her, wondering aloud if I had 'Susannah's talent'. That effectively put me off wanting to use it. Later, my parents gave me a similar paintbox, without any mention of Susannah or her talent, and I discovered I enjoyed painting and was good at it. My father was pleased and encouraged me and I turned out some quite creditable efforts. He bought me some oils later on and I found I liked oil paints even more than watercolours. Susannah, I knew, had never touched oils. She'd stuck to watercolours. I wouldn't use this set of paints. I closed the box, but gently, surprisingly touched by the sight of it. More than any object so far it had made me feel sad. Used paints are sad to me, though I find it hard to say why.

It seemed logical that the next thing I unwrapped should be a painting. It was about ten by eight inches, unframed. The scene was a hillside with some kind of building halfway up. This building, a cottage or croft, was sketched in pencil, and so was a stream, or what I thought appeared to be a stream running past it. It was an unfinished painting, obviously, with only the sky and the top of the hill and some boulders properly painted. I looked at it for a long time, trying to make something of it, trying to have some positive response or even some critical appreciation, but all I felt was depressed. It was a rather drab attempt at a painting, no better than the famous one of the empty meadow. Was it left to me so that it would inspire me to finish it? Or was I intended to track down the place it depicted? But so little *was* depicted. This unassuming hill with its cottage could be anywhere.

The last package had been wedged with some difficulty in the very bottom of the box. It looked square, but when I opened it there was a cylinder of rolled-up papers within the strong cardboard box. I unrolled them. I was looking at reproductions of colour prints. Two of them cut out of some art book; good draughtsmanship, a bit sentimental, probably nineteenth-century, I guessed, but I didn't recognise the artist. One showed a mother in a blue dress cradling and kissing a baby; the other a mother in a cream gown cuddling her baby. They might not be mothers, of course, I told myself: they could be nursemaids. But there was something about the way the babies – both naked – were held that suggested motherhood. I rolled them back up, disappointed.

It was over and hadn't proved traumatic after all. Such a lot of unnecessary angst over what had turned out to be a collection of harmless mementoes. Rather wearily, I stuffed all the wrappings back into the box and put the lid on. I wanted to put the box somewhere out of sight. My cupboards weren't deep enough to hold it without the doors sticking open, but I found a place in my darkroom, under the sink, a compartment empty except for the stopcock taps, where I managed to wedge it. I felt much better when it had been hidden. Some of the objects themselves could stay on display. The hat was already a fixture on the glass head, the necklace in my mirror drawer (one of those wooden swivel mirror stands), the rucksack with the map inside hung on a hook in my bedroom behind the door, the shell sat on a bathroom shelf, the feathers I took out of their plastic bag and stuck in a bottle which also stood on the bathroom shelf. The silver hand mirror I wrapped in a cloth and put in a drawer full of sweaters together with the address book. This only left the rolled-up prints, the paint-box and the unfinished painting. I put them in a pine linen chest which was at the top of the stairs with only a spare duvet in it.

I don't know why, but I had made a list of everything in numerical order. I suppose I thought that once I'd unwrapped the packages I'd forget how they had been numbered and that it might be important. But looking at the little list I couldn't see why the correct sequence should be important at all. Why were those feathers numbered 1? And the prints 11, last? I wandered about for a bit, list in hand, restless and perturbed. I didn't like being made to feel stupid, suspecting that I wasn't spotting connections which someone brighter might make. I was tired too, and hungry, so eventually I put the list on my desk, made myself some pasta and ate it in front of the television, watching the news, but not taking it in. All the time I was looking at the screen I was seeing not the images actually flashing across it but all the things that had been in the memory box, an endless procession of them over and over again.

In bed, it was worse. I was sleepy, but the moment I closed my eyes, ready to drift off, the wretched box was before me, so confident of its power over me. I told myself that now it was stuck under the sink in the darkroom, its contents revealed, it *had* no power any more. But this was not true. The after-effects of opening it were different but still powerful. The fear of some kind of horrible surprise had gone, and so had the terror of being swamped by emotions I hadn't known I could feel, but nevertheless something threatened me still. Susannah had reached out to me through her box, as she intended to, and even if I did not fully understand what she was saying, she had succeeded in making a claim on me. I could no longer reject her. She had forced herself into my mind, where I had never wanted her to be. I had worked hard since I knew of her existence, knew she existed at all as *my mother*, scarcely to think of her. Now I lay in the dark obliged to think of myself as once part of her. I must have been with her when she was choosing and wrapping and arranging the things in the box. I would have been in a cradle or cot beside her bed. She would have hung over me, perhaps talked to me, showing me what she was leaving me, telling me why she was doing it. I found myself, in my half-asleep state, straining to imagine her voice, to see her face looming over mine, to feel the tenderness of her touch . . .

I sat up and switched on my bedside lamp. This was sick. It was also ridiculous. I reminded myself I had been only a few months old and could have no memory of Susannah. There was nothing to recall. But what is memory anyway? Could it be claimed nothing is forgotten, even a small baby's impressions? Could I, in fact, have memories of Susannah embedded in my brain somewhere if only I knew how to log into them? Was the problem only one of retrieval? I slumped there in bed, wondering what happens to memories not remembered. I envisaged them in a kind of vast lost-property room, all jumbled together and crowding each other, clamouring to be let out. It seemed to me that if it is hard sometimes to remember, it is also hard to forget. Perhaps if I went to a psychiatrist, or a psychotherapist, my baby memories would resurface, but I had no intention of doing that. I swore to be stern with myself, sensible. The only important truth was that I remembered nothing and that this had always been a blessing. I had been protected from the pain of Susannah's death. I hadn't pined for her or cried out for her. I hadn't even known she'd disappeared for ever, but had at once accepted my grandmother as a substitute and thrived until Charlotte came into my life.

There was no way of being sure that this cheerful version, in which I had always believed implicitly, was absolutely accurate. Maybe I had missed her. The not crying, the easy transference to my grandmother's arms, need not necessarily signify that I had not registered they were different. I remembered suddenly how my Aunt Isabella had once remarked, in tones almost of disapproval, how adaptable I had been, as though she felt it was neither natural nor right that I had been so docile and had not screamed at my deprivation. She'd seemed to think it shocking how happily I'd given up Susannah, who had loved me with such a fierce passion. Maybe she would rather I had been inconsolable, knowing instinctively what I had lost. I recalled what I'd felt when I first saw the box, that it might be a weapon. She might have wanted me to resent her death. This thought startled me – I had always assumed it must have been a comfort to her, knowing how young I was, thinking I would remember nothing and that therefore her death would not blight my own life. She knew she was going to desert me, but what if, rather than being glad I would not remember her, she had been angry? Perhaps rage had been packed between the layers of her box: 'How dare you not remember me, how dare you say I mean nothing to you, how dare you never call me your mother?' She was not, then, entertaining me or educating me. She was intent on making me examine my attitude to her. I was to take stock and include her in doing so.

I got up, walked about, had a drink of water, went back to bed, but didn't put out the light. Sleep was going to elude me for a while yet, I knew, so that the best thing to do was make myself comfortable and try to be calm. I'm always trying to be calm. 'Calm down,' has been said to me endlessly, by my parents, my grandmother, my teachers, my lovers: 'Calm down, Catherine, for heaven's sake!' What is so wrong in being turbulent, volatile, I wonder. But of course I know perfectly well what's wrong with it. It is tiring, wearing, for other people. They read into my agitation some sort of madness, I think, and it frightens them. They think I might explode and harm them. Or myself. But it runs through me like a stream of hot lava, this bubbling rage I seem always to have within me – rage about things not worth the rage. People said I would learn to control it, or at least direct it, but I never really have. It is me, and I've stopped being ashamed of it. I've stopped wondering where it came from, too, although it used to worry me terribly in case this was Susannah coming out in me. Nobody had ever told me she had a fiery temper, or that she was capable of the kind of rages which regularly overcame me, but, when I felt the need to blame somebody for the state I was in, it was convenient to blame her. I did that a lot, secretly. And once, when I screamed at my poor grandmother that I couldn't help being *bad*, it wasn't my fault, I was *made* that way, I saw the strangest look come over her face. It scared me, and I hurled myself into her arms, and sobbed and said I was sorry for yelling. She just stroked my hair and held me and was silent.

Tony was the only person who succeeded in helping me to be calm when I was angry or upset. He was calm himself, this man I used to love not so very long ago, not so many weeks before the memory box came into my life to disturb me. Tony lived with me for over a year, the year that ended with Charlotte's death. He helped me through my father's death and then through Charlotte's illness. He helped me stay sane, by loving me and tolerating my rage and understanding the misery that was fuelling it. It was Tony who taught me tricks other people had tried to teach me and which I had rejected. I had always been so insulted to be told to take deep breaths, or to close my eyes and count to ten when I was furious about something and letting rip. Tony didn't come out with rubbish about deep breaths and counting, but he did introduce me to yoga and practised it himself with me. I jeered, I sneered, but grudgingly I let him teach me and, though it didn't stop me exploding from time to time, it did make me calmer in general. So did his ideas for making my bedroom a soothing place into which I could retreat. Tony put new lighting in and together we chose a carpet to cover the plain boards: the room became a softer place, less stark, less bare. We painted the white walls a pale apricot and left them bare except for the wall opposite the bed. This was to hold what he solemnly referred to as my 'calming picture'. I humoured him and after great deliberation chose a print I'd always loved.

It's a Cartier-Bresson photograph, 'En Brie', taken in 1968, a classic in black and white. It's the one showing a road leading between fields of what might be lavender, a road broad in the foreground and narrowing to pass through a long avenue of trees, the sort of road so common in the French countryside. The line of trees curves to the left, fading into the horizon. Half the picture is sky. No clouds, just smooth, grey sky. No people or buildings. Many a night, in the half gloom of my bedroom I've stared at that photograph and followed the clear yet mysterious road. Usually, it helped me travel to sleep but that night it had the opposite effect. I felt suddenly alert. I began to turn over in my mind what I would leave in a memory box. Would I put this photograph in it? And if I did, what would I intend it to convey, and what might it signify to the person to whom I bequeathed it? I saw how it would help to think about this. The only way to make sense of Susannah's legacy might be to put myself in the position of leaving a similar one myself. Instantly, I realised the dangers. Presented with a print of this Cartier-Bresson photograph, what might a recipient think? Surely, they would home in on the *place*. They would decide that wherever this road was, I had walked or driven along it and that it was somehow of great significance to me. They would feel bound to find it and then wait for enlightenment to dawn. But it wouldn't. The place, the road itself, was of no importance and going there would have told them nothing about me. I had never been to Brie. It meant nothing to me. What meant something was purely the art of the photograph. It would have been left as a marker of my taste.

What else would I leave? I tried to think of myself, of what I had become, what I was, of my life in general. What would I want the unimaginable daughter to know? What would it pain me to realise that photographs and the testimonies of others had not told her? Susannah had left a husband, a mother, a sister and several uncles, aunts and cousins, who had not only tried to keep her memory alive but who had in their possession a whole archive of material about her. If I had wished, I could have been swamped in it. (My grandmother in particular had seemed determined to tell me what I didn't want to hear – there was no stopping her, and I grew to dread the words 'Susannah used to'.) Hers were all stories in which this Susannah won things, it seemed to me – prizes galore for the best handwriting, the best-decorated Easter egg, the fastest crossword-puzzle solver, the best singer, the best verse speaker – on and on went the litany of praise. She used to work so hard, try so hard, think so hard; she used to smile so winningly, make friends so easily, charm people so completely. All my grandmother wanted, of course, was to bring her *alive* for me, but that was the very thing she could not do. Maybe if she had told me just one story, given me just one example, of Susannah being naughty or spiteful she would have succeeded, but she never did. As a child, I assumed there were no such detrimental tales to tell, and only now do I realise my grandmother may have been censoring Susannah's past, if with the best of motives.

No child of mine would have had all that. There were no grandparents to be keepers of my flame; most of my cousins had faded out of my life. There was only Rory who had truly known me and who was still close. And he would not be trustworthy. Any box of mine would be far more significant than Susannah's – it would have to speak for itself and compensate for the almost entire lack of other voices and evidence. And there would be no husband to safeguard it . . .

That was a stupid thought. If I had had a child there would have been a father if not a husband. I thought about this,

40

getting deeper and deeper into absurd speculation, moving further and further away from my original starting point. I saw I was obstinately refusing to answer properly my own crucial question: what would I put in a memory box if I had to leave one? Good God, it was simple enough. Then I saw why I was being so evasive. It wasn't because I couldn't think what I would need to communicate, but that I was ashamed of what that was. Susannah had had plenty to be proud of. Happy things. Good memories. I did not. I had to confront the fact that I had made a mess of much of my life. I had done things with which I did not particularly care to acquaint those who did not know. Only my childhood, especially my early childhood, was worth trying to encapsulate, my first supremely fortunate ten years or so. I would have liked a child of mine to have known of this happiness, hoping the knowledge of it would please them. But how could I pass it on, if I was obliged to, in the shape of some object to go in a comparatively small box? I thought of our house in Oxford, my lovely childhood home, and I remembered the model my father had once made of it, a doll's house given to me on my seventh birthday, the most beautiful object. I still had it, sitting in a broad alcove halfway up the stairs. But it was too big to go into a hatbox, or indeed a crate. The doll's house could not be part of my memory box. It could only be a memory in itself.

Yet somehow having thought of starting with this house I felt less agitated. It reassured me, the reminder that of course I had something worth communicating of my life however it had turned out. This box business was only, after all, about communication, nothing else. There was no justification for regarding anything Susannah left for me as sinister. I didn't need to sweat and strain for deep meanings. And then I slept.

Chapter Three

I WOKE late the next morning, a Sunday, feeling cheerful. Taking my coffee into the sitting-room, I looked at the red hat on the glass head, the sunlight glancing off it just as I had known it would, and prepared to think differently about what had been in the memory box. I told myself this was, after all, like a treasure hunt, though not the sort Rory had liked to romanticise about, and that I should regard it as fun. I would treat each of the eleven objects as a clue and following these clues, in search of Susannah, I would have a sense of purpose. Indeed, it was a welcome diversion for me even if she could not have known I would need it.

What did I need a diversion from? It was embarrassing to admit the answer even to myself: life, my own life. I needed a respite from life in the manner I was increasingly living it. It wasn't that I was suicidal — suicide never entered my head. I was just tired, jaded. I could find little pleasure or satisfaction in anything I did and I was angry with myself for feeling like this when I had so much to be grateful for. Everything seemed flat and when real tragedy happened, when both my parents died one after the other so unexpectedly, this seemed only to point up how little happiness I had been enjoying anyway before I had real reason to be unhappy. It had been almost a relief to have cause for my vague feelings of despair. What a sorry, un-Susannah-like state of affairs. I had no idea exactly how this had come about. Everything had been so promising but then had just collapsed, and I found myself at thirty-one looking back with disbelief at myself at eighteen, nineteen, so confident and determined.

I hadn't looked ahead much then, didn't have precise plans, but then not many eighteen-year-olds do, except the fortunate few who have always wanted to be doctors or lawyers and see their paths clearly marked. I just assumed . . . I don't, in fact, remember what I assumed. That things would happen, I suppose, that I needn't worry about the future, it would come to me. I never had worried. I never had had reason to worry. Occasionally, my father would enquire, in a mild sort of way, if I'd thought what I would like to do in life. I remember being surprised that he should need to ask at all. Surely he knew that I'd go to some sort of place where I could learn more about photography and then I'd be a photographer. I wasn't interested in anything else, but of course I hadn't thought it out, I hadn't the slightest idea how one became a photographer by profession – I just liked taking photographs. Wasn't that enough? My father didn't think so. He thought I should have a more general education, and either go to university or art college to do a foundation course then a degree. I refused to go to university and only agreed to the basic foundation course because I had heard everyone had a good time doing it (and at St Martin's in London I had a very good time indeed).

There wasn't much photography in the course then, but that didn't bother me. I took photographs anyway, pleasing myself, without a thought about earning a living. I saw no need to. Ever since my parents had given me a good camera, a Pentax, on my tenth birthday, I'd known I was hooked. I taught myself the obvious way, through trial and error, taking endless photographs, and the only help I had was in learning how to print them. Luckily, my school had an excellent art department with photography as one of the options in the sixth form, and I was a quick learner. My father fitted out a little room that had once been a coal cellar as a darkroom for me and he was quite happy to finance what he thought of as my hobby. He bought me a Leica on my eighteenth birthday, more extravagance. But it wasn't a hobby, it was a passion, and I think he was amazed how it came to absorb me. I was soon entering competitions and winning some, and as far as I was concerned that was it, that's what I'd do. Patiently, my father pointed out that winning competitions was one thing, but paying one's bills another. Bills? I don't think I even knew what he meant. You could say that it was his own fault: he and my mother had been over-indulgent. They had never made me realise the value of money. I had never had to work at menial jobs in the holidays to earn pocket money as most of my friends did. They gave me a generous allowance and I actually thought my expenditure modest, on the grounds that I rarely bought clothes or records, failing to appreciate what I cost them in other ways (cameras, films, equipment). A case could be made out (not that I would make it) for my parents being responsible for much that happened simply through being too generous. The curious thing to me now is how little shame or guilt I felt at being the only, spoiled child of well-off parents. I took it all as my due. I seemed to think it was my birthright to be so cosseted, and had no qualms about it.

They financed me through St Martin's and then bought me my flat. As if that wasn't enough, they gave me an income until such time as I could earn enough to support myself. It took me four years and never once did either of them remonstrate and say I would have to get some kind of other job if I couldn't make photography pay. They were utterly, completely supportive and it didn't concern me in the least. All I can say in mitigation of my bland acceptance is that I loved them and showed it. I didn't move away from them, they were never a burden to me, as so many of my friends find their parents (and as Rory with equal cause for gratitude certainly finds his). I loved them, I liked them, I phoned them almost every day and visited them every other weekend. They shared in everything I did and the warmth between us never cooled, or only very slightly. Over men, the two before Tony. My choice of men friends, of lovers, did produce not so much a cooling of the affection between us as an anxiety which had never been noticeable before, even if it had existed (as I'm sure it had). They became a little tense; it made them uneasy when certain men moved into my flat. They were always visibly relieved to hear they had moved out.

Maybe it was men I was tired of, not life. There hadn't been many. Only a few. Only two of any importance. I wasn't good at relationships, that was the trouble. I always grew restless and felt claustrophobic a few months into a relationship, however much I loved the man. It made me wonder, of course, how much I loved them. Could what I felt *be* love, if a great deal of the time I wished they were not there? Didn't being in love mean you couldn't get enough of the loved one? My father and Charlotte loved each other. They never seemed to want to be apart longer than a day. And the happy Susannah had been the same, with my father, so far as I knew, her only lover. Perhaps I am simply a bad judge both of men and of what love is. In any case, my personal life was very far from rich and satisfying and I couldn't seem to sort it out. I preferred being alone.

I realised, though, that morning, how much I wanted Susannah's legacy to touch and change me, to work magic. I knew it was foolish to have such expectations, but I felt that unless I forced myself to make an effort and be optimistic, I would waste these gifts left to me with such love. And there *was* love there, whatever else, I was sure of that. Everything had been wrapped with such care and packed so tenderly. But maybe it was the thought of this love which I had always instinctively feared. If I felt the love, I would feel, too, its withdrawal. Perhaps I had unconsciously been clever all these years to refuse this posthumous love. It could fill me with a resentment and a rage against fate which I had been spared.

That day, I made a plan. I studied the list of objects that had been in the box and resolved to try to trace them in the order in which they had been numbered. 'Trace' was not exactly what I meant, but I could think of no more appropriate word. I wanted to do a sort of study of each object which would involve trying to find out its possible significance first in its own right and then with regard to Susannah. If a trail leading somewhere was intended, then this, I was convinced, was how I would follow it. If there was no trail, if, in spite of the numbers, this was merely a random collection of mementoes meant to serve as the most tenuous of links with a dead woman, then it would be exposed as such.

I regretted having to start with the three feathers, really, because of all the objects they seemed so vague. There was nothing that I had been told about Susannah to connect her with birds. She hadn't painted birds, there had been no books about birds amongst those belonging to her which I had sent to a dealer. A trip to the library next day and half an hour's study of a pretty limited ornithology section taught me that the three feathers were neither rare nor exciting. They were the feathers of the common gull, found all along the sea coasts of Britain. It was unlikely that even an expert would be able to say where they had come from. So, straight away, I felt disappointed. Back home, I held the feathers in my hand, thinking hard. Where had Susannah got them? Was the number 1 to indicate some reference to her childhood? Or those sailing trips with my father? (I remembered only one 'seaside' photograph of her that had hung in my father's study – on a boat somewhere, though no gulls that I could recall.) I got out the oldest of those photograph albums bequeathed to me by my grandmother. It was the sort with thick, black, cardboard-like pages on to which the mostly small square photographs were stuck with strong glue. No snaps of Susannah at the seaside, none at all. A few beside various lochs, but none actually at the coast.

The photograph albums covering Susannah's life were all together. I'd packed them in one box, the two my grandmother gave me and the two dating from when my father had started taking photographs up to and including my own birth. As soon as I opened the first of the albums kept by my father, I found pages of photographs of Susannah taken by the sea. Too many, all too alike, which is probably why they'd barely registered before. He'd had a fixation about getting her in profile, in the foreground, so that the eye focused on the line of forehead and nose and chin and very little else. He must have had her sitting on a cliff top because the background was all sea and sky. And yes, there were gulls, seagulls, white dots, sometimes swarms of them, in this background, though none distinct. Because my father was a methodical and neat man, all these photographs were labelled. He'd written little captions, in italic handwriting, underneath – date, place, everything. These first few pages of pictures in the first of his albums were all from the summer he met Susannah, at the end of which he'd taken her home to meet his widowed mother who lived in Whitehaven. Some of them were taken on trips to places along the coast – St Bees, Allonby, Skinburness – but most at Whitehaven itself.

Did the feathers come from the Whitehaven coast? Well, was it a fair assumption or not? It seemed so to me. Susannah had begun not with any link to her childhood but with a link to my father. In a way, it was the most vital of links since it was to produce me. But it was hard, all the same, to see the relevance of leaving me three gulls' feathers. Did she want me to go to Whitehaven on a kind of memory lane trip? The idea made me feel slightly queasy, but on the other hand I had never been to Whitehaven, or indeed to Cumberland (my father never called his county 'Cumbria'). After his mother died, when I was too young to have any memories of her, though she apparently lived with us in Oxford during each of her last two winters, he never went back, for the reasons I have already guessed at. Cumberland was closed to him. If he'd still had relatives living in Whitehaven, especially a brother or a sister with a family, then I'm sure he would have got over whatever block he had and taken me there, but he was an only child, as bereft of family as Charlotte was blessed and burdened. In his rare mournful moods, he would tell me I was the last of an ancient line of Musgraves and recite poetry to me, lines I think from Walter Scott, in which our name was lauded.

I always liked having a regional surname even if I had never been to that region. 'Musgrave' doesn't have a particularly attractive sound, in fact rather the opposite, but I fancied it went well with Catherine. I dropped the Hope entirely. Of all the things I was grateful to Charlotte for, I was most fervently grateful that she'd changed my name, or rather selected my other name for me to be known by. At birth, I was named Catherine Hope, to be called Hope. Susannah called me Hope. But Charlotte, when she became my mother, when I was still only a little over a year, asked my father if he could bear her to use my given first name of Catherine. My father said he preferred it, and then it turned out that my grandmother, whom he consulted with trepidation, was pleased. Catherine was her own name and she, too, had not approved of my being called Hope. Everyone, then, was glad to reject the name Susannah had chosen for me. Precisely. Hope, indeed. It was unbearable to think of, and when later – much, much later – I did think about it, I hated it. I didn't want to be her hope, I didn't want to think my name had been invested with such symbolism. I was her hope for the future and it had failed. Every form I ever filled out after the time I knew this gave my name as Catherine Musgrave.

I couldn't really see any point in going to Whitehaven just because a few seagulls appeared in photographs of Susannah taken there, but on the other hand it was a town I'd always wanted to visit, if because of my father rather than her, and there was nothing to hold me back from going. I was a free agent. I had no ties. I needed a change. It was early autumn and the weather was pleasant, so I decided to go. But I didn't drive there. I'm not a keen, or a particularly good, driver, and there was something wrong with my car. I didn't want to wait until it was put right – my enthusiasm might fade within the forty-eight hours the garage needed – so I went by train, to Carlisle, and arranged to hire a car up there.

The best thing about train journeys as opposed to car journeys is, of course, that one can read. Tony was always surprised by how much I did read. He said I hadn't seemed a bookish person when we first met. I took this as an insult, not a compliment, and demanded to be told precisely what he meant. Did he mean I seemed too empty-headed to be a serious reader? Too frivolous? Too stupid? He was patient and said no, none of those things, but rather that he thought I was more of a visual person who preferred pictures, films and television as stimulation. And he hadn't thought I'd have the sheer patience that reading demands. I seemed always on the move, always rushing, and he couldn't see me sitting still, turning the pages of any book. Well, he soon learned he was wrong. I read more than he did for pleasure and not what he would have called light stuff either. I love thick biographies and best of all, to alternate with these, volumes of classic short stories.

It was in thinking about what I would read that my mind took a sudden and surprising leap. As I went into my local bookshop I was thinking about how Susannah's feathers would be a good subject, if I were a writer, for a short story – 'The Feathers' or 'The Seagull Feathers'. And then I thought 'The Seagull', and that there *was* a short story, a famous one, with that name. I was wrong, but not so very wrong. It was not a short story I was thinking of, but a play, Chekhov's play. I knew it was ridiculous, but this bizarre idea, that my gull feathers would somehow be explained in a play by a nine-teenth-century Russian dramatist, fascinated me. My father had certainly had Chekhov – and Dostoevsky, and Turgenev – among his books. Who knew if Susannah, obliged to spend so much time resting, had read this play and tied it in with some obscure message she wished to convey?

I suddenly remembered that Susannah had at one time wanted to be an actress. This wasn't one of my grandmother's stories but told to me by my Aunt Isabella. She'd come to watch me in a school play – she and Rory were staying with us and came with my parents. It was *Toad of Toad Hall* and I was the bombastic toad, a part I loved. I overdid Mr Toad's cavorting about and shouted rather than spoke my lines, but I got a lot of laughs and was quite flushed with my success when I rushed to ask my family what they had thought. My parents were full of praise, as ever, but Isabella was tight-lipped and did not hang back from pointing out that she thought I'd been 'showing off a little, just like Susannah used to'. My father quickly said Mr Toad *was* a show-off, it was that kind of part, but Isabella said all the same I'd upstaged the others at several crucial moments – 'just like her mother'. It could all have got very ugly – I was on the edge of tears to be told I had been less than wonderful – but Charlotte smoothed things over and, though I never quite forgave my aunt, no real argument resulted. I think she must have felt a little guilty because later on that evening she said she thought I'd make a fine actress if I toned myself down a bit. 'Your mother was going to be an actress once. She auditioned for RADA but didn't get in and she gave the idea up, luckily. Our mother was relieved, she'd never approved of acting, she thought it brought the worst out in Susannah. And so it did.'

But maybe Susannah had still been interested in the theatre, maybe she'd read plays for pleasure and still had her little fantasies of being an actress, perhaps it was not so absurd that she'd tried, through leaving me the seagull feathers, to direct me to a play, because it said something about her.

There was no one to mock, no one to tell me how silly I was being, nobody to talk sensibly and tell me not to be preposterous. It was crazy enough to connect three ordinary bird feathers with a particular place and look for some revelation by going there, but to seek literary enlightenment through so forced a parallel was wilfully stupid. But I wanted to be stupid. And I had to have something to read, so why not a World Classics cheap copy of *Anton Chekhov's Five Plays*? I was smiling when I bought it, hugging to myself the joke, but once settled on the 10.45 train from Euston and reading *The Seagull* the idea that this was a joke receded. Looking for meanings, I found them instantly. The first line Masha speaks, the second line in the play, is 'I'm in mourning for my life, I'm unhappy.' Then everything Nina says is meaningful in the context of Susannah's situation – 'My heart's full of feelings for you' . . . 'What is to be, will be.' She thinks she is like a seagull herself – 'I'm a seagull' . . . 'Something seems to lure me . . . like a seagull.' And then her final long speech before she runs out through the French window – 'What a life it was – so serene and warm, so happy and innocent.' My eyes were jumping from line to line, picking up odd words, refusing to read properly or to make sense of the play as a whole. I hardly knew what it was about, except that this woman Nina's life appeared to have been somehow ruined when once it had been perfect. And the seagull, or a seagull, with whom she identifies, is killed.

End of my mad notion that Susannah had made a literary reference. I found myself blushing a little as I closed the paperback and stared out of the window. How dangerous it was, this game, because that was what it was turning out to be, a game, one without any rules of play and only the merest chance of an elusive prize at the end. My imagination was enjoying itself, conjuring up absurdity after absurdity, trying to make profound what was simple. I had let some kind of brake off and was freewheeling, my mind rushing down all kinds of strange alleys. Seagulls, feathers, visions of Susannah floated before me dizzily and I felt a kind of physical excitement I did not like. It was a relief when the dreariness of the Midlands gave way to the hills of the North-West and it soothed me to stare out at the smooth roundness through which the train was travelling. I was like a medium coming out of a self-induced trance.

By the time I got off at Carlisle I was sensible again. Which was fortunate, because the drive from there to Whitehaven was not the easy coastal meandering I'd expected, but a fraught business, which involved driving on a difficult, quite narrow road, with very few stretches of dual carriageway, among large lorries. There wasn't much chance to look at the scenery and I had only a faint impression of mountains off to my left for a long way. It wasn't until I was almost at Whitehaven itself, high up on a top road I'd somehow strayed on to from the main road in an attempt to escape the traffic, that I sensed anything glorious about the landscape that corresponded to my father's memories. But then I saw the sea stretching away to a blue line of hills on the Scottish side and on my other side a great vista of soaring and dipping mountains, and I began to appreciate something of the hold his home county had had over him.

What I didn't know, and pondered as I drove into the town down a long and winding road, was whether Susannah had shared his affection. She was a Scot, not a Cumbrian, and surely more loyal to her own hills. And unlike my father she hadn't been a great climber and walker, not possessing, because of her heart condition, his stamina and strength. I didn't even know how many times she had actually been in this area. There was that first summer, when he'd brought her home to meet his mother (not a success – she'd thought Susannah looked 'delicate' – too true), but after that? I didn't know. I thought there must have been at least one other occasion, when they went walking, and there was their honeymoon and the photographs from that in a more southern part of the county, showing Susannah looking incredibly tanned and healthy and far from delicate. I had her map with me, and the rucksack, numbers 2 and 3, and had vague ideas of going on from Whitehaven to explore further if I felt like it.

All the time I was trying to find my way round the town (and I seemed to go in circles, realising I was passing certain buildings twice), I was straining to imagine my urbane father coming from such a place. I couldn't see him belonging at all, and the feeling increased once I'd parked the car in a little turning off the quayside. I tried to see him as a boy, playing on the miserable, muddy patch of dark sand I could make out beyond the wall of an inner harbour, and failed. Then I walked down a sad shopping precinct full of shoe shops with wire baskets of cheap trainers standing outside until I came to a small market place, where the tourist office was housed in a pretty painted old building. It was a relief to reach it. They gave me a street map there, and I followed its directions to Washington Square, where I knew my father had been born and brought up. It wasn't a square at all, but a triangle in the middle of narrow streets and connected to others by a cut. Now here I *could* see my father, sitting sketching perhaps on the bench in the square, drawing the five little trees quaintly lined up on the cobbles, or copying the mural of the George Washington sailing ship, dated 1732, which adorned the brick wall of a house backing on to it. It was so strange to come from the shabbiness of the shopping area, with its dispirited air, and from the forlorn harbour, into this charming enclave and I felt pleased. I stood and stared up at the house where my father had lived, its three windows stacked neatly one above the other, as he had described, with the top window that of his room. It didn't seem to be a private house any more, none of these houses did. There were plaques on the outside of most of them stating hours of business and none had curtains at the windows. But there was still an air of faded gentility around, which was unexpected and soothing.

It was distracting to be conjuring up images of my father when I was here to think of Susannah. I saw how Whitehaven would have confused her, coming as she did from a fairly affluent Edinburgh family who lived in a solid, stone-built house among others the same, in an area where there was no mistaking general prosperity. She'd never lived cheek by jowl with obvious poverty as my father had done here, hidden from it but part of it. This house, his house, in Washington Square was an elegant, Georgian residence but I knew that inside it had been sparsely furnished and always cold, unlike her own overstuffed, overheated home. My paternal grandmother had had very little money after her husband died when my father was sixteen, and she herself had never worked, so she had sold most of the furniture, anything that fetched a decent price, and lived a spartan existence. I thought about knocking on the door and asking to see round it, but didn't. It wouldn't look the same; there was no point.

Instead, I walked along Queen Street a bit and turned down

the next corner into Cross Street. There were several houses in its short length with bed-and-breakfast signs in their windows and I chose one for the cheerful geraniums hanging in a basket outside. The woman who answered the door was not at all cheerful. She stared blankly at me and had to think for a long time before agreeing she had a room vacant and that she could provide me with an evening meal. She told me where I could park my car for the night and once I'd done this I returned immediately because 'evening' apparently meant five-thirty and it was nearly that. Having the meal was a bit embarrassing. There was only the woman, a Mrs Robinson, and me. She didn't eat. I sat at a table laid with an embroidered cloth and she pottered between kitchen and table waiting on me. I was given bacon and egg, which I don't much care for, toast and cake and a large pot of tea. She stood and watched me eat as though I were a creature from outer space and I began to feel like one. All attempts to engage her in conversation failed, or rather petered out quickly. She said, 'You're not local,' a statement so obviously true I couldn't think of a reply. I said my father had lived here, round the corner, and at the name Musgrave she took a brief interest. Yes, she knew the name. Plenty of Musgraves around still. She didn't ask me why I was here, betraying no curiosity whatsoever, so I didn't tell her (though I realised I'd quite wanted to). The moment I'd finished the bacon and egg and nibbled at the toast, she whipped my plate away, saying she was going to choir practice and must get the dishes washed first.

By then it was dark, though only seven o'clock. I was tired, so went to my room, thinking I would have a bath and read until I fell asleep. The bathroom was next to my room, at the front of the house. After my bath, I stood wrapped in a towel, drying my hair with another while I looked out of the clear panes above the frosted glass. The seagulls were everywhere, silvery white in the dark, gleaming in the dull light of the few street lamps. There was one on the window sill, its beak hawked and its legs longer than I had ever thought they would be. The noise they made was not so much a screeching as a high-pitched whistle and it was insistent. I wondered, as I went back to my room – enough to give me vertigo with its swirling patterned red carpet and curtains of pink and yellow stripes – how long the birds would keep this up. Were they governed by the tides? Did they sleep? Would they soon all swoop off and leave the square suddenly silent?

I think they must have done. It was quiet enough, at any rate, when I woke briefly in the night. But then in the morning there was a different noise, rain, heavy rain, lashing against the window and a moaning wind coming through the gap I had left open. The room was cold and I shivered getting out of bed and rushed to pull on jeans and a thick sweater. Mrs Robinson offered more bacon and eggs – I could smell the bacon already frying – and was put out when I declined. I asked if by any chance she had coffee and she was aggrieved, saying of course she did. A large mug of instant coffee was triumphantly produced and I made the best of it. Who did I think I was, coming here with my hoity-toity metropolitan ways and expecting real coffee, black and bitter? She asked if I would like a flask filled to take out with me. At first I said no, but then changed my mind. It looked as if I was going to get drenched. I might never find a café. Watery Nescafé might at some point taste like nectar.

At least I'd come well equipped. I was no novice when it came to being out in exposed places in horrible weather, and had all the right clothing: lightweight but waterproof leggings and jacket, with a hood, and wellingtons. I had a case, for my camera and tripod, which was completely watertight, and I carried a large and, unfortunately, heavy golfing umbrella which I used as a shield when taking photographs in such conditions. Crazy to attempt to take shots at all in such poor light, but I'd had some remarkable successes all the same, some dramatic results in similar conditions. I didn't know why I was thinking of taking photographs that day — it was just automatic, it was what I did, my job. Wherever I went I had a camera with me; it was part of me, sometimes the only part in which I had any pride. Taking pictures had always seemed to help me feel real, to steady myself when I felt I was wavering. The photographs were solid proof that I had been where I thought I had been and seen what I thought I had seen.

And yet I had always known not to trust the camera in this way. I soon learned its limitations, its tricks. Every time I looked at a photograph I had taken I saw the deceit. It was not what was in the photograph that gave the lie to it, but rather what was outside the frame, what was missing. I knew very early on, without being able to articulate it, that photographs are made, not taken. They are created, formed by the photographer, who can persuade the onlooker to see what she wants them to see. As Cartier-Bresson made me see that road in France as a fluid, peaceful surface, enticing me along it in a dreamlike way until I failed to register where the road might be coming from or going to, it didn't matter to him. I knew I would have made a different photograph and might not even have seen the seductive curve he used to such soporific effect. He made something calming and beautiful out of a scene I might turn into something sinister and harsh. It happens all the time, the photographers' emotions as well as their vision forming the photograph.

I wondered often why I had always distrusted photographs of Susannah. Portraits, after all, ought to be safest from the photographer's interpretation — people, straight to camera, where is the room for interpretation? But they are not. Photographs of people are always, to me, sentimental in no time at all. Before the film is even developed, a kind of death has taken place in the subject. The person has changed, they will never be as they were in that photograph again. I look at Susannah, posed so carefully by my father to her best advantage, and all I see is death. Those photographs make me shudder. I don't think, How lovely she looked, how fine her eyes were. Instead, I think, This is a reminder of a life over. So I don't take people, ever. I take landscapes only, and always black and white. Colour is less true, more subject to exaggeration. I automatically distrust a colour photograph. Looking at Susannah's eyes and hair in my father's photographs I think, No, they were not that shade of blue, that shade of gold – that is the colour of the film, of the print, and what can be seen is a mere approximation. Blue eyes, blonde hair, yes, but where is the subtlety? Colour blanks it out.

Trudging through the sodden streets of Whitehaven that morning I took a grim pleasure in my preference for black and white pictures – looking for colour, I would have been dismayed. There was none. Once I was out of the town and climbing a track leading from the quayside to a headland, there was no colour anywhere – grey leaden sea, black gusts of rain, sullen grey sky weighted with huge dark clouds. And everywhere the seagulls, great blurs of palest grey tossed into the sky. Yet for no reason I could think of, I began to feel exhilarated.

Chapter Four

HOURS I lay there, hours and hours all the long, wet day, on my front, barely sheltered by the umbrella, stuck up to the top of its handle in the grass and yet threatening all the time to blow away. I watched the sea through half-closed eyes, the rain driving into the side of my hood, stinging my right cheek even though it did not penetrate the waterproof fabric. The material stuck to my skin, cold and clammy, but I dared not ease it away. The sea before me, far below, was ugly, black and bitter, the tops of the heaving waves a dun brown, like beer, and the white foam and spume not white at all but more a filthy ivory. Every now and again I had another look through the lens of my camera, as protected as I could make it by a smaller transparent umbrella within the larger one, and saw the same — thick clumps of seagulls travelling so swiftly no shutter could cope with the movement and produce more than a blur.

There were hundreds of gulls, driven in great angry gusts back from the sea. They were tossed high above the waves, which kept up a ceaseless crashing on the shingle, all along the battered shoreline. I had never seen anything like this violence of wind and water, full of such fury and menace. The birds seemed at the mercy of these dramatic elements and yet they could not be subdued — again and again they were hurled towards the land, then forced yet higher into the air, only to turn and strain towards the horizon, when their effort would begin again. I couldn't imagine why they did not fly inland and find shelter until the storm was played out. Or let the wind take them where it wanted to. They seemed heroically determined to fly out to sea and would not give up, staying close together, striving as a group, not a stray to be seen. I wondered if they were shrieking in protest but it was impossible to hear them. There was no sound except the roar of the wind and the thudding of the waves. The birds were silenced so long as the gale blew.

There were no boats out there at sea. Behind me, in the harbour, all the bays were full, crammed with boats of every size jostling and jangling in their shelter together. There were no people either. Trudging up on to this headland I had seen no one. I had been granted a privacy and sense of isolation I had rarely known. I was frozen and the rain had found a way into my boots, which were slowly filling with it. But I went on lying there, inert, wondering if this was how people died of exposure, died on mountains or in the wilderness because they became too apathetic to move, because they gave themselves up to those particular forces of nature which threatened to overwhelm them – and were in the end pleased to do so.

In my inner pocket, beneath the layers of waterproof, were the three feathers. It could not have been a day such as this when Susannah found them. The beach below might, for all I knew, be littered with seagull feathers, but nobody could possibly pick them up in these conditions. No sane person would be outside at all. I was not acting in a sane way myself. Any nearer the edge and I could be blown off, sent plunging down into the greedy sea. I knew I had taken no photographs worth having. I hadn't captured anything of what lay beyond the camera even if I had caught a fleeting impression of the turmoil. Everything on film would be flat, unable to record what I felt: a sort of awful fear. I found myself clutching the grass and imagining I was sliding down the slope.

I had never before allowed myself to imagine Susannah's fear, but lying there, reduced to such a pitifully feeble state myself, merely through exposure for a prolonged period to cold and rain, an image began to steal over me. She had surely been afraid. She had known that her heart muscles were failing, they had been failing for years, and that at any moment the main pump of her heart might stop (as it did) without further warning. My grandmother endlessly mourned the fact that, a mere five years later, a heart bypass could have saved her, but at that period nothing could and she knew it. It was a matter of time before she grew weaker and weaker. The fear would have grown, fear of death, fear of the process of dying, fear of leaving me. I felt suddenly paralysed with her imagined fear and ready to weep at the thought of it. I'd never once before felt sorry for her.

It was only with a great effort of will that I switched off this wretched mental meandering and stood up. At once the wind slapped me down on to my knees and I gasped with the shock. Much more slowly, I raised myself again, swivelling round so that the wind was behind me. I think of myself as physically strong; I'm proud of my fitness, but collapsing the big umbrella, struggling to get it out of the ground, was so hard that I was panting before I watched it being torn from my grasp and sent catapulting ahead, a lethal weapon with its spike foremost. My camera bag I pulled over my body, the strap over my shoulder and across my back and chest, keeping the bag itself in front of me. Then I set off, half-stooping, trying to walk slowly but instantly bullied into a jumpy run by the wind. I was soon hot with the strain of trying to hold myself back and the rain, coming towards me as I turned, at last found its way down my neck. Some of the time I had my eyes closed and prayed I would not stumble. Then, as I came down from the highest point, I felt the wind slacken. I hit a pocket of calm between two inclines and rested. The remaining descent was easier, and soon the danger I'd felt on the top seemed absurd. It was only wind, only rain.

I came to the market square, quite deserted except for a few seagulls, and cut through to Queen Street and made my way to where I was staying. The streets were empty, though it was only late afternoon, the gutters running with rain water to such an extent they were like streams. Mrs Robinson, opening the door reluctantly, said, 'You're wet,' in tones of annoyance. She made me take my boots and waterproofs off in her vestibule, tutting with exasperation as the puddle grew on the tiled floor. I apologised and said I would mop it up, and she said that would be a good idea but I'd better have a bath first or I'd catch my death. When I came down half an hour later she had in fact done the mopping up herself. My jacket and trousers hung dripping on the back of the door and she'd stuffed wads of newspaper into my boots. I apologised once more for the trouble I'd caused and thanked her. The meal that night was soup, her own, and kippers, both good. Then I went to bed, paying her bill first and saying I would slip out early in the morning without disturbing her. She still had not betrayed the slightest curiosity about me.

It was only eight o'clock by then, but I was so tired. I didn't even think of reading but put the light out straight away. I could hear the seagulls again. They had come in from the sea with the dark and had taken possession of the rooftops, resting from their labours. The wind did not seem so strong and the rain no longer drove against the window. Mrs Robinson had said the worst was over, and then had gone on to boast that this storm had been nothing compared with what she had known. 'We're used to it here,' she said, with some pride. 'We think nothing of it. If you lived here, you'd get used to it.' Lying there, so drowsy, so glad to be safely in bed, I didn't think so. How could I have allowed myself to be carried away, thinking I'd find significance in the feathers of a gull?

Before I fell asleep, I thought of my flat, my home in London. There would be cars going up and down my road in Crouch End, and the restaurants and cafés all along the Broadway would be brightly lit and packed with people for whom the evening had barely begun. Here, there was no human sound outside. Nobody walked the streets on a night like this. There were no lights to make a nonsense of the darkness – it was never really dark in London. And time was different here. Every hour was felt. Time didn't seem to me to whizz by but to plod on, and yet I was in a town, not a deserted village. Some people would love the peace of it, the absence of noise. They would declare this town wonderfully, mercifully tranquil and extol the benefits of its calm centre. What would have happened if my father had returned here with Susannah, his first wife, and I had been born here? What if my paternal grandmother had looked after me in my early years and Charlotte had never appeared?

I woke up to the shock of strong sunlight coming through the thin curtains. I could hardly believe it, but jumping out of bed and going to the window I saw that the sky above the opposite rooftops was an intense, Mediterranean blue with not a cloud in sight. I was outside in minutes. It was only seven o'clock when I put my stuff in the boot of my car and set off to the sea. I went the way I had come the day before but covered the distance in half the time, walking rapidly where previously I had been obliged to crawl, battling against the wind. The sea that fresh, new morning looked magnificent, not calm so much as swollen, a great, smooth, heaving mass of dark blue, gently undulating and breaking on the shore with hardly a murmur. Already, the harbour was almost empty. I could see the boats bobbing up and down beyond the walls that had protected them, chugging cheerfully down the coast and out into the Irish Sea. I walked along the quay, along the top of the wall, bending like an arm round the inner harbour, loving the worn slabs of sandstone, worn by wind and rain and age more than by feet. I went right to the end and then I stopped beside what I took to be a sort of beacon, and looked towards the headland where I had been the day before, suffering.

It looked so green and peaceful up there. Scores of seagulls wheeled overhead, quite startlingly white now against the blue of the sky and their screeching dominating the air. Their movements, the arcs they made, seemed leisurely, the frantic whirling of yesterday forgotten. They were lovely to watch, exhilarating to follow with the eye, and when one or two landed near me and perched on the sandstone I thought them beautiful, not ordinary at all. Their feathers seemed sleek, they glistened in the sun, and they strutted so confidently to the brink of the wall before soaring effortlessly into the sky. Was this how Susannah had seen them? Had their exuberance in flight made her heart lift? Had she merely wanted me, some time in the future, to share the delight she had felt as a young, happy woman on a morning such as this? It seemed perfectly possible. The feathers did not need to symbolise more than that – the sea, a beautiful morning, the freedom of the gulls and how it made her feel. I took the three feathers from my pocket and caressed them. How brittle they were to the touch, as sharp-edged as the day she had found them, and it didn't after all matter where that was. The points were sharp enough to draw blood if I stabbed them into my hand. I hesitated, then I threw them into the sea. They fluttered towards the water slowly, seeming to stop and rest in the air every now and again, and then one after another came to rest gracefully on the surface and were carried away. I followed their lazy passage until I lost them, until I could no longer see the specks of white, and then I followed instead a swarm of birds racing towards the horizon, low over the sea, crying shrilly.

Suddenly, everything felt so satisfactory. I had made a little ceremony of the feathers, given them back to Susannah, not in any fit of petulance or resentment but in a spirit of acceptance. What I felt I'd accepted was that she'd loved the seagulls, for whatever reason, and the sea they haunted, wherever it was. That morning, I loved them too. I took dozens of photographs and felt so buoyant as I went back to my car, knowing I'd accomplished something. I was hungry, but had no intention of going back to Mrs Robinson, though for the first time the thought of her bacon and eggs was quite tempting. I found a café and made do with toast, lots of it. Then I drove out of Whitehaven and into the fells, choosing a minor road I hoped would be free of traffic. It was. It was the most seductive road with hills ahead and mountains behind them dramatically silhouetted and before them open moorland. I could have driven along it for ever, and as it was, made slow progress since I stopped so often to take photographs. Now, I felt near my father just as watching the seagulls I had felt near Susannah.

I felt my decision to follow the route on the map in the memory box had been made for me. If it had rained again, I would have gone straight back to Carlisle, but the splendour of the morning drew me on. I had filled the rucksack with bread, cheese and apples before I left Whitehaven, packing it with all the enthusiasm of a child. I hadn't intended to use it at all, despising it for what it was, a poor imitation of a real rucksack, but I was in such good spirits the shabbiness of the material and the uselessness of the thin straps no longer put me off. Even its stains seemed distinguished and its flimsiness attractive. I couldn't wait to put it on my back and set off. I watched a few clouds come sailing over the highest mountain as I drove along the side of Crummock Water – was it Great Gable? I wasn't sure – and worried the weather was about to change, but though more joined them, they were small and puffy and white, and the sky was still mostly blue when I parked at Buttermere, just before the village.

Once past the Bridge and the Fish Inns, I walked at first through flat meadows joining the two lakes (or rather separating them) and then crossed a stream and followed a rocky path along the lake for a mile or so. I didn't need to look at Susannah's map. The way was obvious. I could enjoy instead the sight of the rowan trees, thick with red berries, strung in raggedy lines above the lake and the reflections of the fells on the other side showing clearly in the still water. Turning away from the lake, on a path still distinct, I began to climb up a pass but without any sense of struggle – it was easy going. There was a stream cascading down the fellside at a terrific rate, its water startlingly white and frothy as it bounced off the rocks, and I stopped to wash my face, gasping at the icy cold of it. I didn't look back until I got to the top, wanting the full surprise of the vista I knew I would have. I forgot about Susannah when I saw it at last. The lakes were blindingly bright in the sun, but what made me stand quite still and hold my breath were the shadows cast by the mountains. The brutal bulk of Red Pike to my right threw a black cloak over all the green below, turning the limes and evergreens into sludgy browns and darkening the clear waters of the streams. Beyond the shadows everything sparkled, and when the sun began to lift itself, just as I was about to turn away, and rose above the mountain, I saw the blackness fade rapidly and all the hillside seemed to shout with relief. Even the rocks took on colour – the side of Red Pike was not after all black but ochre and silver, the stones full of a metallic glitter, and high up the redness of the soil which gave it its name stood out richly.

Now I did take out the map. From here, Susannah – and, surely, my father – had not gone on towards Ennerdale, as I would like to have done, following the path still, but had turned right, following the valley along the side of Melbreak.

I could see no path, but her directions on the map, the red line, were quite firm. I stepped out in what I thought was approximately the right direction and was soon ankle-deep in mud. I was crossing a marsh, with no track visible through it. But then, after half a mile or so, I saw the path appear, quite broad, stretching all the way down the valley. She didn't seem to have gone all the way down, though. Her route was marked as stopping at the Mosedale Holly Tree. I could see this tree, the only one in what was a most barren landscape and yet far from spectacular. It was, I thought, a stunted-looking tree, hardly worth the importance of a label on an Ordnance Survey map. Walking along the path, which for a while kept high up before descending at an angle, I felt in the heart of the fells, enclosed by them, shut off from the glories of the lakes, but with no feeling of claustrophobia. I liked the emptiness, the dun brown of the bracken, the coarseness of the grass flattened by sheep. I dawdled along, feeling secure and relaxed, my ears singing slightly with the silence broken only by a lone bird and the odd cry of a sheep. When I was level with, but above, the holly tree I stopped and sat on a boulder. There was no one to observe me. For miles and miles I was the only living being and it thrilled me to know it.

I left the rucksack on the boulder and scrambled down to the tree, taking only my camera with me. The holly tree was not stunted at all. It was quite large close up and the shape more like an oak tree. Its roots were strong and between them were large rocks, like seats. I chose one to sit on and felt as if I were under a canopy, awaiting some ceremony. If it had been raining I would have been quite sheltered, and that is how I did feel: sheltered, hidden. The grass was short, the ground almost bare under the tree, a magic circle of smoothness, while outside it all was rough, the grass thick and tangled. I looked up, through the dense branches. There were few berries, but the holly leaves had a sheen on them which gave a brightness. What had Susannah found here? Peace? Protection from the elements? Had she buried something where her red cross stood out on the map? The young Rory would have thought so, but not I. So what other explanation could there be for it? That something had happened here, some moment of revelation? I looked about me slowly, taking in the sweep of the land down to the bed of a stream and then up again towards the pass to Ennerdale, where it narrowed at the top. It was at first sight, and even second, so barren and yet as I stared and stared I saw different kinds of vegetation, different kinds of exposed soil and rocks. I had thought there were no flowers at all, but then looking at the patch of ground upon which I was sitting, and which to anyone walking above it was also surely flowerless, I saw tiny, starlike, frail yellow flowers hidden in the grass and the longer I looked the more I saw. It was a question of looking and finding.

I took out Susannah's map again. Why did the red dots not continue down the valley to Loweswater or double back to Crummock Water? She couldn't have stayed here for ever, she had made her way back somehow. Maybe they had camped, she and my father, and this was where they had pitched their tent – but no, they never camped, I knew that. My father loved climbing and walking, but his love of the outdoor life didn't include roughing it. He liked a comfortable bed at night. I went on sitting there, pondering, for a long time, yet I wasn't feeling as irritated or frustrated as I might have been. If there was a mystery to be solved and I was failing to solve it then that, in this case at least, was Susannah's fault. But I was beginning to think the only mystery was why she had appeared to want to make it into one, with her red cross and exclamation mark. She was teasing me. I could take being teased, taught how to do so by Rory long ago.

Meanwhile, I had to decide what to do. I had, at some point, to go back to my hired car and drive it the forty-odd miles to Carlisle to catch the train home. I couldn't sit under this holly tree for ever ruminating. Going back the way I had come, I could be at the car in little over an hour. Going ahead, and round Melbreak, where I could see a clear path on the Ordnance Survey, would at least double the time. But I chose to do that, disliking the idea of retracing my footsteps and liking the prospect of the unknown ahead. I also felt quite liberated once I'd left the tree. I was free of Susannah's instructions and making my own way and I enjoyed the vague feeling of defiance. And it was a beautiful walk, taking me round the end of Melbreak and through a wood until I came out on to a grassy path so smooth it looked as though someone had taken a lawnmower along it. All the way back to Buttermere I had the lake, Crummock Water, snaking ahead before me and the path stayed so high I had the illusion of flying over it. I had made a round trip and it felt satisfying and complete.

My legs ached by the time I reached the car and I was glad to sit down. The expedition had taken me four hours, but it was still only two o'clock – plenty of time to return the car and catch a train. I took a minor road, marked yellow on the map, over Newlands Haus to Braithwaite and from there skirted Keswick, then drove along the west flank of Skiddaw. I knew Skiddaw was the first of the real mountains my father had climbed, when he was absurdly young, four or five. He'd climbed them all by the time he met Susannah but, of course, she could never climb any with him. The walk round Melbreak to reach that holly tree would have been a triumph for her (was that cross and the exclamation mark to say so, to raise a cheer for her own achievement, never to be exceeded?). She'd never been strong enough for tough stuff. My father, according to my grandmother, had always tried to make her conserve her strength and energy, but she had sometimes resented his protectiveness and been wilful. Maybe the walk to the holly tree had been an instance of this. She'd perhaps wanted me to do that walk precisely for this reason, to show me she wasn't always feeble, that once she had been able to stride out and had shaken off attempts to persuade her not to risk it. She wanted me to know she had pushed herself and relished the effort.

What she couldn't have known was quite how much to my taste that walk would be. As I took another minor road to Carlisle, a wonderful winding road dipping up and down hills through Uldale and Caldbeck, unfenced for the most part and empty, and with sudden views of the Solway, I thought how what I had seen was imprinted visually on my mind and how I would be able to do that walk over and over again in my head for years to come. I had seen everything with a photographer's eye, sharply, in a concentrated fashion, and it had been thrilling. Would she have expected me to have this kind of appreciation? She and my father were both architects, and she was an artist, if an amateur, so perhaps I was wrong and it was exactly what she had expected. She may have decided that unless there had been some mighty genetic muddle I was a child destined to have a highly developed visual sense. But that didn't mean I would also like to walk. The two things don't automatically go together, and I haven't in fact done much walking in the way my father did. I never think of myself as athletic or the outdoor type, though I am perfectly fit and do spend a good deal of my working life out of doors. It struck me, as I dropped down from the fells on to the Eden plain, that I would like to walk more, to walk as my father had done. I would come back and plan longer walks and climb the mountains he had climbed, and I silently thanked Susannah for giving me the ambition to do so. Skiddaw, Helvellyn, Scafell – I'd do them all.

It was odd, in the circumstances, how very much I was being led to thinking about my father. This was his country she'd brought me to, not hers. It was his life, his early life, I was being drawn into, not hers. Why wasn't she taking me to Scotland, or to places known only to her? I didn't need to be told about my father. I knew all about him. I had to control myself, stop the tears coming, just thinking about how *nice* he was. If I'd heard a hundred times how happy Susannah was, I'd heard a thousand times how nice my father was. It used to annoy me, not because I challenged the truth of it (I knew it was quite true) but because 'nice' is such an anodyne word. It was a word our English teacher would not allow us to use. She said it was lazy, hardly an adjective at all, and certainly not one worthy of our using. And she was right, it doesn't convey much. To call my father 'nice', to emphasise his nice-ness above all else, was to make him sound bland and insipid and he was neither. He was clever, kind, cheerful, good-tempered and had a horror of any kind of unpleasantness or confrontation – which is mostly what people meant when they labelled him 'nice'. He got on with everyone and was always popular. But on the last stretch of that drive, blinking back the tears I couldn't quite stop, I remembered something my grandmother had said. One day, when I was about six or seven and she was staying with us, as she often did (she and Charlotte getting on famously, thank God), she took me on her knee and said, 'You have a lovely daddy, Catherine.' I wriggled off, not liking any more to sit on anyone's knee, and said, quite crossly I think, that I knew I had, and my grand-mother said, 'Look after him, won't you? He doesn't like to be alone. That's the only thing he's afraid of. He needed Susannah more than she needed him, he needs Charlotte more than she needs him, and one day he'll need you more than you need him.'

I was far too young for this. It all sounded silly to me, and made me feel uncomfortable without knowing why. But remembering this strange little outburst, which was so unlike my sensible grandmother, I wondered if she had been trying to tell me that my father was not emotionally strong and that the women in his life had to be. Always, because of her health, I had seen the dead Susannah as weak beside my father, almost a burden on him. Yet my grandmother, her mother, had definitely said he needed her more than she needed him. She had been sure, it seemed, that he was dependent on her and not the other way round. I suppose I had gradually, without quite realising it consciously, seen that so far as Charlotte was concerned she was right. When he died, one of the first things my mother said was, 'Thank God he went first.' It embarrassed me, it seemed such a pious thing to say, and I wished she hadn't said it. I never thought of asking why she had.

It was a relief to be on the train at last and able to slump. I didn't read, just looked out of the window, soon seeing my own reflection as it grew dark. The rucksack with the map inside it was on my knee. I'd almost discarded them both in Carlisle station, dropped them into one of the capacious waste bins, deciding they were now of no use and not worth keeping for their own sakes, or at least the worn rucksack wasn't. But at the last minute I'd held on to them, out of pure sentiment. They could go in a cupboard when I got back. But their numbers were ticked off – 1, 2 and 3, all attended to, to the best of my ability. Whether it had been worth it I wasn't sure. The figure reflected in the window looked pretty morose, exhausted too, as though she had been through some kind of ordeal, which in a way was true. My high expectations had exposed me to it. I'd put myself through a process that had depended constantly on imagination and, more than that, having to interpret what it came up with. No wonder I felt drained. A kind of madness had set in and I was at its mercy, unable to stop now I had begun. All I could hope was that the rest of the objects left to me would make fewer demands and lead to more satisfying explanations. Frankly, that contentment I had briefly experienced on Whitehaven's quayside, and the glow I had felt walking to the holly tree on Melbreak, had faded. I was left with that feeling I hated, of something being just out of reach, not quite within my grasp. I was trying too hard and didn't know, as I travelled back to London, whether I had the heart to go on.

I slept for the last hour and dreamed of the shell.

Chapter Five

RETURNING from the north, I seemed to fall into a woeful state of listlessness. I had intended, after I split up with Tony, to go abroad somewhere, but then came those two awful deaths, and day slid into day, week into week; and then there was the box and I'd done nothing about going any further than Cumberland. There was no pressure on me to do anything, that was the trouble. I had no commitments, no responsibilities, no one to demand I pull myself together. I could drift as long as I wanted. It was an enviable position to be in, and yet I found myself wishing I could lose myself in the demands made on a wife or mother. I started to blame Susannah, unfair though I knew this to be. If she'd left me alone, I'd have recovered from my mother's death and at last gone away to revitalise myself. I needed some proper distraction, but I was too jaded, and too confused about the contents of the box, to go in search of it.

There was a message from Rory on my answerphone when I got back. He asked where the hell I'd got to and why I hadn't turned up for that drink we were going to have, he was pissed off with me. I'd forgotten our arrangement, not exactly a firm one anyway, and knew I ought to ring him. But I didn't want to, even though he was the only relative with whom I still had any regular contact, and certainly the only one for whom I felt any affection. Only with Rory did I feel completely at ease. The pattern of holidays changed after I was about seven and, instead of spending most of them surrounded in my own home by my mother's nieces and nephews, I went to Edinburgh to stay with Rory. This, I gather, was my own choice. My parents were none too happy about it, but apparently I pleaded with them and they were as indulgent over this as they were in everything. But they thought Rory was a bad influence. He was by then well known to do silly things, sometimes quite dangerous things, and they worried I would copy him. They were right, I did, or if I didn't exactly copy him I allowed myself to be led by him and admired his daring.

This was not so very extraordinary, but at the time it was thought bad enough. Once, when we were both eight, he took me hitch-hiking. We got a bus to the outskirts of Edinburgh, I don't remember where, and then Rory marched me on to a main road where the city boundary gave way to countryside, and we stood and thumbed a lift, or rather I did. He'd made me wear a pretty dress, which I hated, a white thing with a Peter Pan collar and a sash, thin material covered with little blue flowers, saying cars would be more likely to stop for a girl dressed like that than for any boy. No car stopped as I stood self-consciously following Rory's instructions, but a lorry did. It was a gigantic lorry with wheels so big they towered over us as it ground to a stop and the steps into the cabin were so impossibly high the driver had to get out and come round to lift us in. He asked where we were going and why we were on our own, and Rory came out with incredibly full details to do with sick grandmothers, broken-down cars, lost money and God knows what else. He said we were going to London, where we would be met by our uncle. I hadn't known this and didn't even realise it was all part of the lie. The lorry driver settled us in his cabin, which seemed like a house to us, full of all kinds of funny possessions, like a potted plant with a tiny watering can beside it, and two cushions embroidered in Rangers football club colours, and a tray set as if for tea, complete with a dainty net cap over the milk jug. He was a big man, his overall sleeves rolled up to reveal muscular arms tattooed with pineapples, and, though he talked to us all the time, we couldn't make out a word he said above the noise of the engine.

Quite quickly, it all stopped being exciting and became very boring indeed. We were glad when after about half an hour the driver pulled into a service station for petrol. He said he was going into the café, when he'd filled up, for a cup of tea and an egg sandwich and would we like to join him. Rory said we hadn't enough money (another lie – he had a ten-pound note but had been going to wait until this man was in the café and then we were apparently going to run away and find a more comfortable car to travel in). The driver laughed and said he'd treat us and without asking he lifted me out of his cabin, so Rory was obliged to follow. We all trooped into the café and he settled us at one of the red Formica-topped tables near a steamed-up window, then he went to get drinks and food. We couldn't leave – not that I had any plans to, though Rory did – because he kept his eye on us all the time. We saw him tell the woman behind the counter what he wanted, and then he came back and said he had to ring his wife and he'd be back in a minute. Even then, we were never out of his sight because the telephone was at the end of the room and he faced us while he rang. We saw him talking, but of course there was too much noise for us to hear that he wasn't ringing his wife, he was ringing the police.

By the time we'd finished eating, and he'd been told our names were Jimmy (which was what Rory had always wanted to be called) and Valerie (my fancied name), and that we were orphaned twins, the police had arrived. Half an hour and our real names and address later, so had my Uncle Hector and Aunt Isabella. Hector was absolutely furious. The lorry driver and the policemen were amused, but Hector saw no humour in the situation at all. He proceeded to do a very old-fashioned thing, there and then in the café, much impressing the lorry-driving clientèle. He took hold of Rory, who admittedly was slight for his age and offered no resistance, put him over his knee, pulled down his pants, and slapped his bare bottom hard several times. I remember there was a ripple of noise throughout the café, but I don't know whether it amounted to a collective gasp of admiration or of horror. All I was worried about was whether my turn to be humiliated would come next. It didn't. We were both taken home and put to bed after more shouting from Hector and a lecture from a tight-lipped Isabella. She felt obliged to ring my parents, and I heard the phrase 'anything could have happened' over and over again, plus repeated apologies for Rory's disgraceful behaviour. I was sent home the next day.

Rory didn't improve as he grew older. He was referred to as 'bolshie' by his father and grave doubts were cast over his honesty and integrity and all the other virtues his family prided itself on possessing in abundance. Both his parents were Camerons, though in no way related, except presumably several generations back, and they held their family name in great respect, as proud to be Camerons with all they considered this implied as my own father was to be a Musgrave. Rory, by the age of sixteen, was becoming known as 'not fit to be a Cameron'. He'd disgraced himself in all kinds of ways anathema to them. He was clever, but regularly failed exams; he was never short of pocket money, but was caught shoplifting items he could easily have bought; he got drunk, crashed his mother's car (which of course he was not old enough to drive), dyed his hair green, had his left ear pierced, wore torn jeans and in general did all the classic wild teenager things so objectionable to his deeply conventional parents. The list of his misdemeanours grew longer and longer. My father used to smile, while shaking his head, as he passed on the latest on

Rory from Isabella. He prophesied that Rory would probably turn out to be a hero when he'd finished sowing his wild oats, but in fact he never did finish sowing them. The moment he left his excellent Scottish public school, to which he'd most unsuitably been condemned by his ambitious father, who'd been there himself, he promptly embarked on a life of minor crime.

It was cars at first. He had his own car, given to him on his seventeenth birthday, a perfectly adequate second-hand Volvo, but that wasn't good enough. Encouraged by the youths he associated with and learning from them (though that was no excuse), he stole sports cars, changed their number plates, had them resprayed, and resold them. He told me he had only intended to do it once, for himself, but he got away with it so easily he decided to do it again and then again and make money out of it. But the money wasn't the attraction – though Hector had stopped his allowance by then, so he had to earn a living somehow and had no intention of doing any regular work – and he never pretended it was. He loved the daring of it, the excitement, the pitting of his brains against those of the police ('no contest' he boasted). But he had a little sense left in his head, enough to stop the lark before his luck ran out. Abruptly, he switched to trading in antiques, his own idea this time. The trading consisted of keeping an eye on local newspapers, the funeral notices and will announcements, and then targeting widowed old ladies. He would go and visit them and ask very politely if he could help them dispose of any furniture. Because he was entirely unthreatening, still slight in build and blond and with a cultured Edinburgh accent, and by then dressed for the part in a suit, and a sparkling white shirt and old school tie, he was well received. He bought bits of furniture at absurdly low prices and sold them for absurdly high ones. This was not of course criminal, just a form of cheating, if one sanctioned in the trade. He always knew the real value of what he bought and he always knew the old ladies did not. He said he made them happy by giving them his time and listening sympathetically to their woes. But this kind of thing was only the respectable front for a much more dubious enterprise which, when he hinted at it, I told him I did not wish to know about. Whatever it was, he came unstuck in his late twenties and had to leave Edinburgh hurriedly. Ever since, he'd lived in London, though never for long in the same place.

Rory came to my mother's funeral, which was good of him. Charlotte had never been sure whether she liked him or not, and he had always sensed this and been wary of her. It was only my devotion to him that made her tolerate his visits later on, when she had heard enough about his wicked ways to justify her unease. But he came to her funeral and was kind and tried his best to comfort me. He told me I was not to forget he was my best friend and would always be there for me. I was touched. Touched, but not fooled. Rory's concern for me might be genuine – no, it *was* genuine, I'm sure – but he cared more about himself. I knew that if my needs clashed with needs of his own he would put himself first. Normal, I suppose. He was just a normal man. But ever since the funeral he had been most solicitous and had rung me often, though I knew it wasn't just because he felt sorry for me. There was self-interest there too. Once Tony had gone, I think Rory fancied himself as my flatmate. He hadn't suggested moving in outright, but he'd hinted at it. I'd been very careful to give out clear signals of refusal.

I could never share a flat, or even a big house, with Rory. Not because he is untidy (though he is, horrifically) or because he smokes heavily, but because of his personal life. He has never so far as I know had any relationship lasting more than a couple of weeks, and he says he has never wanted one, this causes him no grief. He moves on from one man to another, in spite of these being dangerous times, and says this suits his taste perfectly. Perhaps, but without being judgmental, it would not suit me. I couldn't bear a constant stream of youths passing through my flat. It wouldn't matter how discreet Rory was, and discretion was not something he was known for, I would hate the presence of strangers. It is hard enough for me to share my living space with someone I love, never mind with those I would not even get to know. Rory ought to have understood that, since he didn't like sharing himself.

It is an odd connection between us. We like to be on our own and find it a strain to share with lovers, however devoted we are to them (not that Rory has ever shown much sign of devotion). We don't like our homes cluttered up with others. The only-child syndrome, perhaps? Always having everything as we wanted it? But I'm sure there are as many only children who go the other way, who cannot bear to be alone and require constant companionship to make up for their years of deprivation. At any rate, Rory, like me, lived on his own but, unlike me, had never bought his own place. He said he couldn't afford to, but I know there were many times when he had the money to do so. He went on living in rooms not his own surrounded by furniture he'd never have chosen, never properly inhabiting anywhere he lived. These were sad places. He never invited me to any of them, but once I tracked him down and turned up on his doorstep and he was obliged to let me in. It was a basement flat in Kilburn, damp, dark and with walls painted a really lurid purple. He'd made no effort to do anything at all to it and just laughed when I shuddered. He said he wouldn't be there long, and he wasn't. I never visited him again. It was too depressing to witness his circumstances.

Maybe he floated the idea of moving in, after Tony left, from kindness. Maybe he thought I would be lonely, considering Tony had lived with me longer than anyone ever had, well over a year. If so, he couldn't have been more wrong. The best thing about Tony's departure was that it allowed me to reclaim my own territory. The relief was enormous, even if it was tinged with guilt. I swear that waking up to find I was on my own remained absolute bliss for weeks afterwards – I'd wake up, stretch out in the bed, realise I was alone, and feel such relief. I don't think I was ever meant to live with anyone, except my parents, as a child. I am too intolerant, too irritable, too fond of silence. I suppose I had survived so long (long by my standards) with Tony because I'd been away on jobs a lot that year, and because he worked late himself, often, and I had whole evenings undisturbed. It was when I hit a spell of a couple of months without any assignments, which can occasionally happen, that things began to go wrong. We loved each other (I think) but I discovered then that, put to the test, we weren't really compatible. It wasn't so much a case of his liking one thing and my another as of our person-alities. The attraction of opposites had been an attraction, but over time, living together at close quarters, it was being so different in temperament that brought us unstuck.

It's odd, but it takes a long time for temperament to show itself, or so I've always found. No one can really be certain of the temperament of another until they have lived with them for a while. Attraction is all about physical things at first, obviously – I mean, you *see* someone, usually before you hear them and before you know them. What I saw in Tony wasn't what he was like. His calmness was not so evident. On the contrary, he seemed particularly sharp and alert, as though he were on the watch all the time, noting things, analysing them. And he spoke too quickly for me to consider he was a settled sort of person of quiet tastes. Then, even after he had moved in with me, it took a while for me to appreciate how extremely solemn and serious he was, about everything, and how (to me) unnaturally patient. Nothing seemed to anger or upset him. I'd drop and break something and swear furiously; Tony would drop and break something (though he hardly ever did, being much too careful) and simply pause for a moment, looking at what he'd done, before going to get a brush and pan to clear it up. It wasn't just a case of staying calm over trivial upsets either – he was the same over important things. He once had a briefcase stolen from his car with incredibly important documents in it which he needed the next day. Did he yell and roar and go berserk? Did he hell. Turned a little pale, did a bit of hard swallowing, but there was no violent explosion of rage as there would have been with me.

At first, Tony's temperament made him the ideal person for me to live with. He balanced my constant state of near agitation and I found this so soothing. It was like having my mother with me again: he could cope with me as Charlotte had always done. But then his studied (except that it was natural) steadiness began to annoy me in ways hers never had. I wanted him to shout at me when I was being impossible, I wanted him not to be so bloody, nobly understanding. And sexually I wasn't sure I was happy with him any more. He was a good lover, if being a good lover means being both tender and passionate and always thinking of my pleasure as well as his own – what more could a woman want? – but I was no longer excited. I persuaded myself, or tried to, that this didn't matter, that sex always gets less exciting with familiarity, but I didn't really believe it. I thought there should still be some spark there whenever I saw him. If I loved him, as I thought I did, where had it gone? In its place there grew irritation with how he was, his habits.

It made me want to move away, though it was Tony who literally had to do the moving since it was my flat. I thought he never would. He didn't seem to see what had happened, how I had reached the stage of trying to be out if he was in and vice-versa. He said things like, 'We don't seem to manage to spend much time together these days,' as though it was something we both regretted instead of something I'd conspired to achieve. Then he put what he called 'my moods' down to my father's sudden death and my mother's illness, and made endless allowances. I had to be brutal and ask him to go. It was as though I'd shot him. His face drained of colour and his expression was incredulous, but he said nothing at all. He just went, with no pleading, and for that I was grateful.

But there was no doubt that the solitude I'd wanted and was so relieved to reclaim was dangerous once I came back from that Cumbrian jaunt. Rory's voice on my answerphone was surprisingly welcome and on impulse I rang him straight away, before I could think about it and wonder if I could be bothered. What I hadn't anticipated was that the moment he heard me he would say he was coming straight round and then hang up. I was so annoyed — it hadn't been what I'd wanted at all — but once he'd arrived I found myself quite glad to see him. Someone, for once, was better than no one, and Rory was better than anyone. 'You look awful,' he said, and laughed. 'So what wild adventures have you been having, cousin mine?' I made him coffee and, because there was no way I could avoid it and make any sense, I told him about the memory box, just the bare facts. He loved it. He demanded to see the eleven objects immediately and I was obliged to get them all out and line them up again, all except of course for the discarded feathers.

'What a joke,' Rory said, and I was cross and said there was nothing funny about this. 'Don't be silly,' he said, 'of course it's a joke, a laugh. You're getting everything out of proportion. For God's sake, Susannah leaves you a box of junk and it gets forgotten for thirty-odd years and then when you open it you start looking for symbolic meanings — it's stupid, you know it is, and what's wrong with you, where's the cold-eyed realist,

Catherine? Chuck the lot out. She probably didn't even know what she was doing, she was so ill.'

'She knew,' I said. 'It was all carefully done. You should have seen the wrappings. And everything was numbered and arranged. It was all thought out.'

Rory lit a cigarette, without asking permission, and studied me. 'Such misery, dearie,' he said. 'I didn't know you cared about Susannah anyway. I always thought it was great, the way you were never a tragedy queen about your *real* mother dying, the way you never brought it up or traded on it, the way you didn't go in for any poor-little-me stuff. What's happened to change that? Why is this dead woman suddenly getting to you? Have you become a born-again Christian or something? Has the Lord spoken to you about your beloved biological Mama you've denied all these years?'

'It isn't funny.'

'I know it isn't. That's what astounds me – you think it's so bloody serious when it *should* be funny. The whole thing is ridiculous. You should treat it as farce not get all worried and mournful.'

'It doesn't feel like a farce. Things left by dead people are creepy.'

'Yeah, *dead* creepy, geddit?' And he laughed, hooted.

'Don't, Rory.'

'Well, for fuck's sake.' Then he peered at me. 'Oh, come on, Cath, you're not *crying*, oh my good gawd.'

I wasn't, not really, but there were tears ready to roll if I didn't control them. I allowed Rory to give me a cuddle and then he said that we both needed something stronger than coffee, and jumped up to open a bottle of wine. When we both had a glass in hand, and I was more composed, he wandered about touching the objects that had been in the box. I hated him doing that. He is always a great toucher, a fidget, incapable of just looking at anything. He has to pick things up, turn them over, examine minutely anything he is interested in. He picked up the shell. 'Don't touch that!' I snapped, but he ignored me and put it to his ear. 'Receiving, receiving,' he chanted. 'I'm ready for the message – loud and clear – here it comes – "I am from the ssssea!" ' He laughed and took it in both hands, running his fingers critically over every bump and ridge. 'It's not such an extraordinary shell,' he said, quiet now. 'Not from any British beach, but there are plenty of these in the South Seas and even the Caribbean. I've found them there, shit loads on Anguilla when I was there.'

'Susannah never went to the Caribbean or the South Seas,' I said. 'She hardly went abroad at all. People didn't, then.'

'How do you know?'

'My dad told me.'

'But what about before she met him?'

'She met him young. She hadn't had time to go anywhere.'

'Well, maybe not. You should check with my mum. But anyway, even if she didn't go somewhere to bring back this shell for herself, someone else must have done. They gave it to her as a souvenir, that's all. It hasn't any other meaning – a pretty holiday memento she passed on to you.'

'Depends who gave it to her.'

'Now that really is looking for messages,' he protested. 'This will tire my poor little brain out. You are actually suggesting, my sweet cousin, that the point of this shell being left to you was that it was given to Susannah by someone she wanted you to track down? Don't be so silly. It-is-only-a-shell. She liked it. She hoped you would like it. End of story.'

I was suddenly sure he was right, but instead of being relieved I was disappointed. Just a shell. A shell from some part of the world to which she had never been but had always yearned to go. Maybe leaving it to me signalled her yearning, maybe she hoped I would be able to go where she had not been able to go. Well, I had. I hadn't been to the South Seas or to the Caribbean but I had travelled far and wide, as she had not, and I intended to visit many more countries. If she wanted, she could come with me in spirit and we'd find other shells like this and bring them back to join this one. I smiled to think of this sentimental fancy, and Rory, mistaking my own self-mockery for a new cheerfulness, which he credited himself with bringing about, said, 'That's better, that's a good little girlie, now.'

He picked up the mirror next. 'Nice mirror,' he said. 'Queen Anne, I think. I'll give you fifty quid for it.'

'So that means it must be worth at least two hundred pounds.'

'Cheeky.' He scrutinised the silver work on the handle and said, 'I wonder where she got it from. There's a mark here I've seen on some of my mother's silver – look, see that curly C, round the stem of the ivy? It probably belonged to our grandmother. It's probably a family heirloom and as much mine as yours.'

'It was left to me, thank you.'

'But maybe Susannah had no right to it. Anyway, you've always denied you're a Cameron. You've always boasted about being a Musgrave: all your precious dad, with nothing of Susannah and the Camerons in you.'

'Maybe, but I do have Cameron genes whether I want to acknowledge them or not.'

'And you have their mirror.'

'So? You're not suggesting Susannah stole it, I hope?'

'No. But if you don't want it I should have it.'

'Should?'

'Just teasing.' He was still holding the mirror when he sat down beside me and held it out in front of him so that it reflected both our faces. 'Remember?' he said, the teasing tone gone, 'Granny screaming, when she saw me looking in the wardrobe mirror, that she thought my reflection was Susannah?'

I remembered. We were both staying with her. Rory had just turned five so I was a bit younger. We'd been dressing up, Rory as a girl and me as a boy. He'd put on a pink, frilly frock of mine which I hated and he adored, and he had a pink ribbon holding back his blond curls. We hadn't been able to tie a bow properly in spite of laborious attempts and it hung down his back. His hair was still quite long then and very thick and he was thrilled because he made such a convincing girl. But seeing him in the mirror gave my grandmother such a fright – she nearly had a heart attack, believing him for a moment to be her own dead daughter. His likeness to Susannah as a child, already remarked on, was apparently uncanny. He had the same colouring, the same shape of face, the same eyes. My grandmother told Rory never, ever, to dress up as a girl again and give her such a shock. He took heed, but only to the extent of never letting her see him do it again. In fact, every time we were together for years and years after that the first thing we always did was dress up as the opposite sex. It went on until we were about eleven, when suddenly I was the one who refused to dress up at all and spoiled the game.

'I remember,' I said, 'but I'm sure you don't look like Susannah now, even if you dressed up as a woman.'

'Shall I?'

'No, you shall not.'

'You are so mean.' He held the mirror closer, fascinated by his own face. 'I'm sure I still do look like her.'

'No, your face is too plump.'

'*Plump*? Don't be gross.' He peered anxiously at himself and felt his cheeks. 'That's bone,' he said, 'good, strong bone structure, not fat. Plump, indeed – the idea. I've just filled out rather charmingly. And anyway, Susannah only became thin-

87

faced when she was ill. I've seen the photographs. Up to the last six months her face looked like mine does now, lovely. It's the hair makes the real difference. If I had a wig, one of those pre-Raphaelite jobs, I'd look just like her still.'

'Why would you want to?'

'Well, she was beautiful. Everyone said so.'

'But she's dead.'

He put the mirror down and turned to look at me. 'There you are,' he said, smirking, 'you've just realised. Yes, she's dead. She's been dead thirty-one years, sweetest, so why are you fretting over an old box?'

I ignored that. 'Why do you think she put a mirror in it?' I asked him.

'Oh, for Christ's sake . . .'

'Please, humour me, Rory. Please.'

'All right. Because it's valuable. And because it is a family heirloom.'

'Not because she wanted me to take a close look at myself, as she looked at herself, and see the resemblance between us, search for it?'

'Have you any whisky?'

'No.'

'More wine, then, it'll have to be more wine. You're driving me to serious over-indulgence. Stop it.'

'You over-indulge all the time, Rory. You're so unhealthy – all this smoking and drinking, and you never take any exercise.'

'I look healthier than you, dear – I haven't got great black circles under my eyes, thank you.'

'I haven't been sleeping well.'

'I'm not surprised. You're driving yourself mad. Trouble is, with Tony gone and as you don't seem to have much work on, you've got nothing else to do but brood over this wretched box. And you were all upset anyway. It came at the worst possible time.'

'I know. I'm going to go away soon. I meant to, as soon as the house was sold.'

'Where will you go?'

'Don't know yet.'

'Who with?'

'Nobody. By myself, of course.'

'I could go with you, if you like. I fancy a bit of sun.'

'I didn't say I was going somewhere sunny.'

'Then I'm not coming with you.'

'You haven't been invited. Why should I want you?'

'Because it isn't good for you to be on your own at the moment, and I'm your best friend.'

'Like hell you are.'

But he was, he is. I've never been good at friendships. I don't put enough into keeping them going. At school, I had plenty of friends but I was never really close to any of them; I didn't go in for best friend pairing off. If I wasn't on my own, I preferred a group. And then after school I didn't make the effort to keep up with anyone. Same at St Martin's. If anyone I'd been friends with there contacted me afterwards I always responded (I think), but I never made the first move myself, and people naturally notice that and get tired of it. So my only close friends came to be lovers and when affairs ended so did the close friendships, inevitably. I don't suppose, for example, that Tony will think of me now as a friend. And with my parents dead (because they were definitely friends as well as parents) that does indeed leave Rory. It was quite like old times, our bickering, and I enjoyed it. 'Come on, then, best friend,' I said, 'I'll take you out for a meal and we can do some more bonding.'

I used to wonder if my lack of interest in close friendships was because my parents were too much my friends when I was young, and then later on, when there were things happening in my life that erected a kind of barrier between us, I had

Rory. I might not see him often, and I might not always know how to reach him even, but the connection between us was so strong it could be resumed immediately. I've always felt comfortable with Rory, completely at ease. Maybe it amounts to a sort of conceit, but I think I know him in a way no one else does, or not to my knowledge. The Rory I know is not the person others see. He projects an image, quite deliberately, of someone flippant and careless, he proclaims his sexuality defiantly and even crudely, and though I have never understood why, I think I understand very well that this is a complicated challenge he's issuing. He dares people to be repelled by him, by his own stridently camp representation of himself, and when they are he imagines he's tested them and found them wanting and has nothing more to do with them. In a weird way I do much the same thing – I, too, like to project an image that tries people's patience and I'm not satisfied until they've put up with my fierceness and hostility and general surliness and still want to know me. Just as Rory can stop acting a part, so can I. But there was something else, something Tony was near to realising. I think we were attracted to each other once, Rory and I. I think that on the very brink of adolescence, when we were eleven or twelve, there was an attraction between us which I may have mistaken for love (because I certainly hadn't realised then that my cousin was gay). Nothing ever happened. It didn't go anywhere. But when I say Rory is my best and only true friend to the exclusion of all others there is that element mixed up in it.

The best thing about Rory is that I don't have to be careful, I don't have to *try* in any kind of way. He's known me all my life and I feel more comfortable with him than I ever have with any lover, which says something (though I don't quite like to wonder what exactly). Familiarity in his case hasn't bred contempt, but instead security. He knows me through and through, maybe the way a brother would have done if I'd had one. I can be rude and bad-tempered and offhand, and he isn't offended. He lets me try to reform him in all kinds of ways and doesn't hold my attempts against me, except to warn me not to try to be his mother when I push him too far. As if. My feelings about his mother, about his father too, are pretty much in agreement with his own. Hector is overbearing, humourless and disgustingly racist and homophobic; Isabella is prudish, cold and utterly self-centred. I would never try to be either of them. I don't know how such people could have produced Rory (and frankly neither do they). There is no trace of either of them in their son. Our grandmother always swore there had been a mix-up somewhere and really he was Susannah's — Isabella did not seem to find this offensive. She was always plaintively wondering aloud where Rory had come from (and in time she got some pretty crude answers from him).

'So how's Tony?' Rory asked, once we were settled in the restaurant.

'You know perfectly well I don't hear from him, so shut up.'

'Poor Anthony.'

'Oh yes? I can't think why he's thought of as "poor".'

'You were horrible to him and he loved you so.'

'I wasn't.'

'You were. Vicious and nasty.' He was laughing and making faces between mouthfuls of bread, but I knew he meant it. 'The dear man adored you and you led him on and then you dumped him. Poor Tony.'

'It wasn't like that. We were just wrong for each other in the end, that's all, and I had to say so.'

'In the beginning, more like, that's what I'd say.'

'Then you'd say wrong, Mr Smart-arse. Don't be so stupid. Why would I have had him to live with me if I couldn't stand him in the first place? You make these stupid remarks without thinking what you're saying.'

'I know what I'm saying. What I'm saying is that you knew damned well he wasn't right for you, but you were attracted to him because he was like your father and you couldn't resist him.'

'I'm not speaking to you any more. You appal me.'

'You amuse me.'

'How sick.'

'Any mention of your dad and you go all frigid and furious.'

'Anyone would if the kind of silly comments you make were made to them.'

'It wasn't a silly comment. Tony looks like your dad. So did what's-his-face, Ian thingy, the one before, and that foreign fellow before him. You only go for men who *look* like your dad and then when you find out they aren't like him, you chuck them out.'

'Did I ask for this?'

'No.'

'And you're drunk.'

Suddenly, he leaned across the table, and taking hold of my hand, even though I tried to snatch it away, he pressed it hard and spoke differently, in an embarrassingly urgent, sincere way. 'I'm not drunk,' he said, 'I'm worried about you. You're messing up your life like I've messed up mine. What are you going to do? Thirty-something, career on hold so far as I can see, no lover never mind no husband or darling kiddies, a poor little rich orphan going potty over the ridiculous contents of a box . . .'

I got up, flung some money on the table – we hadn't actually eaten anything except bread so far – and left the restaurant.

Chapter Six

I WAS used to thinking I never wanted to see Rory again. We were always having these scenes, one or the other of us storming off, one or the other of us feeling smug because we thought we'd come up with some searing home truth. What made me so furious that night was that what Rory had said, about both of us wasting our lives, was *not* true. How dared he make me out to be a sad cow, as hopeless as himself? It was unfair, a lie. I was a professional photographer, with work to prove it, and what was he? Nothing. A dealer in this and that. No wonder his parents despaired. I hated to think I agreed with them in any way, but when it came to considering Rory's lack of career or respectable employment I was bound to. He had, like me, had such a good start in life, he had no excuse.

Next morning I woke feeling ashamed of myself. There was, after all, some substance in Rory's summary of my situation, even if he hadn't got it right in every particular. Hadn't I admitted to myself I was in the doldrums, tired of the way I was living, with my lack of enthusiasm for anything? It was the manner in which he said it that so angered me, the way he lumped me with himself, when our cases were quite different. And the stuff about my father and how I was attracted to those men who looked like him was true. I'd realised it myself, even if I liked to think the men never had. It's common enough, for heaven's sake, a cliché, girls wanting to love their fathers, but I'd resented all the rest Rory had come out with. I might have been attracted to Tony, and the others, because of their physical similarity to my father, but I never for one moment thought they were actually like him, so there was no disillusionment. I knew from the moment I met him that Tony, for example, was quite unlike my father. Tony is a very solemn person, very serious, whereas my father rarely had a smile off his cheerful face. And Tony didn't talk much, whereas my father was a great chatterer – his idea of hell was being stuck in a railway carriage with someone who wouldn't talk to him. Tony would've been that someone, buried in a book and not wanting to be disturbed.

It hurt that Rory hadn't seen how much I had thought I loved Tony, that he'd had the nerve to imagine my relationships were anything like his shallow, sexual encounters. Rory didn't seem to have loved anyone, ever. It was nothing to do with his being gay; it was to do with being Rory – selfish, reluctant to commit himself to anything or anyone at all, greedy for what he was given and offering little or nothing in return. But I knew I was wrong to say to him, as I had often done, that he had no excuse. He did have an excuse, or at least there were extenuating circumstances to explain his attitudes. His parents had been good parents only in the purely material-istic sense, looking after his physical welfare faultlessly, clothing and feeding and housing and educating him to the highest standard. But emotionally they'd failed him. Rory says he always knew he was gay (though I don't quite believe him) and by the time he was seventeen he had told them so. It was a brave thing to do, especially with parents like his. They'd not only been disgusted, they'd absolutely refused to believe he knew what he was saying. He'd been reading suggestive books, seeing suggestive films, mixing with the wrong sort. In a marvellously contradictory statement they told him at one and the same time he was wrong, and that he would grow out of it, and never to come to them again talking such nonsense. He never did.

I'd been Rory's champion then, outraged at my uncle and aunt on his behalf, but gradually I'd come to acknowledge that not everything about Rory's instability could be blamed on their rejection of his sexual nature. They'd made him suffer, by denying he could feel as he felt and trying to force him into the mould they wanted, but he hadn't helped himself. Everything he did from adolescence onwards looked like defiance: 'Look at me, see how bad I can be!' It was childish and went on being childish long after he was an adult. He said his parents didn't love him and never had (though I never thought that last bit true) and then he seemed determined to make sure no one else would be allowed to. It didn't make him happy, even though his nature was to be light-hearted and pleasure-loving. Underneath, and not so very far underneath, all the prattle there was a wistfulness for something more meaningful. Or so I thought.

At any rate, I never stayed angry with him for long. I rang him up that day and got his answerphone, upon which I left a sharp message telling him he was an absolute pain but that if he wanted to come with me wherever I was going – not that I knew where that would be – he could and I'd pay providing he didn't come out with any more rubbish, any more of his wonky psychobabble. I felt better the moment I'd done it. He'd been right about another thing. Being on my own wasn't, for once, the best thing for me. Whatever else, Rory had succeeded in making me think of Susannah's box in a more rational way. I didn't feel so challenged any more and was prepared to accept, if I had to in the end, the possible insignificance of its contents.

But not without more effort to find the opposite. I had the urgent need to get away, and soon, and, without any job on at that moment to guide me, I had to decide myself where to go. It was almost November, the weather was turning cold, the nights drawing in, so it made sense to indulge Rory by going to the sun somewhere. Sun, blazing sun, is not good for my kind of photography, but then I wouldn't be choosing the destination for that reason. I thought about Africa – Malawi or Mozambique maybe – but the thought of all the inoculations I'd need and the anti-malaria precautions put me off. Still turning over various possibilities in my mind, I went to pack. It didn't much matter where I was going to go, I always took almost the same things, give or take a jacket or two. I often packed before I knew where I was going, sometimes as a sign of intent to myself – packed, I had to go, no dithering allowed. So I went to my bedroom and started selecting light trousers and shorts and several loose cotton shirts and a sweater and so on, and rolling them all up to shove in a bag, the sort that could go with me on any airline as hand luggage. Pulling stuff out of a drawer, I saw the address book I'd put back there after Rory had finished looking at everything.

I hadn't studied it thoroughly before, and Rory himself had hardly glanced at it. Picking it up again, it struck me how worn it was, which I hadn't noticed. The pattern, the peacock feather pattern on the cover, was quite faded in parts, as though the book had been left out in the sun often. She must have taken it with her wherever she went. This puzzled me all over again. Susannah hadn't been able to travel much, but maybe my father hadn't known where she'd managed to go before she met him. What about her earlier student years? She hadn't met him until their final year. I ran my finger down the index and saw several letters of the alphabet seemed to be missing. The 'L', the 'P', the 'Q' and the 'R' were all torn off. I looked at those pages first. There were no entries at all written on them. So why tear the letters off? I felt that rising irritation I'd felt before, a sort of agitation, because I might be making something out of nothing but I couldn't know if it *was* nothing, if things like torn-off letters *were* meaningless. The book was old. Paper can be fragile. Tiny letters get bent and torn and come off an index such as this.

Trying to control myself, to stop being on the lookout for signs, I turned to 'E'. No names, of course, as I'd observed before, but there was no mystery here. The Edinburgh addresses here were known to me. One was Rory's parents', one my grandmother's, one some Cameron relatives I remembered visiting even though I couldn't remember their names. So she did put in personal addresses and not just hotels, as I'd first deduced. 'W' had my father's old home address in it, so this book had still been in use when she met him. 'V' had an hotel in Venice which I knew of, and also another in Vienna, a city I hadn't visited. Did she think I would trail round all these places in her wake, thirty years on? Surely not. This address book seemed to serve only as a record of all the places she'd visited. The places, not the people, were important. It was a diary of place, of memories in the form of places. How odd. Was she trying to show me once more that contrary to anything I might have been told she hadn't always been an invalid, that once she had had energy and strength and had been around? Was she afraid I'd have the wrong fixed image of her?

She hadn't been far, though. Flicking through the book, I could see she hadn't been out of Europe. Except there was one place name I didn't recognise — Bequia. It sounded middle-Eastern, or perhaps African, but I'd never heard of it. No hotel was written above it. The entry just said 'The Cabin, Friendship Bay'. I didn't think an hotel would call itself a cabin. But 'cabin' didn't sound European. It sounded American or Canadian, but she'd never been across the Atlantic so far as I knew. I got out my old atlas, bought for me years ago by my father, and looked up Bequia in the detailed index.

97

It wasn't listed. No Bequia. There was a Beqaot in Jordan, and a Beqoa in Israel, but no Bequia. Intrigued by then, and praying it didn't turn out to be some obscure town in the Balkans, I rang the travel agent I always used. She had no problem with Bequia. 'It's in the Grenadines,' she said. 'Bequia', pronouncing it Beck-wee, 'is a lovely little island, one of the prettiest in the Caribbean.'

It couldn't be. Susannah had never been to the Caribbean. I knew that for a fact. But did I? With my studied lack of interest in her history, I had never grilled my grandmother or my aunt about her early life. They had wanted to tell me but I hadn't wanted to listen. Though I was sure that if I had been told tales of her going off to the Caribbean in her youth, that would have registered. She hadn't had any money, so how could she have gone so far, especially in the Fifties? All these European cities in her address book, and there were not so very many, must have been visited by her when she went hitch-hiking with girlfriends. I'd heard about that, had it shoved down my throat that Susannah had had to work as a waitress to pay for *her* holidays, whereas I was spoiled. It was one of my Aunt Isabella's running themes – Rory and I had never had to slog our guts out to travel abroad as she and Susannah had. Too true. But Isabella had never mentioned a trip to the Caribbean and I was convinced it would have been too big a thing not to be mentioned. I was suddenly excited, sensing at last a real mystery here for me to solve. Forget seagull feathers and rucksacks – this would surely yield more, this little entry in a battered address book.

But then I cautioned myself. This address book was old. The Bequia address had been written down something like thirty-five years ago, maybe more. The trail (I couldn't help thinking in such schoolgirl terms), if trail there was, was cold. If I was going to go off to this island it was no good expecting to find anything at all. I could use the address as an excuse to go there, but nothing more. Well, I thought that quite satisfactory. I wanted to go somewhere sunny and I'd never been to the Caribbean — frankly, it had a poor image in my mind, one of vulgar, flashy beach resorts and a lot of calypso singing. I didn't even need to tell Rory why I'd fixed on Bequia, I could say my travel agent recommended it, he wouldn't care.

The atlas had the Grenadines all right. I was surprised and pleased to see they were so far south, almost off the coast of Venezuela, and nowhere near either Jamaica or Barbados (about which I knew next to nothing, but where my notions about the Caribbean came from). I went straight out and on my way to the travel agents stopped and bought a guidebook. The guide said Bequia was only seven miles long but that this made it the largest island in the Grenadines. It had quiet lagoons, good reefs and long stretches of nearly deserted beaches. A large percentage of the inhabitants were of Scottish descent (did that mean Susannah had known someone there?). There was one village, Port Elizabeth, on a bay known for its safe anchorage. This bay had been a haven for pirates in the seventeenth century, among them Captain Kidd. Rory would be ecstatic.

He was. He came over again that evening, the unpleasantness of the night before forgotten, and we were both almost hopping up and down at the thought of jetting off to the West Indies ('Don't say Caribbean,' Rory pleaded). It hadn't been as simple to arrange as I'd hoped, which was annoying — I wanted to go there and then, without delay. We were going to have to wait two whole days before we could get a plane to Barbados, from where we could get a much smaller plane to Bequia. I said I'd meet Rory at Heathrow and he went off immensely pleased with himself to pack, under strict instructions to make sure he had only hand luggage. I knew Rory. Unlike me, for him holidays meant clothes, absurd amounts of them, and that meant a proper case which would have to go in the hold and slow us up horribly on every arrival. Once he'd gone, I rang Isabella. It seemed only logical. My father was dead, and might never in any case have known where Susannah had been before he met her, and so was my grandmother, who certainly would have done. That only left her sister, Isabella. It was worth a try.

I always felt uncomfortable whenever I rang my aunt, or even when she rang me. Both were rare occurrences, and usually happened because one of us had some specific news. Either that, or it was New Year greetings or Happy Birthdays. Isabella was scrupulous about both. She always rang me on 1 January and on 12 June, my birthday. I'd thank her and we'd have a few minutes' strained chat before hanging up. The last time I'd rung her it was to tell her Charlotte had died. She wasn't close to my mother, and had always resented the fact that I insisted she *was* my mother, referring to her as 'your stepmother' whenever she mentioned her, but still, I felt I had to let her know as well as Charlotte's own family. She was surprisingly sympathetic and told me I was welcome to come and stay with her any time in Edinburgh. 'Treat our house as your home now,' she urged, and actually sounded as if she meant it, though she must have known I'd never put her to the test. She didn't come to the funeral, but then I'd said there was no need to. Plenty of Charlotte's family were there and she would have been swamped by them and I'd have felt responsible for her. Rory himself looked lost among all the Fraser cousins, but it was his presence that meant most to me. I'd so lost touch with the Fraser tribe, whom I'd once adored, that I hardly knew how to talk to them. Fortunately, my silence was put down to grief, which was genuine enough.

So I rang Isabella and told her I just thought I'd let her know I was going away for two or three weeks, maybe a bit longer. She was pleased, said it would do me good, I'd had a rough time and she'd been wondering how I was recovering.

She asked where I was going, somewhere nice and sunny she hoped, and when I said Bequia, she gave no sign of recognition, just expressed a vague interest without seeming to connect this unusual destination in any way to the dead Susannah. I let her ramble on a bit, about my taking care to use a good quality sun-screen cream, and then I mentioned I had an old address book of Susannah's which listed a cabin in Bequia. She was silent a moment, and then said, 'Does it? Where is that exactly? Is it America? She had a vac job in America once, I remember that.' I said no, Bequia was an island, one of the Grenadines, and gave her the description the guidebook had given me, the bit about the safe harbour and so forth. There was another, longer pause, into which I read either confusion or some struggle to remember. 'Aunt Isabella?' I prompted. 'Did Susannah go there, then, can you remember?' 'All I recall', Isabella said, 'was that she went sailing, her first year at university. I never knew who with – some well-to-do person she got in with, some gang she was invited to join. But I thought they sailed round Scotland. I can't believe they went that far, never.' Trying to sound very sensible and not at all excited, I pressed on. 'But she would have told you afterwards, wouldn't she? Wouldn't she have been full of it, if she did something so daring?' A sigh came down the line. 'She'd have told my mother, but we weren't good friends at that time.' A famous feud between the sisters had been hinted at by my grandmother, but I decided it would not be diplomatic to pursue this. And now that I'd been given every encouragement to believe Susannah might have gone to Bequia – well, I convinced myself I had – Isabella had served her purpose. We moved on to Rory. She always used phone calls, whatever they were ostensibly about, to enquire if I knew how her son was. He almost never called her and she rarely knew where he was to call him (not that she would necessarily have done so). I said he was well, and coming with me, I was treating him. She loved the idea – for once, she would be able to visualise him safely in my company and not in that of the decadent crowd she imagined he spent his time among.

I didn't tell Rory, when we met up at Heathrow early in the morning, that I'd rung his mother. There was no point in starting our jaunt off in the wrong mood and any mention of either of his parents invariably made him sullen and irritable. He was in great form, looking very smooth in brand-new white chino cotton trousers and black T-shirt, quite the male model as I immediately said, with a sneer of course, and he'd obeyed instructions about hand luggage only. He had always been a congenial travelling companion, very relaxed, very keen on observing other people, just as I was. I knew we looked like a couple, which is no bad thing if you are a woman. It prevents any hassling from lecherous men, and stops people of either sex latching on to you because you're alone. I could have done with Rory on many of my trips and quite liked his being taken for my lover. Nobody could possibly guess that we were related. So convincing was our partnership that we had sometimes registered as a married couple, if we needed to in more staid establishments, and very often shared a room and even a bed when travelling. I don't like sharing a bed with anyone, but if I have to, Rory is perfectly acceptable. He's a peaceful sleeper, no tossing and turning or snoring.

I'd made it plain, that evening he came round, that he was going to have to behave himself. Twice, on previous excursions together, when I was not paying for him and had no hold over him, he'd behaved outrageously and I hadn't forgotten. Once I'd had to bail him out of jail – and the other time collect him from hospital, where he'd had to have stitches for a deep cut over his eye. The anxiety he caused me that second time had been enough to make me swear I would never go anywhere with him again, and up to then I never had. I'd made it clear that if he didn't take my warnings seriously I'd ditch him and cancel his ticket home. He'd said he didn't know what all the fuss was about – he'd been young and stupid the last time we'd travelled and now he was old . . . well, older, and very, very wise. He was going for the sun and the adventure and the pleasure of my wonderful company and he would neither get drunk nor indulge in sexual encounters. He said he'd given up sex, just like me. I said I hadn't given it up, what a ridiculous idea. 'Well,' he beamed, 'let's just say we're both resting, darling.'

We flew Club Class, a hideous extravagance. Rory was delighted. 'Oh,' he murmured as we went into the Club Class lounge and sank into the deep armchairs with a drink in hand, 'I've always wanted to be a little rich boy and leave all the riff-raff behind.' I laughed, but thought how my parents would have disapproved. They were well off but never travelled Club Class or stayed in expensive hotels. They had none of Rory's taste for luxury and up to then neither had I. In fact, I'd prided myself on always travelling the cheapest way possible and had endured many a long haul cramped in Economy when I could have afforded better. I had never wanted to *seem* rich and my parents were pleased about this, feeling, I expect, that their example was being followed, their standards upheld in this respect at least. But now I was done with all that. I had decided it was a silly sort of self-denial when I had the funds to fly in comfort. It was spoiling Rory, though, to include him. I should have made him travel Economy. It slightly annoyed me that he took Club Class as his due, betraying no sign whatsoever of any embarrassment at my abundant generosity.

'Why aren't you telling me this is too good of me?' I asked him, only half jocularly, as we boarded the plane and were shown to our luxurious seats.

'You can't be too good,' he said, smartly. 'I'm worth the best.'

'Don't push it, Rory,' I said.

'Oh come on,' he said, 'don't be petty. You know I know you're loaded now.'

'So that makes it all right, does it?'

'Don't you think so? I mean, if you'd scrimped and saved . . .'

'Then you'd insist on going Economy?'

'No, but . . .'

'But what?'

'But I'd be ever so humble and grateful. I'd get down on my knees' – and he got down on them there and then and I could see the other passengers thought he must be doing something terribly romantic such as proposing – 'and kiss the hem of your jeans and show you the hair shirt I was wearing and refuse all wine and food, and . . .'

'Oh, stop it, you idiot,' I said, slapping him none too gently.

He is such a taker. I am not. I don't like taking from anyone. I'd rather be a giver, though not for any worthy reason. It's about control, obviously. If I give, I control; if I take, I am controlled. If someone offers me something for free I am at once suspicious. Rory never is. The more people have wanted to give him the happier he has been to take, and their motives have troubled him not at all. Nor has he ever worried about having to give something back in return. 'No such thing as a free lunch' is a saying which mystifies Rory. Of course there are free lunches, he's spent his whole life trading on them and so far has never recognised any obligation to pay them back. He has become notorious for never returning hospitality and when I have tackled him about this meanness he has defended himself on the grounds that he is a charming guest who sings beautifully for any supper he is given. Such confidence.

Rory slept most of the way across the Atlantic, even though

it was a daytime flight, but I didn't. I sat with Susannah's red hat on my knee, thinking about her. I hadn't worn the hat to travel in, just held it in my hand. Rory had noticed, of course, but had said nothing. He could have pointed out with justification that it wasn't a very suitable hat either to take on this kind of holiday or to match what I was wearing (jeans, a sweater). But he didn't, maybe thinking any reference to it would result in another lot of boring ruminations about the box, and I was grateful. The hat felt comforting to hold. The velvety material was so soft, as I turned it round and round, and I began to think of Susannah wearing it. She certainly wouldn't have worn it when, as I was determined to believe, she'd sailed to the West Indies. This was a city hat, a Seventies hat, I was sure, worn with a long ethnic skirt and a lot of beads. And yet I'd chosen to bring it with me now. I hadn't planned to. I'd looked round my sitting-room before I left it, a last look to check windows were closed, and it had caught my eye, perched so attractively on the glass head, and I'd snatched it off on a sudden impulse.

I wondered who she'd been with when she went, in whatever way she did go, to Bequia. With a man? Several men and women? I tried to think of the people outside her family whom I'd heard mentioned as her friends. There was a Gillian who'd lived next door in Edinburgh. I'd had her pointed out to me by my grandmother when she'd insisted on showing me photographs of Susannah and Isabella as little girls. 'I wonder whatever happened to Gillian,' my grandmother would say, which seemed to suggest the friendship hadn't survived. Then there was Lorna. She'd been at university with Susannah and was her bridesmaid, together with Isabella, when she married my father. Lorna, I knew, had been a real friend right up to the end. I'd met her, at my grandmother's, when I was about six and I'd been uncomfortable while she held me on her knee and reminisced about this dead woman who was supposed to have been my mother. I think she was disappointed at my total lack of interest, as she was bound to be, but she went on sending me birthday and Christmas presents right up to when I was eighteen. Lorna, I was sure, would still be very much alive. I didn't have an address for her, though I knew she'd emigrated to Australia, but I was fairly certain I could track her down. Lorna would know, surely, about this Bequia jaunt. She might even have been on it herself, though my memory of her, a child's vague impression, was that she was too sensible to go off on what must have seemed a wildly adventurous trip across the Atlantic.

There must have been a man, or men, involved. I suspected a crew of women only wouldn't have sailed so far in the Fifties. And who had the money to finance the voyage? There must have been someone with money, and I felt it more likely to have been a man. A man with a rich daddy who let him have his yacht. Susannah could sail, though, I knew that. She'd learned as a child with her uncle, who'd taken her round the Scottish islands, her and my grandmother and Isabella. My grandmother told me she and Isabella hated it, but Susannah loved it and went again. Maybe she crewed for some rich young undergraduate. Or maybe not. Maybe he was a boyfriend, even a lover, someone she knew before my father, and she didn't have to contribute to the cost. But wouldn't Isabella have known afterwards, even if they weren't the best of sisterly friends at the time? Or had my aunt been concealing something?

My head began to ache with the strain of trying to concoct some reasonable scenario and I envied Rory, who slept blissfully on at my side. I reminded myself that Susannah might never have been to Bequia. An address in a book didn't prove it. There was no real evidence that Susannah had been where I was now going, and I had repeated this over and over to myself since deciding to book the flights, but suddenly, halfway across the Atlantic, I began to blame her for leading me on. Why couldn't she have left me alone, or been clearer? What would have been wrong with a little note stuck in the address book – 'Dear Catherine' (no, it would have been 'Dear Hope') – 'I kept this little book because these are all the places I had holidays in and maybe some day you'll visit them and think of me. I loved Bequia, in the West Indies, best. It was so thrilling sailing there – yes, sailing – with . . ' What was the point of being so enigmatic? I felt like waking Rory up and yelling at him and only just stopped myself. But the old anger I'd originally felt about the memory box resurfaced and I became so agitated I had to walk up and down for a while in the narrow confines of the aeroplane. A stewardess asked if I was all right and, shamed, I sat down again.

I put the red hat on, and the dark blindfold provided by the airline, and tried to lull myself to sleep. I must live in the present. It was the only way, but controlling my urge to leap ahead into the future, or speculate about the past, and never live in the present, was almost impossible. Tony had complained about this all the time. He'd found it so wearing, the way I endlessly anticipated what was going to happen or fantasised over what already might have happened – he said it was imagination gone mad. But the present had never seemed a real place to me. It was useless, dull. Everything exciting lay in the unknown, the future, where anything was possible. Susannah knew that. The future was where she had wanted to be, with me. My head seemed to grow hot and I felt the perspiration standing out on my forehead, but I couldn't take the red hat off. Its soft crown covered my hair as it had covered hers, the material caressing my head as it had caressed hers, little messages of memory breathing through the fabric to me. My eyes behind the blindfold were tightly closed, but I began to see her in this hat, smiling, holding her hands out, and slowly I began to lift my own, only to drop them as Rory said in my ear, 'Are you practising yoga, or what?'

I took the wretched hat off and scrunched it into a ball and thrust it into the flap of the seat in front of me. It could stay there, I didn't want it. Rory, wide awake now, said, 'Temper, temper,' and I told him to shut up. 'It suited you,' he said, 'you should wear hats.' I told him I had always hated hats, that I hated them now, and would always hate them. 'Well, goodbye red hat, then,' he said, lightly, but he squeezed my hand affectionately, knowing how I always got going with my strings of hates − hate this, hate that − when I was particularly miserable and upset. We ate yet another meal, drank yet more wine, and after that I surprised myself by really sleeping until we were about to land in Barbados. The next four hours were hellish. The LIAT plane which was supposed to take us on to Bequia was delayed with engine trouble and we had to wait in a hot and crowded airport until another was found. We ended up flying in a chartered plane so small it took only six people, including the pilot, and it was fortunate we had only hand luggage, because the minute hold and the other three seats were taken up with goods being transported to the island. The noise was awful, the claustrophobia acute. We seemed to fly so slowly over the open sea, and not all that high above it, only very occasionally passing over land, over islands that were mere dots of rock surrounded by rings of white foam. I looked down and tried to imagine a yacht slipping through these blue-green waters and wished I had thought to enquire if we, too, could actually have sailed rather than flown this last stretch of the way. And then the pilot gestured and shouted over the roar of the engine and we saw Bequia ahead and a landing strip improbably short. 'Here we go!' he shouted, and I closed my eyes.

Chapter Seven

IT was the quietest airport I had ever known. One uniformed
woman was on duty and that was all. She checked our
passports and waved us on through the completely empty
building, quite a sizable building too, not a shack but newly
built of modern materials. Outside, there were no taxis or
buses, nor any clue as to how to get ourselves from here to
wherever on the island we were going (but where was that?).
We saw a narrow road, leading up a hillside that rose above
the sea, but there was no one and nothing travelling along it,
and no sign saying where it went. 'Bliss,' Rory said, and sat
down, his back against the wall, his face lifted to the sun.
Typical. He waited contentedly for me to take charge. And I
did. I'd seen a telephone inside and went back to the one
official to ask if I could use it. She said yes. I went to see if
there were any cards pinned up beside it by taxi firms or
hotels, as there usually are, but there were none. It wouldn't
have been much use if there had been because I discovered
the phone was broken. I went back to the woman and said
so and she agreed. I asked if she knew how we could get
transport, and she said, 'Where you goin'?' 'The town,' I said.
'No town here,' she said.

But there was a village, a thriving village, all strung out
round Port Elizabeth bay when we found it. We walked. It
took over an hour, nearer two, but it was a beautiful walk
over the spine of the island with spectacular views of the bay
from the top. The road was good and it was empty for the

first couple of miles except for others walking. All along the way it was like walking through a garden, with brilliantly coloured foliage and flowers cascading down the banks on to the road, and to the right we saw the hillside dropping away to a long, curved beach, in terraces of greenery. From the highest point on the road we could see the sea on both sides, calm and blue on one, choppy and dark green on the other. Rory moaned a bit about the weight of his bag and the soreness of his feet, but even he was struck by the loveliness all around us and the lack of man-made horrors. We passed hardly any houses and those we did pass were low and painted white and half-hidden by every species of climbing plant.

It was downhill from the halfway mark and an even better road, wider, twisting and turning gracefully to Port Elizabeth. There was only one street, running along the waterfront, the sea coming right up to the boards alongside it. The houses were brightly painted and decorated in yellows and reds and greens, all higgledy-piggledy jammed together with only a sombre bank interrupting the colour. There was a huge ship moored next to the long pier sticking out into the bay and we saw scores of small boats cramming the sea beyond it. The bay was clearly a haven for yachts, its arms enfolding them so completely there was no swell on the sea. We had no idea where to go but there were several cafés along the seafront, so we went into one and asked for bed-and-breakfast places and were directed to the very end of the street, to a little wooden house painted green with white shutters, its crenellated top a startling purple.

This is where we stayed a whole month, in one room looking out over the harbour. We shared a large wooden bed, perfectly big enough to stick pillows down the middle and never knock into them, and not much else. There was no chair, no cupboard, nothing else to share. But we did have our own slot of a bathroom with a shower that spurted cold water erratically, and a lavatory. So we were lucky. It suited us fine. We were hardly in it, except for a few hours at night. It was an outdoor life from the moment we woke up and went to have breakfast next door, sitting looking out at the boats and often sharing a table with the yachties. These came in all sizes and nationalities, coming in to shore in their dinghies, buying supplies, treating themselves to a drink, and then going back. Was this what Susannah and her friends had done? I thought the place could hardly have changed and that what I was seeing would be what she had seen and where I sat might very well be where she had sat. I only hoped she felt as fit and well and relaxed as I soon did.

But even if she sailed here, the address in the book had named a cabin and another bay, so once she'd arrived she hadn't stayed on the boat. Was she ill? What was she doing, with a heart complaint, going off on such a voyage? What had my grandmother said? But maybe that was the point, to prove to herself she could do it and had got over her childhood poor health. There were lots of certificates showing a certain kind of sporting prowess among the memorabilia my grandmother had saved for me and used to insist I looked at. It was obvious that though she didn't go in for contact or team sports (I was glad, I remember, that she didn't seem to have played hockey, which I loved and was good at) she had done well at anything not quite so physically demanding. She swam, she played golf, she could ride well. She obviously chose to defy medical opinion and scare her mother, and for a while she had succeeded. Was Bequia the high spot of her good health? Maybe she felt so strong, in this glorious climate, that she'd stayed on; maybe the others had sailed on but she'd stayed behind, in this cabin place. Alone? I didn't think so. And not for long. She'd never missed a year at university, so whenever she had come she would only have had three months, four at a pinch.

But I'd promised myself not to be obsessed by Susannah, only thank her for bringing me here. It was just what I needed. Rory and I spent our time walking – more like ambling – to other beaches, or taking little water taxis to them. There were beach bars on a couple of them where fish was cooked every day, the morning's catch, and we sat for hours eating and drinking, then lay on the sand and slept. I didn't even take photographs the first week, though I was never parted from my camera. At the end of the second week, I managed to hire a car, more like a small truck, open at the back, and we rode round the rest of the island as far as roads would permit, which wasn't far. There were few tarmac roads and they soon ran out. It was when they ran out and we carried on along dirt tracks, until these became impossible, that Bequia was at its most mysterious. On the far side of the island from where we were staying, the road ended at a beach, heavily shaded by trees, where a fisherman had established a sort of hospital for turtles. He took the baby turtles as soon as they had hatched and cared for them until they were big enough to fend for themselves, then he returned them to the sea. We talked to him, and he let me take photographs and I got some unusual shots which I knew would come out perfectly.

We spent the day there, on the Atlantic side of the island, Rory as content as I was, and strangely silent. He pointed out what I'd been thinking myself – how like parts of Scotland the scene before us seemed. Parts of Arran, parts of Skye had looked like this when we went on holiday there as children. Neither of us knew the names of the trees we were now looking at, but we knew they were not palms or coconut trees, nor trees associated in our minds with the West Indies. They looked more like fir trees. The grass was long and rough here, growing thickly between outcrops of rock, and, though there were no mountains behind us, the land rose gradually to the north and had a rugged look. The sea broke quite violently along the headland and we watched the waves crash on the rocks and thought about shipwrecks. We used to play at being shipwrecked as all children do, given the chance, given the right setting, only we played it not wanting to be rescued – our game never ended with 'Ship ahoy!' It was the being-resourceful part we liked, trying to build a shelter and find provisions.

We returned again and again to that place, drawn by the isolation and the curious sense of familiarity. 'I could be a good person here,' Rory said one day and, though I laughed, knowing any 'goodness' wouldn't last long, and how bored he would become put to the test, I knew what he meant. Rory's problem is one of temptation. He succumbs so easily, and here there would be nothing to tempt or provoke him, not, at least, until he turned away from it and, inevitably, went in search of what it lacked. He never mentioned going back to London and neither did I, but I thought about it. I thought about my turtle photographs and about developing and printing and selling them to a magazine. I felt I was going to be proud of them and I realised I wanted them to be seen. It was a very long time since I'd felt anything of the sort and the pleasure of it, of some interest in my work, warmed me as much as the sun did. I wished Rory had something to cheer him. All he would go back to would be more of the same, not a single satisfying thing about it. But I wasn't going to act the concerned mother, though the opportunity was there.

I felt that here, if anywhere on the island, there must be the cabin to which Susannah had referred, but there was no sign of one. I asked the fisherman and he pointed to a wooden house set back from the beach and named a couple of others not far away, but none were called cabins nor ever had been as far as he knew. I asked people all the time, in cafés and bars and on the water taxis, but, though some knew of several cabins, none knew of any called *The* Cabin, which served as an hotel or similar. I always took care to enquire when Rory was out of earshot, feeling some odd need to be secretive, and one day, when he'd gone off to buy us bread and fruit, I managed to get our landlady to myself so that I could ask her in detail about where I might start looking for a cabin that had been there thirty or forty years ago and had taken in guests. At first she said she'd no idea, she'd only come from St Vincent herself ten years before, but then she gave me my first bit of help. There was a woman called Gracie Monroe, an elderly Scottish woman who lived at the top of the island and had done for as long as anyone could now remember. She might know of this cabin, and if she didn't then nobody would. I asked for this woman's telephone number but she had no telephone and, as for address, it was simply 'Miss Gracie's' and I'd have no difficulty finding it — all I had to do was follow the road to the top of the island and I'd see her house, just the one house there, all by itself.

I don't like calling on people unannounced, just as I don't like being called upon, but there was no alternative. By that time, Rory and I were often separating and spending a few hours on our own (God knows what he was up to — I didn't ask), so there was no problem about that, but in fact I almost asked him to come with me. He loved door-stepping and would be in his element and useful to me. But then I thought I had a better chance of establishing some rapport with an elderly woman if I were on my own — two women together sort of thing. So I went alone, following the road as instructed until it turned into a track and then stopped abruptly at a gate. The gate was flimsy, not much of a barrier at all, but as I got out of the car a huge dog came hurtling towards it, barking furiously. My landlady had said nothing about a fierce dog. She'd said Miss Gracie loved all visitors, that she was crippled with arthritis and loved company because she could no longer get about. I stood by the gate and waited. The dog stopped barking and, putting its paws on the top of the gate, wagged its tail. But I was not reassured enough to try to get past it and went on standing there, uncertain what to do. At last, after several minutes of the dog and me practically eyeball to eyeball, I saw a young black woman coming slowly down a path which I could see led from the gate to a flower-covered stone house some distance away. She was wearing a red dress, the colour of the hibiscus on either side of her, and she was singing.

She patted the dog, and without speaking to me opened the gate. 'You come see Miss Gracie?' she asked, smiling and gesturing that I should follow her. I said yes, I had, and was it convenient to call now, uninvited? 'She always glad to have a visitor,' the woman said. 'She lonely now, she don't walk far, she eyes poor, she don't read much.' We walked at a very leisurely pace back to the house, my companion resuming her singing and swaying a little as she walked. I had to try hard to walk slowly enough not to get ahead of her. The dog bounded along and I saw another, smaller dog come out to meet it. I tried to make conversation but the singing continued and I gave up. Turning a slight bend, we approached the house from a different angle than the one I had seen from the gate, coming towards a terrace facing towards the Atlantic side of the island. At the top of it was a flight of wide, shallow stone steps out of which, all along the rims, grew masses of tiny purple flowers. There was an air not of neglect but of abundance only just controlled about the whole garden, a feeling that at any moment nature would explode and reclaim steps and house and paths, and go back to how it had once been before man had interfered.

On the terrace there was a white basket chair, in which sat

an old lady with her feet up on a broad stool covered with a cushion.

'That's Miss Gracie,' the young woman said, and then raising her voice she called, 'Miss Gracie! A lady visitor from England for you! Come see you now!'

I hadn't said I was from England, but I suppose this did not take much deducing. Miss Gracie's eyes had been closed as we approached, but now they opened and she smiled and said, rather disconcertingly, 'About time, about time. Sit yourself down, here, close by, or I won't hear a thing.' Her accent was unmistakably Scottish and what's more it was an Edinburgh accent, with what Scots call a 'pan-loaf' sound to it (meaning posh, or cultured, a pan-loaf being a superior kind of bread). So I sat where she indicated, on a stool at her left side, and said, 'Good afternoon,' and gave her my name, and told her my family was from Edinburgh, that they were Camerons on my mother's side. (It was the first time I'd ever referred to Susannah as my mother and even as I said this I resisted the words.)

'It's a wee while since I was in Edinburgh,' she said, 'but I mind it well, oh I do, I was born and bred there.'

Her breathing seemed laboured, and I wondered if she was going to be up to much talking at all and whether I would exhaust her if I tried to get answers to the questions I wanted to ask, but she seemed eager enough, and her eyes, if as poor-sighted as her maid had said, were nevertheless bright with intelligence and curiosity.

She observed me closely, looking me over quite deliberately, taking in my camera case (though she could not know what was in my ordinary-looking canvas bag), and her glance flick-ering over my hands several times. Was she looking for a ring, a wedding ring, I wondered? She asked me if I liked Bequia and I enthused, and the maid brought out a jug of lemonade and she urged me to have a glass of it. 'You must drink plenty here,' she said, 'in the heat, you know, and not the hard stuff either,' and she laughed. We both drank, and then she asked me some obvious, polite questions – was I by myself, was I staying long, where was I staying – and I let her finish before venturing any of my own. I asked her first how she came to live on Bequia, and she sighed and said it was a long story and she hadn't the energy to go over it all but that she'd come out here to get married and the man she was engaged to, whom she'd come out to join, had died before they could marry. She'd been ill with the grief and shock and then when she was well enough to go home again she found she hadn't the heart to return. 'There was nothing calling me back,' she said. 'I had no family left there. I thought I might as well stay in the sunshine, near Douglas, for a while, anyway.' The 'while' had grown and she never had gone back, not even for a visit. 'I had the means to stay, or it might have been different,' she said. 'Douglas had provided for me before he was taken. He took no chances. And the folk here were awful kind, they took to me.' She'd started a little school – she was a schoolteacher, Douglas a clergyman – to occupy her, and to bring her into contact with children because she would never have any of her own and she loved them. 'And here I still am,' she said, smiling.

All this had taken a long time to tell, with many pauses and sips of lemonade, and I thought she might need to rest, even to sleep, but almost as soon as she had finished she said, 'Now tell me about yourself, I'm wanting to know everything.' But I didn't know how to begin. I'd practised in my head what I would say, how I would lead on to Susannah and the address book, but I stumbled as I began to tell my tale and all fluency deserted me. I started again, but realised I'd oversimplified the story and that all its complications were needed to make it mean anything. Suddenly, I found myself blurting out, 'My mother died when I was six months old' – exactly what I had been determined not to begin with, however true it was as a beginning. I'd thought it too much like a plea for sympathy and had hated the idea of seeming to beg for it. But instantly Gracie patted my arm and her face creased even more with concern for me. 'Oh, the poor lassie, the poor lassie,' she said, and I didn't know whether she meant me, now, or my dead mother, then. 'Was it the cancer?' she asked, and I told her about Susannah's heart condition and what had happened, so far as I knew. Then, with Gracie's attention so concentrated, I plunged straight into the story of the memory box but left out my rejection of it and implied that it had been lost until recently. Gracie was enthralled, her cheeks became quite flushed and I was worried I was over-exciting her. Her mouth formed 'oohs' of astonishment and her eyes widened when I got to the bit about the address book. I'd brought it with me and held it out to her, but she shook her head and said she could read nothing now, not even with her spectacles. I said there was nothing much to read, only the name The Cabin, and Friendship Bay, Bequia.

Gracie's face grew calm, almost blank in expression, when I asked her if this meagre address meant anything to her. She seemed to have withdrawn from me and I didn't know what to do to bring her back again, or even if I should try to do so. I hesitated, and then said something about how I thought Susannah may have come to Bequia, the theory that she'd sailed here in the late Fifties, and somehow stayed on. At this, Gracie opened her eyes again and frowned and said that struck a chord, but she didn't know why. She held her head for a moment, as though listening, and then shook it and sighed. 'It was a long time ago,' she murmured. 'Lots of young folk came in their boats – it's a great place for the boats – but we didn't see them up here. There was just us, and the German man with the hut.' I didn't dare interrupt her to ask if 'us' simply meant herself and a maid, but stayed quite still and let her remember whatever she wanted to remember, relevant or not. 'He was a German man, but who was before him in that hut? Poor whites, a family of them, locals, but Bequians look down on them, they don't mix, they never did, the black Bequians and the poor whites... The German man left. When?' (I hadn't asked when. I wasn't interested in any German). 'Oh, I don't recall. Then there was a soldier, yes, there was, after the war was over in Europe. I knew him. He introduced himself, he was a gentleman, but I can't mind his name. He had a boat, the soldier. He married a Bequian girl – now, what was her name? – names are the devil... she had a baby...'

On and on Gracie rambled, her voice low and monotonous but perfectly distinct. I strained to identify anything in what she said which might relate to Susannah, but there seemed to be nothing at all. She'd never heard of Susannah, or of a cabin. It was all hopeless. I sat there feeling numb and miserable, and somehow ashamed that I'd come at all to harass this sweet old woman, but trying to stay alert. She was still describing the soldier and his wife and children when for the first time I heard the word 'cabin'. 'The hut burned down,' she was saying, followed by details of the fire, recalled astonishingly vividly, 'and he built a proper cabin, he built it himself.' (Yet when I'd asked her she'd said she'd never heard of any cabin up here. Had I planted the word in her head?) 'He'd lost his money and they had to make a living somehow and they took in visitors in the nice new house... Not many... It was a long way for visitors to come. They stayed down in the port... it didn't pay much... But they looked after them well in their house, the beds were clean and the food good... They went to England in the end... They said they'd come back to visit but they never did... Too far, it was too far... I had Christmas cards from them for years, mind.' I risked asking, 'And their cabin?' 'Cabin?' Gracie said. 'Their house?'

'Oh, their house burned down, just like the hut had done . . . caught fire, nobody knew how . . . the blaze was spotted too late . . . my house is stone . . .'

She stopped, and this time did fall asleep, deeply enough to snore. Should I just go? But I didn't want to tiptoe away without thanking her and without saying goodbye. I got up and walked very quietly down the steps of the terrace, slipping off my sandals so that I would make no sound. The garden I'd been facing for the last hour was not so much a garden as, I now realised, a fenced-off area of open hillside with little distinction between what grew inside and outside it. I recognised bananas growing wild and other fruits, fruits that looked something like pineapples but were too small. There was a slight breeze blowing not from the sea but towards it, carrying the scent of herbs of some kind. When I had walked to the furthest extent of Gracie's land, almost to where the hillside rolled down to the sea, I had a magnificent view stretching all the way to some smudgy-blue outline of another island far off. I stood there so transfixed I was unable to get out my camera, though the sight cried out for it – all that dazzling sea, all that enormous sky, and that thumbprint of another island. I tried instead to fold away into some deep recess in my memory what lay before me, looking hard, hard, and imprinting everything on my mind instead of on film so that I could take it out when I was back in grey, dismal London. And as ever, in a way that was becoming automatic, I wondered if Susannah had done this. Lying on her bed, weak and ill and afraid, had she conjured this up to console herself? Maybe. Maybe not. It didn't really matter. All that mattered was that I had seen this, I would treasure it.

I walked back to the terrace, resolved to find the maid and leave her with my thanks to pass on to Gracie, but Gracie was awake and waving her hand, though she could not have seen me until I had mounted the steps. I slipped my sandals back on, and said how beautiful I found her garden and how lovely the view over the sea was, and how I envied her. I said it as a compliment, not thinking how she might interpret 'envy', but I saw I had said the wrong thing. 'Ah, I'm not to be envied,' Gracie said, suddenly sad, 'I'm not to be envied by you, no, I'm not. You've all your life ahead. There's the envy.' To my alarm, I saw tears squeeze out of her eyes and she dabbed at them with the edge of her sleeve. 'Oh please,' I said, 'don't cry, Gracie, I'm so sorry, I didn't mean to . . .' But I couldn't think what it was I hadn't meant to do or say and was reduced to holding her hand anxiously. The few tears were soon over, though, and my hand pressed, to show me I was forgiven, I felt, for whatever I'd said, and after a while I thought it safe to begin to say my goodbyes and express my appreciation of her allowing me to talk to her. She ignored this and said, 'Your mother died?' I said yes, a long time ago. 'Do you cry for her?' she asked. I said I didn't, I hadn't known her and I'd loved my stepmother and there had never seemed anything to cry about. 'You don't cry for your mother?' Gracie repeated, seeming incredulous. I said no again, firmly.

I thought she had probably forgotten the little history I'd given her, and certainly forgotten all about the box and what had been in it, but she then said, 'I'm thinking what your mother was meaning with her box. It would be the pain of knowing she was leaving you. I watched my Douglas, and he knew he was leaving, and the pain was something awful. He couldn't bear to talk of it to me, but he didn't need to, I saw it plain.' Her own expression became one of pain as I watched her, silent myself partly through embarrassment and partly respect for what she was struggling to say, her eyes tightly shut and screwed up. 'It's a terrible thing to be with someone you love when they're dying,' she said. 'Terrible, terrible . . . he held my hand so tight . . . he found no peace in the going, no comfort in everlasting peace . . . he was desperate to live, he wouldn't believe anything was his God's will.' More tears bumped down her wrinkled skin and I hunted for a tissue in my pocket and pushed it into her hand. But she didn't seem to want to use it, only to let the tears run their course. 'I'm sorry,' I said, 'I didn't mean to bring back sad memories.' She opened her eyes then and smiled, even gave a little laugh. 'Oh, you weren't bringing them back,' she said. 'They never leave me. I'm a silly old fool, I like to have them. I keep Douglas living that way, you see, thinking about him, thinking about the good days as well as the bad. I cry, but it's better than feeling nothing, it keeps him here, with me.'

I left soon after this, feeling faintly nauseous and disturbed. The maid had come out with another young woman and between them they had helped Gracie to her feet and she half walked, was half carried, into the house. Upright, she was taller, even though bowed, than I had guessed and I saw that once she had been a big, strong woman. I didn't know her age, but suspected she was well over eighty. How many years, then, had she been keeping Douglas alive? Fifty? Sixty? I'd forgotten to ask her when she first came to Bequia and how old she had been then. It was horrible to think about, her determination to go on remembering a man dead so long, and I realised as I walked back to the car how lucky I had been that my own father had not behaved like that. He'd found Charlotte, maybe *allowed* himself to find her, and Susannah had not been kept alive in the way Gracie kept her Douglas alive, clinging on to him because she had nothing else, and now never would have. The dead have to die, they have to be let go. I was sure of it. And yet I hadn't myself let either of my parents go. I thought about them every day still, many times a day. It was only Susannah, whom in my conscious memory I never had known, that I was happy to surrender to death. But now she was fighting to come back, to fill my head with images of her I had never had and had not wanted to have, and any moment I was running the risk of feeling the pain of loss Gracie still felt for Douglas and which I had never felt for Susannah.

Driving slowly back the short distance to Port Elizabeth, I thought about this other pain Gracie had described, not of the loss itself but of being with a person who knows they are dying and who refuses to be reconciled to this because they have someone to live for whom they cannot bear to leave. Me. Susannah couldn't bear to leave me. I tried to imagine the situation Gracie had conjured up – me in my cradle, Susannah holding my hand and willing herself to live *for me*. Torture. And myself, a baby, oblivious to it, doing nothing to comfort her, as Gracie had tried to comfort Douglas. My father had once said Susannah never, ever admitted she knew she was likely to die, not in so many words. Her memory box was the only form of admission and even then she never actually said what it was she was preparing it for – the future, my future, 'in case', but not necessarily a future after her death. Pretence had been the name of the game and my father had played it with her, refusing to acknowledge she was likely to die, just as she had wanted. What had it done to her, this knowing and yet refusing to know? I wondered whether, if she had had a disease to which a time limit could be given (cancer, say, when a prognosis of terminal within a certain number of months could be given) she would have acted differently, or would she have refused to accept that prognosis too? It was impossible to know and yet these kind of questions nagged away at me.

I was beginning to change my mind yet again about the motive behind the memory box. Maybe it was a sort of insurance policy: if I prepare for leaving my baby I will never have to. That was why there was no written explanation of the contents and why they seemed so haphazard. They were haphazard, selected in panic, however carefully wrapped and numbered and packed. She was clutching on to solid things as a kind of ballast against screaming hysteria. This wasn't a treasure hunt, there was no treasure to be found at the end of it, it was a piling up of defence mechanisms, the building of a bulwark against terror. And I was now pulling it apart, tearing it down, exposing the great hole it had hidden, and I was falling into it. I was letting this dead woman possess me. She had been, in the midst of her fear, so clever. She was emerging to tell me I was half hers, to show me that if she could not live herself she would live in me. However hard I tried to deny it, my genetic inheritance was hers. I might not look like her, I might not act like her, but sure enough there were genes in me that were hers. It was a question of cells. She was in me, somewhere, and she had known she would be. I was the one who, until lately, had refused to admit this. I was doing the pretending, as I had done for over thirty years.

I felt shaken, and once I had parked the car, I walked along the boards beside the sea, not wanting to see Rory yet. I wished I knew about the science of genes, how many cells, or letters, or whatever they are called, go to make up the DNA alphabet. I was ignorant. But I recalled vaguely from school science lessons that women carry more genetic information than men. Susannah would have bequeathed more to me than my father, whatever the physical evidence to the contrary. I knew too, or thought I knew, that characters are not inherited even if families think they are, think some offspring is exactly like a parent in personality. We'd all been surprised by this at school, which is how I'd remembered it, and somehow relieved. And relieved as well to be assured by our teacher, who for once had us attentive, that environment acted *with* genes and so genes could not entirely dominate. I had wanted only my father's to determine what I was, hating to think of that other inheritance because it couldn't be Charlotte's.

So, how was I like Susannah? Or rather, what, genetically,

had been her influence – no, was still her influence – on the map of myself she had made of me with my father? Did it matter? I had never wanted to find out. If I, in turn, had had my own child, maybe I would have wanted to. Susannah would have been passed on through me to him or her and I think I might then have been curious to know what I was passing on. Not that anybody could tell me, unless it was some measurable disease or defect. A heart defect. I knew I didn't have one. There had been a great deal of neurotic checking of this when I was a child, which, although I hadn't understood then what it was about, I'd sensed was connected with the dead Susannah. There was always such relief on my father's face when the doctor pronounced me perfectly sound, and I'd hear him apologising for bringing me to be examined yet again and the doctor would reassure him with words like 'in the circumstances' and 'I understand, what with her mother . . .' My grandmother, too, was always looking at me anxiously – did I tire easily? Was I very pale? Did I get short of breath? Did I have a blue tinge round my nostrils? . . . No, none of them. That part of my genetic inheritance was sound and nothing to do with Susannah.

I was moody and difficult the next couple of days and began to plan to leave Bequia. 'We can't stay here for ever,' I snapped at Rory. 'I don't see why not,' he said. I told him I wasn't made of money and that he had exaggerated notions of my supposed wealth. He retorted that we were living on Bequia far, far more cheaply than in London and he could probably get work here and fend for himself. I sneered at the use of the word 'work' by him. He didn't understand the meaning of it. What would he do? Wash dishes, wait at tables? He said he'd be quite prepared to do either or both if he could support himself like that. I told him to go ahead, but I'd bet he would need a work permit before long. In the end, he came back with me, though swearing he now had an ambition in life and would return under his own steam, for ever. We had a last day swimming from our favourite beach and to please him, and to make up for being so edgy, I took his photograph. He loves having his photograph taken and is always complaining because I'm not interested in portraits – 'I'd make such a wonderful subject.' He posed himself on a rock on the hillside not far from Gracie's house and didn't guess I was moving him so that I would get more of the background – the trees, the great sweep of ocean below, that same distant smudge of an island I'd seen earlier – than of him. I wanted it as a memento of where Susannah might have been.

It was only as I took it that I realised how, with his hair grown longer in the month we'd been there, and curly with all the sea water, he would look just like her from the distance I'd chosen, only his head and shoulders in shot.

Chapter Eight

THE photographs of the turtles were as good as I knew they would be and I had no trouble placing them. They immediately earned me other commissions and suddenly I was busy and enjoyed being busy. There was no more drooping round my flat, or lying on the sofa staring hopelessly at the shell (which now had another alongside it, almost identical, which I'd brought back from Bequia), and I had no time to think about moving. Nor did I have any time for Rory, who disappeared again from my life as he so often did. That was the pattern of our relationship – periods of closeness then spells when we didn't even ring each other, and when sometimes Rory changed addresses and I didn't have his telephone number.

But his mother rang me, just before Christmas. Ostensibly, she was ringing to ask if I had enjoyed my trip, but there was such suppressed excitement in her usually doleful voice that I suspected there must be some other reason for the call. There was. Hector had had a letter from the Prime Minister, saying he was 'minded' to confer a knighthood on him for his services to industry and in recognition of his work for disabled servicemen, if he was minded to accept. Hector was very minded indeed to accept and Isabella was ecstatic. She told me twice this news was absolutely confidential and I must tell nobody whatsoever, and was rather hurt when I carelessly wondered aloud who I knew who would be interested. She said she'd rung Rory at the last telephone number she'd been given but only got an answering machine and the voice on it hadn't sounded like his. She wanted him to know about the honour his father was to receive and to say she hoped he would rise to the occasion and accompany them to the Palace when the time came.

I doubted if he would, though I didn't say so, but what seemed remarkable to me was that Isabella was extending this invitation at all. I would have thought she and Hector would have wanted to keep their errant son a hundred miles from this investiture in case he disgraced them. But in any case I didn't know where Rory was and I too only had the telephone number she had, so I couldn't help. Isabella hadn't finished with me, though. She and Hector were coming to London and they wanted me to dine with them at the Savoy, where they always stayed. It was to be a private celebration and they wanted me and Rory to join them and 'show some family solidarity for once'. That was rich. There hadn't been much solidarity from them. But when she then asked me too, in due course, to accompany them to the Palace, and I instantly refused, I felt so mean I accepted the invitation to dinner and promised to try to track down Rory. 'You will dress nicely, Catherine, won't you?' Isabella said. 'I know what you and Rory think about dressing smartly, but for Hector's sake do him the honour, will you? No jeans and jumpers?'

It was a bloody cheek, giving someone of thirty-one instructions on how to dress, but I let her get away with it. In fact, I thought I would shock her by really dressing up, by arriving for our date in knock-out splendour, all glamour and glitter. The only problem was that I hadn't the clothes. There was nothing whatsoever elegant or glamorous in my wardrobe. I needed Rory for my own ends now – he would know what I should buy and how I should look – but, like his mother, when I called his number I got only a voice that was not his. I would have to manage on my own. I can't remember how I came to think of the necklace I'd found in the memory box but suddenly I did. I'd imagined I would never wear it, since it cried out for some sort of beautiful dress and all that went with it, but now I saw it could be my starting point. I got it out and looked at it closely. The stone was an emerald, so green was the obvious colour to go for. Susannah had once worn it with a green dress. There were two pictures of her wearing it in the albums, one on her wedding day, one at some function later on. On the wedding-day photograph, the green glittered above the neckline of the ivory satin gown and matched the trailing ivy in her bouquet; in the other, the green of the dress was a darker shade of emerald and the stone did not stand out so noticeably. Maybe I should go for white, or cream, or even pale grey . . .

I supposed at first it would have to be a dress and one with a generous neckline to show off the necklace. The whole point of such a piece of exquisite jewellery was to allow it to dominate, and to do that it had to sit on a bare throat with enough space for the pendant in which the emerald was set to lie just above the cleavage. Both Susannah's dresses had had quite low and wide necklines which had perfectly offset the necklace. I had no such dress. I had never wanted such a dress. Every garment I possessed had either a high neck or a modest V-neck. The idea of going out to find and buy a dress which would flatter the necklace but in which I would feel acutely uncomfortable did not appeal. But I would have to shop for something, and so I went out full of gloom to do the looking. I hate shopping for clothes. I like to shop for things for my flat, for furnishings and furniture and household things, but not for clothes. Charlotte loved to shop. She could spend whole days trailing round shops looking for nothing in particular, even though no one would have guessed she had any interest in how she dressed (she had no taste at all and always looked ordinary). But I couldn't and didn't. I bought things in chain stores, in a hurry, and when I liked something I bought it in threes so that I wouldn't need to bother again for a long time. This meant I was an innocent when it came to designer clothes. Rory, on the other hand, was an expert, bandying around the right names with nauseating familiarity. When he raved over some garment he'd purchased, at great expense, for the name, because he or she 'cuts so beautifully', I infuriated him by saying it looked straight out of Marks & Spencer's to me.

I had no idea where to go. For two days I wandered round Harrods fingering dresses, thousands of them, millions of hideous *frocks*, and in the end had to leave empty-handed. The very department 'evening gowns' were in made me feel out of place – the thick carpet, the slightly perfumed air, the racks of bewilderingly similar clothes, the glassy-smiled assistants, the mirrors (in which I could see my slouching, scruffy self).

It brought back memories of shopping as a young teenager in Oxford with my mother – picture us, Charlotte in her pleated skirts and boxy jackets, so way out of fashion they were a fashion statement in themselves, and me in jeans and big, baggy sweatshirt, protesting that I had no need for a dress or, as she put it, 'a pretty skirt and a little top' for some wedding we had to go to. Charlotte would drag me towards a garment covered with sprigs of flowers – most of her own things were covered with sprigs or spots or whirls of some terrible pattern – and I would just glare, or turn on her my most practised look of incredulity. Forced to try something on, I would go into the changing-room and deliberately sabotage whatever I'd been given – I'd ruck it up round my middle and yell, 'Too short,' or jam the zip and say, 'Too tight.' And I did find myself smiling as I wandered round the shops, just at the memory of my mother's face, all puzzled and concerned, and my own silly performance.

It's a wonder the Harrods assistants didn't think I was some sort of terrorist as I lurked there looking, I should imagine, impossibly sinister and scowling at the clothes I was fingering with ludicrous distaste. I knew I was making faces to register my disgust, a one-woman pantomime with no audience except for them. Leaving the department, I found myself laughing idiotically as I entered the lift, recalling my eleven-year-old self hissing at Charlotte that I wanted to be a bag lady when I grew up and wear the same old clothes all the time and not have to fuss about weddings.

I gave up on Knightsbridge and moved to Bond Street and tried to take an interest in boutiques, intimidating though they were. It was no good. I wasn't in the right frame of mind, I didn't have the right attitude. And then, passing one small shop near the top end of New Bond Street, I saw in the window a white trouser suit. It was very simple, almost severe, but the material looked soft. The pants were wide-legged and the jacket long, fastened with two buttons just on the bust, giving it a generous neckline. In my obsession with dresses like Susannah's I'd overlooked this alternative and yet the town was full of such casual chic.

Oh, the joy of finding the right clothes! The moment I put those pants and jacket on I felt terrific and bought them in five minutes flat, not caring in the least that they cost what amounted to my entire clothes budget for the last two years. Thank God, I was sorted. But once home, and standing in front of my long mirror with the suit on and the necklace, I realised I wasn't. Clothes, fine. Necklace with said clothes, excellent. But hair? Disaster. I hadn't been to a hairdresser for ages. It was a mess. I'd simply chopped bits off when the fringe grew too long and tied the rest back with an elastic band. Not good enough. I have thick, strong hair – there's nothing wrong with my hair and it's always in good condition, glossy, and the colour is fine, a deep dark brown – but with the white suit and the necklace it looked all wrong. My hairstyle, or lack of style, insulted the outfit. I picked up the silver hand mirror and turning away from the sight of all of me in the long mirror I looked at myself close up. Make-up, that was another lack. I wore none. Fine, in jeans and T-shirt, but dressed up in the new clothes my features seemed to vanish. I felt so bad-tempered, resenting what I knew to be the truth, that having faced the ordeal of shopping for clothes I'd now have to find a hairdresser and seek advice about bloody make-up. All this to please my aunt and uncle, whom I didn't even like – what had I started?

More than I'd been prepared for. I knew, when I set off to the Savoy, that the necklace had somehow taken me over and changed me, the necklace and all that had had to go with it. I didn't feel myself. I was a stranger, hailing a taxi, and I saw in the cab driver's eyes the kind of recognition I normally never received. I was suddenly a sophisticated woman who would be treated as such. I moved differently. My new garments didn't feel awkward or uncomfortable but instead like a marvellous disguise hiding my imperfections, giving me supreme confidence in my own attractiveness. It was quite thrilling and I was almost in awe of this creature I'd made myself into. The necklace felt heavy and cold round my neck. I was acutely conscious of its weight, though it hadn't felt heavy in my hands. The pendant, with its emerald glowing, seemed to cling to my flesh and I couldn't help fingering it constantly, lifting it up and being surprised when I let it fall back and felt it on my skin. I wondered how long fingerprints last. Would Susannah's still be on the pendant if she, too, had fiddled with it as I was doing?

My hair was in an elaborate French pleat, pulled right back from my face, the fringe gone, my forehead visible for the first time in my life. I'd always had a long, thick fringe to hide behind and now I felt exposed. Make-up (only eye make-up) had made my face look strange to me. My eyes beneath my newly revealed forehead, odd in itself, were bigger and my nose appeared smaller. I felt my old face had melted and had hardly been able to look in the mirror before I left without wanting to go back to the self I could recognise. It occurred to me I did not have to go back to that self at all if I did not want to. I could look like this every day. Many women did, and do. They take time and trouble and of course spend money and they look beautiful and the world treats them differently. Susannah had looked like this. When I was first making a business of sticking to jeans, etc., just before my grandmother died she had said with sadness – and it was that sadness which hurt, not her words – 'Your mother always dressed nicely, always. From a wee thing she loved clothes, she had the knack – and you won't even try. Just look at yourself!' I knew it had been commented on, when my father married Charlotte, that he had certainly gone for a different style of woman from his first wife. Charlotte never looked elegant in spite of her efforts. She looked cosy. She looked how I, as a child, liked her to look.

But as my taxi battled its way down the Strand I reflected that the raw material was never there for Charlotte, whereas it was for me. She could never have looked like Susannah, however well dressed. She was short and dumpy and her cheerful face round and bland. But I, although not like Susannah, had a better chance of appearing elegant if I wished, as I had wished for that evening, than Charlotte ever had. I had height, I was slim, I had strong features (good cheekbones and a straight nose). I was worth dressing, as I had just proved. But what kind of woman had Susannah been that she had been famous for looking groomed even in a dressing-gown? We would have had such fights over how I chose to look, I was sure, whereas Charlotte and I never did, or only rarely, on those occasions she felt bound to register some mild protest at my more slovenly gear. Susannah might have wanted to turn me, her daughter, out in her own image, as a woman who could wear, with ease, the necklace she'd left. And yet she'd proved something by forcing this jewellery on to me. I was capable, after all, of relishing my own appearance.

My aunt and uncle were astounded. They were sitting at a table by the window overlooking the river when I arrived and I had a long walk over to them. I saw them look towards me with that blank stare given to arresting strangers and then had the gratification of seeing them literally start and confer with each other – was *this* Catherine? Hector stumbled to his feet and embraced me rather more convincingly than usual, and Isabella kissed me on the cheek instead of pecking at the air to the right of it. Hector boomed that I looked splendid and called for champagne (though to toast his own success rather than any beauty of mine). The moment I was seated, I saw Isabella's eyes were fixed on the necklace. I touched it, provocatively, while I studied the menu.

'Your mother did that,' Isabella said, frowning, 'always playing with it. I never did.'

'You wore it?' I asked, surprised.

'Of course. It wasn't always hers. It was our mother's. We both wore it, when we had occasion. Susannah just had more opportunities than I ever did. She wore it so many times I think she thought she owned it, but she didn't. A little unfair, but there you are.' She sniffed, and smiled a little too brightly and began whispering about Hector's knighthood and telling me when it would be announced, reminding me to buy *The Times* that day. I ate my smoked salmon and my Dover sole and drank the champagne before moving on to the Chablis, and tried all the time to warm to these relatives of mine. They had aged since I last saw them, quite dramatically, especially Isabella, and I felt I should be able to call forth some sympathy for their grey heads and lined faces and slightly shrunken forms, but I couldn't. They irritated me, as they always had done. I had nothing in common with Isabella except genes. I smiled politely as she prattled on and thought suddenly that this was even more weird than the realisation I possessed Susannah's genes. I could see and hear and judge Isabella. Genetically, where did we touch? I longed to be told. I wanted someone to read our separate DNA codes and say there, and there and there. She is your mother's sister, and there and there and there she is you, you are her.

I felt more connection with Hector, as ever. At least he had not been indifferent to Rory, as Isabella had so often seemed to be. He had had some physical contact with him, if only of a negative sort, taking hold of his arm to shake him, or pushing his hair out of his eyes because it annoyed him to see his son so tousled and wild. Isabella didn't even have this minimal connection with Rory. She seemed, indeed, to move away whenever, as a child, he drew near and looked as if he were going to touch *her*. She recoiled from his runny nose, telling him to wipe it but not wiping it herself, as most mothers of a small child would do, and if he had dirty hands and made to hold her own hand she would literally step backwards. She always seemed to find him repugnant and yet he was such a very attractive child whom others loved to cuddle, the kind of sweet-faced, blond, blue-eyed boy who looks like a little cherub. Her attitude had always been bewildering: the only clue I had to her behaviour came when my grandmother once told me that Isabella had never got over wanting a girl. Rory himself, when he was old enough to appreciate what effect he appeared to have on his mother, also reckoned he had been doomed from birth not to be loved by her and that it wouldn't have mattered what he'd been like.

It wasn't something I had ever been able to discuss with my aunt. I was never, in fact, able to discuss anything with her. Sometimes I even wondered if my hostility to the idea of

Susannah being my mother stemmed in part from my dislike of her sister. And yet I knew they could not have been alike. On the contrary, from everything I had been told and pieced together they were opposites. Isabella envied her sister for being everything she was not and my birth had apparently been the final blow. Susannah had everything she wanted – but then, of course, she died. She did not have life. I had often wondered if that had made my aunt feel ultimately victorious and had dissolved her feelings of jealousy when it was too late, but that was utterly beyond discussion even now. I would never know. I would never learn the reality about Susannah from her sister, because she tried to mention her as rarely as possible. I would have to mention her name myself and it was still hard to do that. But as that meal went on, and the chat was all of charity organisation concerns and the weather and the purchasing of a new car and other banalities, I grew impatient with my own connivance. When Hector, at the end of the main course, and pudding having been rejected though we were waiting for coffee, left the table to make a phone call, I could curb my impatience no longer.

Apropos of nothing, I suddenly said, 'Why didn't you like your sister? Why didn't you and Susannah get on?'

'Really, Catherine!' Isabella protested, as though I had sworn at her. She flushed, too, and looked around as though worrying that anyone had heard me.

'What?' I said. 'It's a reasonable question, isn't it?'

'We're having a celebratory dinner,' she said. 'It isn't appropriate.'

'When would it be?'

'Not here, not in public. Really, you're spoiling Hector's party. You're usually so sensible, you've always been sensible about your mother's death.'

'Sensible?'

Still Isabella was looking furtive and angry, and now she

leaned over the table and in little more than a whisper, more of a hiss, said, 'She had died, and you never carried on about it. You knew it was a blessing that you had no memory of her. You took to Charlotte and that was that. Sensible. Why start all this up now?'

'Is it wrong?' I said, determined to continue now I'd begun. 'Why hold it against me that at last I'm interested in Susannah?'

'It does no good.'

'How do you know? How do you know it wouldn't do me some good? Why not be pleased I want to know what I refused to know before? My grandmother would've been pleased.'

'She's dead.'

'That's the trouble: everyone who could tell me anything is dead, except for you.'

'There's no point to it. You'll only upset yourself.'

'I'm not in the least upset, I just want to know more. I'm thirty-one, Isabella. Think about it: I'm her age, the age she was when she died. And I've just opened that box she left me – I expect you knew about it – a few months ago. Don't you think it makes sense, it's *sensible*, to ask you about my mother however much I've blocked her out all my life?'

At that moment, Hector came back and coffee arrived. It was fortunate, really. I'd spoken much too sharply and that was no way to get anything out of Isabella. But as I drank the coffee, and the mundane conversation with Hector resumed, I was aware that my aunt was not as furious as I thought I'd made her. She seemed more shaken perhaps by the mention of the box than angry, and twice Hector asked her if she was feeling tired and had to be reassured she was not, or not excessively. We went to the ladies' powder-room together and when I came out of the lavatory she was sitting before a mirror in the empty room, quite still, looking at herself. I asked, as Hector had done, if she was all right. 'You've distressed me,' she said; 'you've ruined the evening.' I said I was sorry, that I hadn't intended to. 'I don't like to talk of Susannah,' she said. 'I never have done. It was a waste, a great waste.'

'What? Her death?'

'Oh, her death, of course, but what went before.' She sighed and closed her eyes against the sight of herself. Suddenly, she looked even older and more frail. 'She never liked me. She was my big sister, but she wanted nothing to do with me. I wanted her but she didn't want me. It was as simple as that.'

I didn't speak. Frankly, I found it hard to believe my aunt had wanted to be close to anyone except maybe her dog. She'd never even seemed too keen on old Hector, though he was devoted to her. But there she was, making what for her rated as an intimate confession. She got up, turning away from the mirror, snapping her handbag shut. 'But when she died', I risked continuing as we walked towards the door, 'did you feel differently? Did everything change, did you feel sorry . . .?'

'Sorry?' Isabella said. 'No, I did *not* feel sorry. It was she who should have felt sorry, for the way she treated me, for what she did, never acting as a sister should.' She crashed through the door, quite back to her old self. I tried to say I hadn't meant was she sorry for how jealous she'd been, but that I'd been going to go on to say had she regretted things hadn't been different between them, but there was no opportunity. She'd had enough of me, she wasn't prepared to listen any more. We were back at our table and Hector was waiting and from there we swept to the door and parted company. I left them in the hotel and found my own taxi and sat in it all the way home feeling confused. I felt I'd been handed some kind of indictment against Susannah, the first attack I'd ever heard made on her. She hadn't been a good sister, though there had been no clue as to her exact failings, and Isabella still burned with resentment all these years later. I wondered about her obviously high expectations of sisterhood. With no sister of my own I was hardly in a position to understand what she had experienced or expected. But I found, as I turned over in my mind my aunt's words and how she had said them, that I wanted to defend Susannah without knowing why. Why should she have loved and been close to a sister like Isabella?

Somewhere in Isabella's head were millions of memories which would be of use to me in this struggle of mine to understand what her dead sister was seeking to do to me, but she had thrown away the key to unlocking them. Either that, or she was deliberately obstructing the flowing of memories she did not want me to share. I took off my finery, got into bed, and then lay for hours thinking once more about the nature of memory, only this time about how selective yet random the system of remembering was in my own case. I'd always been bothered by the recurring memories of what seemed absolutely banal. It was these kind of memories, which had no apparent significance, that puzzled me. I was always thinking of a certain corner in Edinburgh. Into my head would flash a wall, the side of a house, and the view of a cobbled street. I was certain nothing had ever happened to me on such a corner and, though I could not have led anyone to the exact place, I felt it was familiar. There was something ridiculous about how often I saw the wall, the cobbles, the blank emptiness of this harmless scene. Why had it been tucked away? And if my memory had salted away such an inane scene, what else had it got in there? Did I have somewhere memories of my first six months, of Susannah? Back to that again, to that wearying straining after lost impressions and all the time wanting to know was it simply that I could not retrieve them or that they weren't there? It maddened me not to know.

To steady myself, I moved on to trying to sort out my first definite memories. I'd always thought my first concrete memory was of dropping my doll on the garden path and screaming when I saw her china head was shattered. Charlotte had just married my father, so I was nearly two. She herself always remembered this incident because it was the first day she had had total charge of me on her own – my grandmother had gone home the day before after supervising the handover to her care. Charlotte was nervous, so this little mishap had seemed to her like a bad omen, but apparently I was easily comforted, the doll sent to be mended, and another accepted as a substitute. Everyone says two is too young to be sure a memory is 'true', and that it is more likely that what is recalled is an adult's telling of the memory, but I believe mine to be what I myself do remember. But my next early memory is far more vivid and it involves Isabella. I was five. It was a summer's day, in the garden of our Oxford house. Rory and Isabella were staying with us. I had a plastic teaset and I'd set it out on the paving stones at the back of the house (later replaced by mellow old bricks, but I can see those slabs of York stone quite clearly). Rory and I were sitting there cross-legged on the warm stone and I was pouring 'tea' for him out of the tiny red plastic teapot, which had a white lid with a little red knob on it, into cups so small and light that they tipped over easily and took hardly any liquid. Charlotte was somewhere in the house making lunch and my father and Isabella were sitting having a drink, their chairs, old-fashioned deckchairs, some distance away from us. I can call up the dazzling light, the heat, the sound of water being poured, and I can even feel the sticky plastic handle of the fiddly teapot, so hard for me to hold securely in my podgy five-year-old hand. The scene is mundane but the reality of it extraordinary – I can always be 'in' it whenever I want.

I visited this memory again that night, enjoying it as I always did. It ended, as ever, with Isabella saying, 'The image of mother, it's so unfair.' And my father saying, 'She isn't an image.' All the times this memory had flashed unbidden into my head, rather than being called up by me, I had disliked what Isabella had said and liked my father's reproof, or what I took to be a reproof. It pleased me to have him correct her. I liked to hear him say I was my own self and not an image of anyone else, especially someone dead. But that night, after what Isabella had said hours before, I found myself halting and checking the familiar memory. Something was wrong, something jarred. I began at the beginning again . . . stones . . . heat . . . teapot . . . voices . . . It made me sweat to try so hard to catch a meaning I'd never thought of. 'The image of mother . . .' But was that it? Had Isabella said 'the image of *her* mother' or 'the image of mother'? I'd always taken her meaning to have been '*her*' mother, but I'd never remembered that she'd said 'her'. Did she? Again and again, I went over it. No, she had not said 'her'. She had said 'the image of mother, it's so unfair.' I felt panicky, realising this; the whole memory was slipping and sliding out of control, Rory's face was hidden, the light was dimmed, the heat receding . . . and yet why on earth did it matter?

I'd been told that when Susannah died, Isabella had wanted to adopt me. She'd thought not only that my father should be grateful but that it was her right to claim me. It was my father, not my grandmother or Isabella herself, who told me this when I was grown up, with some indignation as well as amusement. My father said she had brought considerable pressure to bear, pointing out that a man on his own with his living to make was in no position 'to rear' (as she'd put it) a baby girl. When he had vehemently rejected her offer, which had sounded more like a demand, he'd pointed out that her mother, my grandmother, had said she would be more than happy to have me live with her during the week when he was working and he'd take over at weekends. He could afford a nanny and she would do all the actual looking after. But

Isabella had gone on the offensive at once, saying that he was taxing her mother's strength and that at seventy-two she was not up to the demands made on her by a baby and then toddler even if there was a nanny as well. The responsibility would be hers and my father was taking advantage of her and asking too much. Her health would suffer and her life would be shortened. There had been a horrible argument only resolved by my grandmother discovering what Isabella had been saying and more or less telling her to mind her own business. Then, of course, within a very short time, Charlotte had come along, solving everything.

Isabella had always implied that my father had only married Charlotte to give me a mother. She'd hinted this to me when I was about thirteen and staying with her and I'd been shocked not because of any fear that this might be true but that she could be so wicked as to make it up. I knew my parents loved each other: there had never been any doubt about it. But Isabella couldn't bear the fact that they did – why, when she had Hector? – and what was worse she couldn't bear my devotion to Charlotte. She was always sniping away at her and it was all because she felt if Charlotte had not come on the scene she would in the end have been able to take me over as she had wished. She'd almost managed it anyway before Charlotte rescued us all. The nannies had come and gone, three within the first nine months, and Isabella had come rushing to fill the gap on each change-over. My grandmother was relieved and appreciated the rest it gave her until someone new was found. Isabella had taken me to her own house every day and petted and played with me (and pretended I was hers, I think). Rory naturally suffered accordingly, though since he was only a baby himself, a mere four months older than me, perhaps not too severely. My father, working so hard then, had no alternative but to allow this to go on until he had found a new nanny, and when he had it was only reasonable to let Isabella hand me over gradually. This 'gradually' was, each time, spun out and led to trouble with the new nanny and the whole business was fraught. I suspect that marrying Charlotte was not the only relief for him but so was leaving Edinburgh soon after. Isabella never forgave him. Once we were all in Oxford, she had lost me. All she was left with was Rory, and she used him to draw me back as I grew older. I loved him, not her, and she knew it.

I have no memory, of course, of all this tension and if it is there I have no wish to regain it. Loss of memory, or failure of some period to imprint itself on the memory, can be a blessing too. But having thought about all this that night before falling into a disturbed sleep, I woke next morning convinced I had more choice than I'd realised about what I wanted to regain from the recesses of my mind. I was surprising myself all the time by my new determination to use the contents of the memory box to discover things not about Susannah but about myself. Her objects were acting like triggers, whether she had intended them to or not.

And I still had several to pull.

Chapter Nine

At the end of January, I had to go down to Cornwall to clear out my parents' cottage. I'd only been there once since my father died, to fetch things Charlotte had wanted, and not at all since she herself died. The cottage had never meant much to me, though it was pretty enough. It had only three rooms, perched one on top of the other in a slot of a building with a wooden deck at the back overlooking the Fowey estuary. This was where my father had come to sail and where he'd tried, and failed, to make a sailor of me. I only had to step on to a boat to be sick. He, of course, was a great sailor and so, I'd been told, was Susannah – genes on both sides which should have made me completely happy on water but which had failed to pass through to me.

There was the one good photograph of my father and Susannah on a boat. Most of those photos of them together in the early years of their relationship were small and blurry, unlike the studies taken of Susannah alone. Someone had used a cheap Brownie camera to snap them; but that one photograph which was clearly the work of a professional had hung framed in my father's study for as long as I could remember. It was twelve by fifteen inches, black and white, glossy. Every detail was defined, the strands in the coiled rope lying on the deck of the boat they were on, the shine on the metal fittings, the grain of the wooden planks – all superbly visible. It had been taken for a yachting magazine for which my father had written an article, on the conversion of MFVs (Motor

Fishing Vessels). He was in the forefront, beaming straight to camera, and Susannah was in the background, sitting with her back against the mast, legs drawn up, elbows on knees, head between her hands, looking very serious. All the time, even when that photograph was taken, her heart was clogging up and she was often breathless and tired. But my grandmother said she wouldn't face facts, indeed simply denied them. She was a fighter. She was going to lead the life she wanted to lead. She was going to be normal.

She should never have had me, never have thought of having a baby. I'd heard that said as a child and had resented the insinuation that somehow I had caused her death. But they were fair enough, those words. Of course she should never have had me. She wasn't fit enough. The pregnancy and then an agonisingly long-drawn-out birth (Isabella had once foisted the details on me until I'd walked out of the room) had weakened her when she was already weakening, or rather her heart was. She'd even breast-fed me for three months against all advice. She must have been mad. What did she think she was doing, risking her life, or at least her health, to have a baby? It can't have been because my father persuaded her. He'd never have done that. I'm sure he would have wanted to avoid any risks.

He was never a risk-taker himself. But maybe, before he came into Susannah's life, she was involved with someone who was, someone who encouraged her to be reckless. Going off to the Caribbean as she had done, sailing there, was, I had come to realise, incredibly reckless. My father would never have considered it. Sailing round the coast and islands of Scotland was about his limit, or later to the Scilly Isles. He didn't even sail to the Mediterranean, never mind the Caribbean. But someone else did, and Susannah had leapt at the chance, responding to the idea of an adventure which was dangerous in itself but especially for her. I began to see this as a steel-like thread running through her and I wondered if it had frightened those around her. It was strange to think she might have been frightening. I found myself thinking about it a lot, and speculating about who she might have scared most. Not her mother. My grandmother was not a woman I could imagine frightened. But my father? Very possibly. I'd scared him myself sometimes, with my outbursts of temper, and he'd do anything to placate me. And maybe Isabella. I don't know why that idea came into my head, considering I've always thought of my aunt as formidable. It was something my father once said, I think, which had never struck me as significant before, something to the effect that when he first met Isabella she had seemed so timid beside Susannah and he couldn't believe they were sisters. 'Of course, she's changed since then,' he'd added, and laughed.

At any rate, I'm sure it was Susannah herself who made the decision to have a baby, unless becoming pregnant was an accident. Possible, always possible, and abortions were against the law then (I think). Or if it was an accident, if I was a mistake, maybe she couldn't contemplate abortion even if it had been obtainable. Who knows? Who wants to know? (But that was what was becoming so irritating – increasingly, I did, I wanted answers to questions I'd never asked and which no one could now answer.)

Whatever the history of my conception, I'd been wanted most passionately. Photos of Susannah pregnant showed a woman radiating joy and those taken with me in her arms have an ecstatic quality of an almost religious intensity. She looks as if she worshipped me. There is not a flicker of anxiety in her face, not a hint of concern that she might leave me motherless, yet in six short months all that changed. Life, her life, became so fragile that she assembled her memory box. It was so frustrating not to understand precisely what had happened. I was ignorant, muddled, and wished I had a doctor friend who could explain about Susannah's type of heart disease. I could, I suppose, get her death certificate and see what was written on it, but I haven't done so yet. I had once asked, though, where she was buried. It was one of the very few direct questions about her that I ever did ask, as a young and rather ghoulish teenager. The answer was that she wasn't buried at all. She was cremated and her ashes scattered in the Firth of Forth.

My father had apparently said he'd like his scattered from the deck of their cottage on to the Fowey estuary. Charlotte and I had been going to make a pilgrimage together to do it, but then she fell ill and I had to go and do it on my own, at her insistence. I hated the task. Probably that was why I had taken against the cottage, or at least it was a strong contributory reason. I'd rather his ashes had been left in the Oxford garden, but Charlotte said no, he had wanted to be part of the sea just like Susannah. I didn't argue, it didn't matter. But going down there now to do a final clear-out took me back, of course, to that terrible period of time between the two deaths and I couldn't wait to be away. Luckily, there wasn't much clearing to be done. The cottage wasn't like the Oxford house. My father hadn't wanted two proper homes, just a place to sleep when he was not on his boat, so there was only the most basic furniture and none of that of much value. It didn't take me more than a couple of hours to sort out the clothes and books and the one or two personal items, like the tele-scope mounted on a stand at the window, which I'd once bought him. The new owners were delighted I was leaving everything else behind.

I felt no regret as I left it and drove off into Devon and then on to Dorset, where I had a commission to photograph some churches for a magazine. I enjoyed doing rural winter scenes, when the landscape looks barren, but is full of the kind of unexpected detail I like. Winter suited my style best and I always felt confident. I was feeling pretty confident then anyway, happy to be working regularly and resolved to have a break from thinking about Susannah's box. I hadn't finished with it, but at least (or so I told myself) I'd finished being obsessed and distressed by my inability to understand the significance of its contents. It wasn't going to rule my life. Whenever I went back to my flat, I was always surprised to see the shell on the bathroom shelf, the rucksack hanging on a hook behind the kitchen door, to find the necklace in my drawer — all these little bits of Susannah. It was like having the most self-effacing of guests, but one whose presence was nevertheless everywhere.

I stayed in small hotels or bed-and-breakfast places where there were few other guests at that time of year. Often, I had dining-rooms to myself and always I had the full attention of the proprietor or landlord. They had a certain curiosity about me entirely owing to my equipment — my cameras and other paraphernalia fascinated them and gave me some status, even if they weren't sure what that was. I always had plenty of offers of help to load my car, and remarks would be made about the bags and boxes being too heavy for a young woman to lift on her own. 'You'll ruin your child-bearing organs,' one hotelier joked, impertinently I thought, but he beamed as he insisted on helping me, though I'd told him no assistance was needed. I smiled politely and resisted the retort I'd like to have made, which was that these were organs which would never be used. Not the sort of response one can easily make, really, without causing embarrassment. I can't have children, I'm pleased to say. That's not quite true: it is *unlikely* that I will ever conceive a child, and I think of myself as unable to.

It is a long and, I suppose, sad story, but it can be reduced to a brief explanation and has never in fact been a matter for sadness so far as I am concerned. When I was eighteen, I became pregnant, through sheer carelessness. I don't blame the boy, I blame myself. Anyway, having done such a stupid thing I didn't want my parents to know. I wanted to protect them from the suffering my foolishness would cause. So I had an abortion without telling them – not so difficult in 1982. I had money, and I had friends who'd gone through the necessary system.

The abortion was perfectly straightforward, or so I thought, but then I got some sort of infection afterwards, again through my own carelessness, I expect (or at least it never occurred to me I might not be to blame). I had a horrible few days in hospital – luckily when my parents were on one of their very rare holidays abroad – and afterwards I was told that my Fallopian tubes had been damaged. At the time I didn't care. So long as I wasn't in pain, I didn't care. The doctor who broke this news, which he obviously thought likely to upset me, said I might care a good deal later on, 'when you want to have babies'. Conceiving, he said, would be difficult. I'd need my tubes blown and one of them was likely to be permanently blocked. He seemed offended instead of relieved by my calm acceptance of this information.

I have never yet wanted to have a baby. This is so hard to explain that I don't try to. Most of the men I've had affairs with have never needed to know the whole truth. Tell a man he has no need to worry about contraception because you've taken care of it and he is delighted, merely assuming you are on the pill. But, of course, sometimes, only twice to be precise, I have had to explain. When an affair has become more than that, when there has seemed every possibility of it becoming more permanent, even a question of marriage, then it has been time to confess. And a confession was what it always felt like, something I dreaded because of the possible reaction to it. And it certainly caused a strong reaction – concern and caution in about equal measure. Men do want children, or the two I loved did, and wanted them more than they had realised up to that point. Forced to accept that, if they stayed with me, the chances would be slim, they discovered that children had been very much in the scheme of their lives, however little thought they had given the subject until required to. Once the significance of what I had to tell them sank in, they reacted with barely concealed dismay. Their professed love for me began to wither, especially when I said I didn't want to have my tubes blown or anything like that.

I was shaken by their reaction. It seemed that I was no longer a proper woman to them once I'd said I couldn't give them the fruit of their own loins – oh, wonderfully biblically put, but I fell into such flowery language when going over the matter. Tony would say I was being monstrously unfair. He always swore his love for me had nothing to do with any children we might, or might not, have and that it made no difference to our future together. And, of course, being Tony, he pointed out that nothing had yet been *proved*. I pushed him, though, I insisted that he should answer honestly this question: if it turned out that I really was barren, would he still have wanted children? He said yes, but that it was irrelevant to how things were. He wanted me, that was enough. But it wasn't enough. He lied, I knew he did. He was very family-minded, coming as he did from the kind of family Charlotte had belonged to, large and close. Everything began to go wrong between us from the moment I told him about the state of my wretched tubes and my reluctance to have treatment. He was determined to think he could persuade me to test the truth of what I'd been told.

I was surprised how often I found myself thinking of Tony while I was working on that trip. Something similar had happened with another man, years before, when I'd got to the same point of telling him, but after we parted I'd hardly given him another thought. I forgot him, and couldn't believe I'd felt about him as I must have done to tell him something so intimate. But I hadn't forgotten Tony. I thought of him a lot, wishing we were at least friends. He'd said, very quietly, that being 'just friends' would make a mockery of what there had been between us, and could still be, if I had not been so pig-headed and stupid. The parting had been painful to him, and he had never understood why I'd broken things up, and the only way he could deal with it was by never seeing me again, so I shouldn't talk to him about being 'friends'. I'd told him not to be so melodramatic, that it didn't suit him and wasn't like him, it wasn't reasonable and civilised, and he'd said that was how he felt, I could label his feelings how I liked. There were limits, he said, even to his tolerance.

I admired his attitude in a way. I like decisive people, and Tony was always that. He had a lot of other qualities, too, which I admired and I kept thinking of them on the long drives I was making. Tony had principles but he wasn't self-righteous or dogmatic. He loved his work – he is a solicitor, in a practice handling mainly legal aid defence cases – and had a sense of purpose about it, something which I, of course, lacked. I worked only because I liked to. Pleasure and fun took the place of purpose, and any satisfaction was always merely personal – not for a moment do I ever think my photographs serve much purpose. We used to argue about what Tony called my aimlessness, the way I was never striving towards a goal but was apparently the complete hedonist. It irritated him that I didn't, as he alleged, put my talents to better use. He thought that by choosing to photograph land-scapes I was choosing the soft option. Photographs, he argued, should have more than beauty about them. They should make some moral point. I used to jeer at him, and tell him his high-mindedness was a pain, but I quite liked his efforts to direct me into raising my standards and thinking more carefully about what I was doing. He maintained that inside the I-only-do-what-I-like Catherine there was another person, one who would welcome being made to do more than that. He said I insisted on being superficial and that I needed something to anchor me, to stop me drifting about.

I thought more and more of what Tony would have made of Susannah's box. He wouldn't have scoffed, like Rory; he wouldn't have said the contents were of no significance, just junk. He would have gone the other way and probably driven me mad with his theories and the intensity of his concentration. Puzzles appealed to him. He liked things to be complicated and even when they were not, had a habit of making them so. It used to infuriate me when he deliberately turned something simple and straightforward into a nightmare of possible hidden meanings. But apart from being intrigued with what was in the box the best thing about it, from his point of view, would have been that it forced me at last to think about Susannah. He had been fascinated (unnaturally so, in my opinion) by the fact that my 'real' mother had died when I was six months old. He said it could not have helped but affect me profoundly and would not accept that I hadn't been affected at all, that Charlotte was my mother and the dead Susannah a blank.

He'd met Charlotte, of course. While we lived together, it was inevitable he would meet the parents who were so much part of my life. We went to stay with them in Oxford for the weekend before my father died and they were successful visits. Charlotte liked Tony and got on better with him than my father did; she was more drawn to his seriousness, whereas my father found it a bit daunting and was perhaps perplexed as to why it appealed to me (though he never said so). Charlotte thought he had 'lovely manners' and 'listened properly', not the most flattering reasons to give for liking someone but, since manners and paying attention to what others said counted for her, not trivial either. But Tony thought Charlotte dull. He said she was quite sweet but boring and that never in a million years could she have been my mother. Even if he hadn't known she was not, he swore he would have guessed. I was annoyed and told him not to be so ridiculous, the world is full of daughters who resemble their mothers not one bit either in looks or character, and I immediately reeled off a list of those we both knew. But he was adamant. Somewhere, if you knew them well enough, you could always see at least a glimmer of the mother in any daughter. I denied this, and then I turned to asking what his point was anyway. He said that in my case it meant there was a missing link and always would be and it was of great importance to his understanding of so many things he didn't understand about me.

He liked to look at photographs of Susannah and then study my face and compare them. I hadn't, at that time, photograph albums in my possession, but he saw the photograph in my father's study, the one with Susannah in the background on the boat, and that started him off; then he found a couple of others around the Oxford house (Charlotte had always made a point of having them displayed quite naturally with all the other family photographs). No one among all the people who had known her had ever seen any resemblance between Susannah and me, but Tony found one after his diligent study. Only he saw what he claimed to be identical shaped ears, pointing solemnly to our well-shaped, round lobes and then to my father's lack of any lobes at all. It was nothing, but he acted as if it were something. Ear lobes, for heaven's sake. But he did have to concede that in general I did not look at all like Susannah. Unfortunately, he chose to say this in front of my father and to go on to ask him how he thought, looks apart, I might all the same be like her. My father didn't like this. He replied, quite curtly for him, that he had no idea. He said Susannah had died many years ago and he couldn't remember enough about her now to be sure of comparing anything about me with her.

Tony didn't believe him. He said my father must be reminded all the time of his dead wife and that it must be natural to look for a mother in a daughter. I defended my father vigorously and pointed out that since, apart from not looking in the least like Susannah, I had not grown up with her and had not automatically picked up her mannerisms, and had instead inevitably adopted many of Charlotte's, how would he be reminded of her? I reminded him that Susannah had had a Scottish accent and that I did not, so my father couldn't hear her in me either. Environment, in my case, had won the contest with heredity. But Tony wouldn't accept this. Confronted with how disturbed I became over the memory box, I knew he would have felt vindicated. What was all my angst about if not a long-put-off search for my 'real' mother? And why, Tony would've asked, did I want to find her *now*, at this point in my life, when my other mother had just left me? In his opinion, it would all have been obvious and satisfyingly neat. I struggled, knowing this, hearing Tony in my head so irritatingly clearly, to articulate, if only to myself, what was coming out of dealing with the box. I was not looking for my 'real' mother, I absolutely rejected that, but I was looking for myself, that was true. He would have liked that. I was glad not to be saying this out loud, when I would certainly have stumbled over the words, but instead imagining the conversation I might have had with him. In my own head, I could try, and try again, to grasp what I meant. I had some kind of impression — I took this slowly — that something in me had never properly connected. With what? I didn't know. An ugly simile came into my mind: I was like a plug looking for a socket and until I found it the current couldn't flow. Tony would have *really* liked that.

On that headland in Whitehaven, beside the holly tree on Melbreak, putting on the red hat in the aeroplane, what had I felt? Plugged in? Nothing so plebeian. What, then? A *frisson*, an excitement, a sensation not unlike vertigo, of being shaken and turned upside down. I had shivered on all those occasions, I had felt disembodied for a few seconds, and when this inner upheaval had subsided there had been a sense of disappointment that some profound truth about myself had evaded me. I would never have said this aloud to Tony, but it struck me that for some strange reason I might have said it to Rory. He had always empathised with my restlessness and sense of disconnection from life. Tony had never known what I was talking about. Tony never felt restless or disconnected; he was never waiting for something to rescue him from waiting. And he had no missing link. He knew exactly who he was and where he came from. He'd been so eager to introduce me not only to his parents (his father, a solicitor, his mother a schoolteacher), but to his brother and his two sisters and even to various aunts and uncles – he belonged, like Charlotte, to one of those tribe-like families and he was proud of it. Such families seem to me smug. I couldn't wait to get away from Tony's clan and it offended him. He accused me of being stand-offish and said I hadn't tried to fit in. Quite right, I hadn't. Why should I want to fit in to a group I found alien?

Tony's mother never did like me. She would deny it, naturally, but I think she made her mind up about me before ever she met me. She had liked the woman with whom he had had a five-year relationship before he met me, someone who had gone to school with him and whose family lived in the same county. This woman had been ideal in his mother's eyes, a teacher, like herself, an infant teacher in a local school. Then I came along and spoiled everything, including the conventional marriage everyone had anticipated for him. But I tried so hard, I know I did. I didn't want to meet Tony's mother, but he was so devoted to her it had to be done. I dressed up for the occasion. I got out of my jeans and jumper and wore a dress, just a simple summer dress, a plain cream-coloured thing. I wanted to look as innocent and unthreatening as possible. Demure, that's how I thought I should try to look. His mother was trying hard too, I think, determined to smile and welcome me warmly, but I saw the doubt in her eyes. Afterwards, I found out that Sarah, the girl before, had been a Susannah-like creature – slight, blonde, very pretty – and there was I, as tall as Tony, and, in spite of my cream dress and well-brushed hair, not at all demure. She couldn't bring herself to say how lovely it was to meet me. Instead, she said how much she'd heard about me and, to me, in my paranoid state, that sounded as though she had heard things she didn't like. I wasn't a nice, safe, worthy teacher like Sarah, but a freelance photographer which sounded arty and unstable. And I hadn't known Tony at school and my family hadn't mixed with his all their lives, with our mothers meeting at parents' evenings. I didn't have the kind of background Mrs Crowther was familiar with. She was probably as nervous as I was but it didn't show. 'How did you and Tony meet?' was her first direct question and when I said in an aeroplane, that he'd picked me up somewhere over the Channel on the way back from Paris, I knew I'd said the wrong thing. The truth, but wrong. Her Tony did *not* pick people up. He was a gentleman, who wouldn't do anything so vulgar. She didn't, of course, say any of that, but she stopped smiling and raised her eyebrows and was visibly taken aback. 'Not quite a pick-up, Mum,' Tony said, carefully. 'We just were sitting next to each other and got talking. All quite natural.' If I had left it at that things might have been OK, but I didn't, I had to jump in and say, 'Of *course* it was a pick-up! You even accidentally-on-purpose knocked my bag over to give yourself an excuse to pick everything up and talk to me.'

Oh God. The tone was set and I had set it. My real awkward, prickly self broke through at once in spite of all my vows to be sweet and gentle. Who could blame Mrs Crowther for thinking her darling son had been ensnared by an ill-mannered, abrasive hussy? I tried desperately to make up for this unfortunate beginning, but it was no good. I failed to fit in. Maybe if, that first time, I had just had to cope with the parents I would have managed to redeem myself, but there were so many other relatives there, all invited to Sunday lunch to meet me. My only small success was playing football with Tony's nieces and nephews in the garden – it was a relief to get outside and I dashed about energetically in spite of my too-tight dress and I think the children liked me, I *think* they did. It rained later in the afternoon and we played Scrabble and I did quite well, surprising Mrs Crowther with a wider vocabulary than I think she'd given me credit for. She queried my 'shandrydan' and when I said it was some sort of old, rickety carriage with a hood and that I'd come across it in a caption to a photograph she raised her eyebrows and picked up the dictionary. There was a rather tense silence while she looked it up and though she said, 'Clever girl, you're right,' I felt I hadn't been clever at all: I'd been a show-off.

I was exhausted by the time we left, and depressed. I couldn't understand how quiet Tony could come from such a family, all so hearty and noisy, so jolly and extrovert. I never liked visiting them and it never got any easier. I sent Mrs Crowther flowers after that first time, and always wrote and thanked her after each visit, but I was only doing what Charlotte told me to do. I simply couldn't connect with Tony's mother and he could never understand why.

I was thinking as I drove into Hampshire what a relief it had been, once Tony and I had parted, when I'd realised that I need never see the Crowthers again. I expect they felt the same way about me. I didn't stay long in Hampshire, only a day and a night, and I suspected the photographs wouldn't be as good as the others I'd taken in Dorset. I hadn't felt confident taking them and even began wondering, in a fanciful way, if it was because I didn't like being on Tony's patch. He always said he'd leave London in a few years' time and go back to where his parents lived, or near there. I'd been appalled to hear it. Long before we had reason to split up I'd heard a warning signal: don't get serious because you could never be a country solicitor's wife. It would have driven me mad, that kind of settled, safe, cosy existence. I like to move on, move around, all the time.

Driving back finally to London, on a cold afternoon with a threat of snow behind the dull sky hanging over the bleak countryside, I found myself wondering if that was after all entirely true. Did I really, still, want to move on all the time? Surely I was more centred on my home, my flat, than a true wanderer would be? And once I found a house that attachment would increase. Then I had a fleeting new thought about the memory box: it wasn't a box reflecting a woman focused on domesticity. Not exactly a startlingly original observation, but it made me consider for a moment what kind of daughter Susannah would have wanted me to be. I was beginning to think she would have wanted someone different from the daughter Charlotte wanted me to be, that she would not have brought me up in the same way. I had never let myself think before that Charlotte as a mother was anything less than perfect – she was so kind and gentle, so wrapped up in my welfare, so determined always to put me first and forgive me anything. Love had never been more unconditional than the love she had shown to me. I felt I was betraying her in some way when it entered my head that maybe Susannah would have treated me differently and that it might have been better for me. Was Charlotte what I had needed, however great her devotion to me?

My father had not always thought so. Sometimes he had criticised her for what he called 'over-indulging' me (carefully avoiding that unpleasant but more accurate word 'spoiling').

I'd heard him say of me, 'She needs to learn not to be so selfish', and, 'She needs to discipline herself.' He accused Charlotte, too, of letting me flit from one thing to another without her insisting on any kind of continuity or stability, and told her this was bad for me. That phrase – 'bad for her' – was said quite a lot when I was a child and not only by my father. My grandmother used it frequently. She also suggested to Charlotte that I needed a tougher approach: 'Catherine needs to finish what she starts sometimes,' she said. So far as I can recall, Charlotte never made any reply to either of them. She didn't argue with them, or tell them, as she well could have done, to deal with me themselves if they didn't approve of how she treated me, but I always had the sense that she didn't agree with them. She never made me carry on doing anything I said I was bored with. My boredom was enough. She would always try to find me something more interesting to do and was never angry. 'You give that child her head,' my grandmother would say, 'she'll get out of control if you're not stricter, she'll think she never has to settle to anything.'

Did I ever get out of control? Not while my grandmother was still alive, but perhaps I came near it for a while later. I was expelled from one school for a ridiculously silly reason. All I did was spray paint on a wall. True, it was a newly white-washed wall and, true, what I sprayed along it was vulgar and maybe a bit cruel, but at the time I saw no harm in it: I thought it was funny, and the cartoon I did at the end of what I'd written I thought quite talented. We had this games teacher called Miss Henn and a science master called Mr E. G. Gannon. We all hated both of them. Miss Henn was a bully who forced girls who had no athletic ability at all to try to do backward flips off a high box and regularly reduced them to tears, which she seemed to enjoy. I was never one of her victims but I couldn't bear her malicious attitude. And Mr E. G. Gannon – he always wrote his name like that, complete with initials – was a bully of another sort. He liked to sneer at pupils, using heavy sarcasm to humiliate them, and we all dreaded his lessons. Well, it was known that Miss Henn and Mr E. G. Gannon went out together – they'd been seen walking in the Botanical Gardens, holding hands (which of course made all of us thirteen-year-olds feel sick because he was fat and she was ugly). I sprayed on the new white wall the words 'HENN LAYS E.G.G.' and I did a cartoon of the two of them with Miss Henn lying on top of Mr Gannon. She had very bushy, red, coarse hair and a big, powerful bottom so that was simple enough to caricature and he was bald and wore enormous horn-rimmed spectacles and had a droopy moustache, so there was plenty there to identify him. A stranger couldn't possibly have recognised that my crude outline was a representation of those two teachers, but the whole school did.

When the headmistress asked me *why* I did it I remember shrugging and being unable to answer and I suppose that made my little crime more heinous than ever. 'It was a joke,' I said, which maddened her further. She said she would like this 'joke' explained to her because she failed entirely to see any humour in my actions. I had ruined a newly painted wall, and would most certainly have to pay for it to be repainted, and I had hurt two innocent teachers very much. '*They* hurt people all the time,' I blurted out. But the headmistress didn't want to hear my excuses. She wanted me to apologise profusely to the two teachers and then she might consider allowing me to remain in her school. I refused. My parents were angry with me, but I presented myself so convincingly to them as the champion of the underdog that they were not as furious as perhaps they should have been. My father did say, rather wearily, that writing rude words on a wall was no way to register any kind of protest, but he was so annoyed with the school for expelling me that he didn't go on about it.

So, as I said, it was fairly silly. I got into another school without too much difficulty and behaved myself. But I went off to London the moment I finished 'A' Levels, and lived in a squat for a bit (not long), took drugs (not many) — I suppose all that kind of pretty normal late-teenage behaviour could be called getting out of control. (And becoming pregnant, of course, but nobody knew about that at home.) The whole of that period was in any case short-lived and I was no more wild than a good many of my contemporaries, and unlike most of them I never broke off with my parents. They always knew where I was, if not exactly what being where I said I was amounted to — the address they had sounded perfectly respectable and they would never have envisaged a filthy, boarded-up basement. I never fell out with my father and mother, nor made enemies of them, and even then I never let a week go by without ringing them up. I call that quite remarkably exemplary behaviour, in the circumstances.

But it is true that though I deny I was ever *out* of control I felt no one was *in* control of me, especially not myself. It scared me. I remember feeling dangerous, as though I might do anything and not be able to stop myself even if I wanted to. My life up to then had been so neat and tidy, so safe and secure and predictable, thanks to my parents. I'd never had to look after myself, except in the most trivial of ways, and suddenly I was among a group of people my own age who didn't care about me and who couldn't look after themselves, never mind me. Most of the time they weren't even interested in me, whereas I was used to being the focus of a most intense and loving interest. This absence of attention did odd things to me. It excited me at first, it felt thrilling, but then I began to fear the freedom I'd snatched and had to pretend I didn't. A lot of energy went into this pretence and it changed me. I'd always said what I thought in the past, but now I had to struggle not to say I hated the way we lived and despised most of the people I was with. I'd only landed in the squat because of a friend at school whose brother lived there. We'd gone to visit him one Saturday just after 'A' levels, and I'm sure he spotted my potential as a source of money – probably his sister had filled him in on the fact that I had plenty of pocket money and never needed a holiday job. But I wasn't stupid, it didn't really take me long, once I'd moved in, to realise I was being used. We all shared everything but I was the one, sometimes the only one, who had anything to share.

At first, I was quite proud of this. I had the money, I hadn't done a damned thing to earn it; I was lucky, therefore it was only fair I should subsidise those less fortunate. I approved; I believed that single-handed I was righting some kind of wrong. And, of course, it made me popular – how generous I was, how liberal. But doubt set in pretty soon. I remember lying on a dirty mattress, barely able to see because the electricity was cut off and the last candle had been used, my head aching from lack of air and from the noise of heavy metal music playing at full blast in the room above us, where a whole band squatted complete with Alsatian dog. It was like being in a prison, and yet I knew I'd put myself there and that I *could* get out. All it took was will power, which for the first time in my life I didn't have – because of the drugs, I suppose (though I was a cautious user, compared to the others, and never took heroin or LSD, nothing more than cannabis really). But I was not well and that, too, was such a shock to my system it made it harder yet to leave. After two months had gone by I felt ghastly most of the time – I distinctly remember the terror of trying to haul myself up from that disgusting mattress and finding I couldn't, that I had to flop back, I was so dizzy and weak. 'Poor baby', that was what the boy I was with said, and not kindly – 'poor little baby, all on her own without her mummy.' I think I cried, with humiliation as much as anything.

What kept me there, apart from feeling ill and determination to pretend I was liking it, were the good days. The bright, sunny summer days when we went into the garden (completely overgrown of course but still a garden and really more attractive because the grass was thick and the trees unpruned and heavy with fruit) and for once someone had bought proper food and was cooking it on an open fire and we all sat in a circle round it and the music was just one guitar and we all sang. Sweet. Then there were other good days, when we would go out as a gang, to a festival, and everything seemed wonderfully free and easy and fun. Life in a comfortable suburban home such as that of my parents seemed ludicrous then – this was much better, it was what I wanted. My fears evaporated and I didn't worry so much about feeling strange and complicated and having to hide this from the others because they wouldn't understand. How could they, when I didn't understand myself? I began, on those happier days, to think I could train myself to tolerate dirt and disorder and the lack of privacy and all would be well. But I never succeeded. I got pregnant, I had the abortion, survived the infection, and went home, shocked out of my inertia. My mother was pleased to see me. She hadn't the faintest idea how I'd been living or what had happened. She said only that I was very pale and too thin and needed looking after. She didn't pry, to my relief. I think she was afraid to. Charlotte was basically a timid person and was always determined to think everything was fine.

Would Susannah have done? Would she have been able to look beyond my pallor, my loss of weight? Would she have been able to tell how near disaster I'd been and how greatly I was in need of a different kind of comfort than good food and rest? Charlotte did pretty well after all, just by being there, ready to take me back and restore me to health. Why suppose Susannah could have done any better? Why suppose it would have been a good thing to do any better? I don't know, at this distance of time, what precisely I mean by 'better' either. Talking. I think I must mean that with Charlotte there was no possibility of real talk. I wanted, always, to protect her from the uglier aspects of my life. Would I have wanted to protect Susannah? What difference would it have made that she was my biological mother, *she was me*, in a way Charlotte couldn't ever be? Kind, trusting Charlotte, around whom I ran rings, may have been dangerous for me in ways I never suspected. I bewildered her with my fierce love for her and yet by my erratic behaviour, so different from her own. She defended me when I had no defence.

I wondered where all this was going. In the direction Tony had always wanted it to go, that was where, the direction I had always refused to take. Slowly, as another person emerged, with the aid of her box, from behind the image I'd had of her, I was falling into the trap of believing I was going to solve a problem I couldn't even describe.

Chapter Ten

IT felt like an act of pilgrimage, almost an apology, to go to Oxford again soon after my trip to the West Country. I'd thought I would never go back there. God knows why I was feeling apologetic, but it was something to do with the first wavering doubts I'd been having about Charlotte. I felt shabby and soiled by them and so, on what would have been her sixtieth birthday, I drove once more to Oxford and put some roses on her grave.

Charlotte, unlike my father, had not wanted to be cremated. She had time to think about such things and she was adamant. No matter how environmentally wrong it might be, she said she wanted to be buried. Her family would have had her taken back to Edinburgh and buried with her parents but, again, her long time dying had given her the chance to think about this too. She wanted to be buried in Oxford, where she had spent her happily married life and where she had been a stalwart member of so many organisations connected to her local church. She left all decisions about a gravestone to me, apart from telling me she would like one. My father had wanted to be blown out to sea, but she wanted to be tucked up, all neat and tidy, just like herself.

I'd chosen an angel, what else? Perhaps embarrassingly Victorian, but then there was something decidedly Victorian about Charlotte in that her virtues were more of that era. And she had liked slightly fussy things, a taste anathema to my father and therefore rarely indulged. The angel was moulded in white marble, a full-length figure with her arms crossed modestly across her chest. On the plinth of this statue I had had engraved the words 'In memory of CHARLOTTE, beloved mother of Catherine' and then her dates and the fact that she was my father's wife. When she was buried, at the actual funeral, there was nothing of course for her family to see, and once the angel was in place I doubted if any of them had come to see it. They all lived too far away and it would be unlikely. So no one, so far as I knew, had read the inscription and taken exception to it. It was a lie in stone for someone, say, of Isabella's way of thinking, but she would never see and be outraged by it. It had pleased me to have those words carved – 'Beloved mother . . .' The world should be told that some mothers are made mothers by the act of birth and some by their own dedication and overwhelming love for a child. Charlotte had always said that being my mother, becoming my mother, was the most fulfilling part of her whole life. All I had done was to pay tribute and acknowledge this.

It's true what they say, about having a grave to visit being comforting and important, however ludicrous the idea. It didn't make me shiver, to imagine Charlotte's rotting body under the grass. On the contrary, it steadied me, to know what was left of her was there, quite dead. I sat on a bench for a few moments opposite her grave and wondered what I would have felt if Susannah had been buried and I had had a grave to visit. Would I have gone, now, and sat thinking about her there? It might have given me some feeling of reality about her. But it might have had another kind of effect, a harmful one. I thought again, sitting beside Charlotte's grave, of the dying, of the pain and distress, and it was awful to recall even though I could remind myself it was long since over. If I had sat beside Susannah's grave I would have been forced not to remember her dying, because I had nothing to remember and torture myself with, but forced to *imagine* what it had been like. I'd only begun to do that recently, in odd flashes of speculation, since opening the box, and I had quickly dampened them down. I felt shivers go through me whenever I thought about being with her at the moment of death. I'd been with Charlotte, but that was different. We'd said our farewells, I knew what was coming. But then, with Susannah, I had been a baby. I was not in her arms, my grandmother had said, but lying in a cot beside her bed. They found her dead, with her hand in mine, thrust through the bars of the cot, my tiny hand warm, clutching her dead fingers in my sleep, her face pressed up against the side of the cot to be near me, my breath making the strands of her hair flutter a little . . . it was horrible to me to think of the scene and so I never had done.

But I did then. I thought of Susannah straining to be near me, clinging on to me for dear life, and myself oblivious. No harm had been done to me, I knew nothing about the dying. I was told I did not even whimper as my hand was detached from hers. There was no possibility of my experiencing any kind of shock. In the Baby Book Susannah had kept (one of those cosy little volumes with a naked baby cooing 'My Records' on the cover) my grandmother had written for the second day after Susannah's death 'first tooth cut'. She'd tried to keep these pathetic entries going: and so my first tooth was of enough importance in the midst of her grief to have to write it down. So while Susannah was dying I was cutting a tooth – the juxtaposition struck me as farcical. This same book had been passed on to Charlotte in due course and she had seen no trace of the absurd about it. To her, it was like a holy book. I was nearly two before she started making entries herself, but once she did she was indefatigable. She had recorded my first clear sentence in red, with a line of exclamation marks – 'Want choclick, Mama!' The 'Mama' was underlined. Maybe I hadn't said the word at all before that, or had I only said it to my grandmother? I'd hardly have known to call my grandmother granny, so presumably I'd called her 'Mama'. But do babies only know the word from hearing mothers say it to them – are they just imitating what they are coaxed to say? My, the mysteries of motherhood. At any rate, finally some few weeks after the handover, I said the magic word to Charlotte and she was thrilled. She loved the mother word, all versions of it, Ma, Mama, Mum, Mummy, all of them. Yet I know I never used it as much as other children. Once I'd mastered her name, I liked to call her Charlotte, I suppose because I must have liked the sound and was proud of being able to say it. And perhaps because I was imitating my father and I wanted to call her what he called her. But I was aware, all the same, that Charlotte preferred Mummy. She always smiled delightedly whenever I raced across the playground towards her yelling, 'Mummee – Mummeee!' When I'd thrown myself into her eager arms and she was hugging me tight she'd say, 'Mummy's got you, Mummy's got you,' and I'd hear the pleasure in her voice. But she never stopped me calling her by her Christian name. She let me choose my own way.

I'd never called Susannah anything, that was for sure. What had she had from me? Gurglings, I suppose, and smiles. I imagined her face bending over that cot, pale and wasted, dark shadows under her eyes, and I heard her shallow breaths and, worst of all, I felt the sweat on her slippery fingers as they held my own . . . It was a tableau I had taken care never to reconstruct, and Charlotte's graveside was no place to begin to do it, and yet as I got up from the bench and began to walk away it wasn't the birds in the trees above I was hearing, or the crunch of the gravel on the path under my feet, but the creak of the cot as I moved and the whimper I was making in my sleep. I saw the room I had never seen, with the curtains drawn, the light dim, and this poor woman hovering over her baby and dying . . . Mawkish? Of course. I laughed at myself as I stumbled out of the churchyard, but I let the tears that had gathered in my eyes leak out down my face. I didn't need enlightenment as to why I was wallowing in sentiment now, but I couldn't work out how it connected with my earlier feelings about myself. All I felt was that it did. I was getting nearer to something important and I knew it had been a mistake to break off from concentrating on the memory box.

Still, the space I'd given myself through working again and enjoying it had made me a little more objective. Back in my flat, I realised there wasn't much left that had been in the box to concentrate on. So many of the objects had been already dealt with – the feathers had been thrown into the sea, the red hat left on an aeroplane, the rucksack and map used. The shell? It still sat there but held no mystery any more now I'd walked on beaches full of similar ones. I'd worn the necklace, to great effect, and looked at myself in the mirror, and I'd followed up an address in the address book. The sum total of all this was not negligible, but nor had there been any blinding revelations, and I hadn't reached any useful conclusion. All I had left, though, were those things I'd thought the least interesting – the paintbox, the incomplete painting, the prints cut out of a book or a catalogue.

They were still in the box. I got out the painting and paintbox and set them out on my bed. They were as uninspiring as I remembered. Was that why they were numbered almost last, 9, 10? Or was it because they were the most important? Guessing games again. I picked up the painting and propped it up, looking at it first from a distance and then scrutinising it closely. It was as unexciting as I'd first thought, showing a stretch of moorland with what looked like heather growing on it, and a hill behind with a stone cottage just visible, halfway up. The moorland in the foreground had been neatly painted, though the heather was clumsily suggested, but the hill was only sketched in, in pencil, and so was the building. What puzzled me was trying to decide what on earth it was that had captured Susannah's imagination enough for her to want to paint it – for I was quite sure this half-finished effort was her own. There was no signature on the painting, but the whole style was reminiscent of the famous meadow watercolour. There was nothing particularly striking about it, nothing to make anyone wish it had been completed. It could be virtually anywhere in the British Isles, on any of the high ground in England, Scotland or Wales. There were no distinguishing characteristics to pinpoint the location. Even the heather didn't pin it to Scotland – plenty of heather elsewhere. Why on earth had this unfinished watercolour been left to me?

Completely baffled, but at least calm, I turned to the paintbox itself. An ordinary Winsor & Newton paintbox containing the usual small blocks of paint, twelve of them, six either side of the slot for the brush, and the brush lying there, its bristles (good quality) cleaned of paint. The red paints had barely been touched. I touched them. I put my finger on them, rubbing it over the still shiny surface. They felt firm, solid. The browns, greens and yellows were worn down, as were the black and purple, corresponding to the colours already used in the painting. Not by much, though. She had been sparing with the paint. This painting of Susannah's was on a real artist's board. I turned it over and saw the name of an Edinburgh art shop stamped on the back. It seemed likely that this was a Scottish scene, one she had painted, perhaps, while she still lived at home, before ever she met my father. There were moors within easy reach of my grandmother's house – I'd been taken to them by her myself as a child, with Rory, and heard tales of her taking her own children there.

So, an unfinished, not particularly well executed watercolour of an unmemorable country scene, probably in Scotland. Surely the most significant thing about it, then, must be its very unfinished state. Quite pleased with how cool and rational I was being, I put it to myself that something unfinished needed to be finished. Therefore it had been left to me with the hope that I would go ahead and finish it. Now, to do so I would need to locate this scene and go there and prop up my little easel and get painting. I was feeling quite the ace sleuth by then, basking in my own cleverness. But I wasn't going to act on it. I'd had enough of tearing off on wild-goose chases, however enjoyable. Instead, I went and filled a jam jar with water, took the painting through to the kitchen, and dipping the brush into the water started to fiddle with the green paint. I dabbed a bit on and saw of course it was the wrong green, a mismatch made worse by its freshness. I played with the two greens on offer, mixing them on the lid, and added a bit of brown and a bit of yellow and a dab of black, and then I tried again. Better. Still not an exact match, but better.

It was odd that she'd started with the foreground. Nobody ever does that. First thing we were taught in art lessons was to start at the top and work downwards. She should have begun with the sky, which would be grey. Any other colour would look wrong. A pale, misty grey, very difficult to capture. I stroked my cleaned brush over the white and then the black and applied it to the painting. Too deep. It needed more white. I put the brush down and stared again at the painting, now with my own inexpert marks upon it. One thing, I couldn't really ruin it since it showed little talent. And yet I felt I was doing just that, ruining it, defiling whatever of hidden value had been there. I was rejecting what I had decided was her purpose in leaving it to me: to encourage me to seek this place out in order to complete the painting as faithfully as I could. I had to be *there*, where she had been. Anything else would be cheating.

Still I resisted the crazy idea of trailing round Scotland looking for a likely stretch of open moorland – good God, I'd be spoiled for choice. But then fate took a hand. I was asked to do a job for the Scottish Tourist Board, which involved taking photographs not for a gaudy colour brochure but for a specially commissioned book called something like *Hidden Scotland*. I was to search out places not on the usual tourist beat and try to capture 'true wildness', making the shots as dramatic as possible. They'd wanted Fay Godwin, but she wouldn't even consider it – she did her own books and had her own projects – so I felt flattered to be next in line after someone whose work I'd admired so much. If ever I were good enough to have my own exhibition I'd want it to match her superb 'Presences of Nature'.

Tony always said how unexpected it was that I lacked that kind of ambition (to have an exhibition, he meant). He maintained that on the surface I seemed the ambitious type – opinionated, even aggressive in manner. He couldn't understand why I didn't channel my energies into getting together a body of work which would justify some kind of public display and through being exhibited would raise my status, not to mention my bargaining power. He thought I frittered my talents away on commercial jobs unworthy of them. In fact, I take only those assignments that appeal to me and, as he well knew, the money is irrelevant. There was nothing wrong, that I could see, in working for commercial concerns.

So, I have no ambition in the sense that Tony wanted me to have. I never said so to him, but my only ambition is to keep on doing what I like and get nearer to satisfying myself. That's the hardest thing to do, satisfy myself. I'm always just missing, not exactly perfection – I don't think perfection exists, or even that one should expect it to – but missing what I had intended to capture. Sometimes it's just a question of a shadow here, a darkening where there should have been more light, or of a very slightly wrong angle – something technical like that. Technique is important and mine isn't of the highest standard. I understand the technicalities – I am not one of those photographers who haven't been trained properly in the use of a camera – but I am too impatient to profit from my understanding. I tend to rush, to follow my eye too quickly. This captures mood and atmosphere, but it damages the standard of the result. One day, I always tell myself, I will take time and try harder and I will be satisfied. But I never do.

I didn't think I would do it on the Scottish Tourist Board job either, but I was quite confident I could satisfy them, if not myself, and that was enough. I thought I would start off around Edinburgh and base myself there. So it was a logical next step to ask Isabella and Hector if I could stay with them. Isabella was as surprised to hear my request as I was to find myself making it. I hadn't been near their house for a long time, a fact much resented by my aunt. Once Rory had left home, there was no attraction. I still went to stay with my aunt and uncle so long as he came home in the school holidays, but when they were over, that was it. Rory left school at seventeen – he refused to stay any longer – and after that he came and stayed with us sometimes in Oxford. My grandmother was dead by then, so there was nothing to take me back to Edinburgh. Probably this upset Isabella and seemed like a calculated insult as well as siding with Rory, but I didn't see it like that. I couldn't really believe she wanted me to visit her anyway when we had never really got on and she was surely as conscious of this as I was. The odd phone call, the obligatory Christmas and birthday cards with maybe a note inside, and that was enough in my opinion.

After she'd finished getting over the surprise, she seemed pleased, and was more welcoming than I would ever have given her credit for, when I arrived after my long, exhausting drive. I'd almost forgotten how much I liked their house in Heriot Row, how elegant it had always seemed compared with our Oxford home with its Edwardian heaviness and large suburban gardens. A town house like Isabella's and Hector's in the heart of a city like Edinburgh was exciting and different. I'd loved the noise of the cobbles, and the old-fashioned street lamps, and the friendly look of a terrace as opposed to houses like ours so disdainfully separated from each other. Isabella put me in Rory's old room at the top of the house, overlooking the street, and I was startled to find it virtually the same as when I used to share it with him. The bunks had gone, to be replaced with a brass bedstead, but otherwise nothing had been touched. Everything of Rory's was still there, even some clothes hanging in the cupboard. His posters were on the walls, of Jimi Hendrix and Bob Marley and other musicians he'd liked in his teens, and his collection of fashion magazines gathered dust on a shelf. Photographs of actors stood on the chest of drawers – he adored Richard Burton, which I'd always thought puzzling – and there was what looked like a cash box beside it which I knew contained make-up. I tried to open it to check, but it was locked. I thought it peculiar that Isabella had kept this room unchanged, that she hadn't cleared it out. It felt like a dead person's room, like a shrine, and I couldn't help wondering if it meant Rory's parents had closed their minds to him. Or perhaps it was just a sign of laziness. People in large houses can become lazy in that way; they can afford the luxury of leaving rooms untouched and not going into them. My parents did it in Oxford. I can't think either of them went up to the top floor from one year's end to another after the cousins stopped coming to stay. Charlotte sent her cleaning lady up to give that floor a good going over every now and again and that was it. Now I realised Isabella must do the same – there was no dust on the surfaces, no smell of neglect.

The windows had obviously been opened regularly and the bed aired. It was made up with fresh sheets for me and there were flowers on the bedside table.

I missed the bunks. God, how Rory loved them. He slept on the top one, I on the bottom. Those bunks hadn't been at all necessary for reasons of space – the room was easily big enough to take three, never mind two, single beds – but Rory had pleaded to be allowed them and for once was not told to be sensible. He'd wanted them so that he could pretend he was at sea. First he'd clamoured for a hammock, but when told that really was silly (no reason given) he switched to bunks as the next best thing. When he'd moved on from pretending he was a sailor on the high seas, he liked to imagine he was floating. He'd lie on the top bunk and convince himself he was suspended in the air and no one could touch him. Lying below him, I always felt buried alive, trapped, and I worried too that he would fall through the bottom of his bunk and land on me, crushing me to death. I'd get breathless during the night for fear of this happening and often tipped myself out on to the floor and slept there rather than go on dreading possible suffocation. Rory did once offer to let me sleep in the top bunk, but when I climbed the ladder I knew it wouldn't work. The very sensation of being up in the air which he liked made me panic. I preferred to be near the floor. So he was always on top and I was below, always pretending I only fell out accidentally.

And yet I missed the bunks, in spite of these far from happy memories. The new bed was very comfortable, but I didn't sleep well the first night, thinking about Rory. Lying in his old room I considered his accusation more carefully, that he'd never been loved by his parents, away from his own bitter attitude. Never been loved? Never been touched much, as I had been, but did that mean 'never loved'? It was so hard to tell with people like Isabella and Hector, people not given to visible signs of emotion. Who could be sure that their seemingly cold façade signified a lack of love? Their anger with him, which I had seen often enough, was possible to justify, but which came first, his own bad behaviour or the feelings of rejection he claimed had triggered it?

But what was clear enough in my memory was Rory's announcement that he was gay and his parents' open horror at this news. He'd insisted I should be there when he told them, saying that otherwise he wouldn't have the nerve. I told him I thought it was wrong to have me as a witness, it would only make it harder for Isabella and Hector to accept. My presence would embarrass them. It was something Rory should do on his own, but he said he couldn't and wouldn't. 'Why don't you tell them?' he actually said and seemed to imagine I'd consider it. He maintained he'd tried loads of times to tell them, but they didn't want to hear and always deliberately misunderstood what he was edging towards, or else left the room just as he got going. 'They'd take it from you,' he'd pleaded. Why he thought that, I don't know. I was only just seventeen myself, a girl – they would on the contrary think I didn't know what I was talking about and if I managed to convince them I did they would be shocked at my knowingness. It was an impossible suggestion and I said so. But then Rory was in such despair I agreed to be there, as he wanted. I didn't understand his burning need to tell them, but he said it was driving him crazy, that it was something he had to get out in the open and have done with, then he'd know where he stood. Half of him, I think, wanted to be thrown out of the house, a never-darken-our-door-again situation, and the other half wanted to be told they'd always known and it didn't matter. But either way he wanted a dramatic showdown and was determined to get it.

I went to Edinburgh as soon as I'd finished school, for two weeks. Rory hadn't bothered to write more than his name on most of his school exam papers – not that his parents yet knew that – and hadn't a hope of passing anything except maths. Maths came naturally to him. He hadn't had to do any work yet he reckoned he knew enough to pass that one. At any rate, he was in great spirits, the weather was brilliant, and we had a good time. His parents had taken a cottage on the coast near Berwick-upon-Tweed and I went there with them all for the second week. Rory and I slept all morning then went off in the afternoon to find somewhere to smoke. It was still beautiful, sunny weather and we lolled in the grass near the sea talking rubbish about what we were going to do in the holidays – or in Rory's case, now he'd left school, or so he said. I was leaving on the Saturday and he decided he'd make his announcement (that was what he referred to the breaking of the news as, really pompously) on Friday evening, after supper. We were going out to a restaurant about five miles away, a place famous for its seafood, and Rory said that would be the best time, 'when they've stuffed themselves and Dad's on the whisky'.

I hardly touched the lobster, I was so nervous – far more so than Rory. He was so charming that evening, and his manners perfect. He was extra solicitous, helping his mother off with her coat, pulling her chair out for her before the waiter could, inviting his father to tell us about his latest deal (which usually had us yawning rudely) and in general being a son anyone could be proud of. He looked at his most handsome, too, his blond hair brushed till it was quite smooth, his shirt properly buttoned up and his school tie (which he loathed and never, ever, wore outside school) neatly knotted. He'd even put a suit on, though his mother had said he didn't need to and ordinarily he had to be bribed to wear it. I saw people admiring him, and I saw that Isabella saw them and that she was gratified. We looked a lovely family group, just what she wanted us to look. And yet she was very far from being stupid and I saw a certain wariness in her expression as she looked at butter-wouldn't-melt-in-his-mouth Rory. Hector was entirely taken in, doubtless thinking Rory had at last seen the error of his ways, or that the discipline of his school had worked this miracle, but Isabella wasn't. She waited, and so did I.

We got back to the cottage about ten o'clock. 'Early start tomorrow for you, Catherine,' said Hector. 'You should be off to your bed.' I said yes, I should be, ready to chicken out at the slightest encouragement, but Rory leapt in to say let's have a farewell drink before we go to bed. He got Hector's favourite malt whisky out, and filled glasses for us all. Even Isabella drank whisky occasionally and she didn't demur. I saw her noticing what I noticed: Rory's hand shaking slightly, though not enough to spill the whisky. He was agitated, clicking his fingers and whistling and walking about the small room, with his drink left standing on the table. Suddenly, he snatched it up and drank it in one go and said, 'I have an announcement to make.' Both Hector and Isabella smiled. I expect Hector thought he was going to say he'd decided after all to stay on at school and take Highers (the equivalent of our 'A' levels), and Isabella thought he was going to say he'd decided to take the boring job she'd fixed up for him for the holidays, helping in an old people's home. What Rory, in fact, then went on to say wiped the smiles off both their faces rapidly. 'I want you to know', he said, 'that I am gay. I-am-gay. A homosexual. There is no doubt about it, I've always known . . .'

'Don't be disgusting!' Isabella said, then without another word she got up and left the room. 'Mum!' Rory shouted after her, but she was out of the room and up the stairs and had gone into her bedroom all in a moment. Hector sat there stupefied, then he groaned and put his glass down and covered his face with his hands. 'Dad?' Rory said. 'Oh my *God*,'

Hector said, his voice muffled, 'my *God*, why did you have to . . .' Rory looked at me. He had a funny, twisted grin on his face, as though to say, 'Told you so.'

'Uncle Hector,' I said, 'it isn't anything terrible.'

He dropped his hands and gave me such a baleful glare I flinched. 'Keep out of this,' he said. 'I don't know what you're doing here, to hear this.' His fat face was horribly red and I thought that any moment he might have a fit (if I'd known about strokes then I'd have been sure he was on the edge of one).

'She's my witness,' Rory said. He, on the other hand, was white-faced, a little muscle working away in his left cheek and his eyes so narrowed they'd almost disappeared.

'Witness?' Hector said, incredulous. 'What the hell do you mean, *witness*?'

'She's a witness to what I've told you,' Rory said, 'so you and Mum can't pretend I never did. I've told you I'm gay. That's that. You know. I've been trying to tell you for years and you'd never . . .'

'Oh, shut up!' Hector roared. 'Stop all this. I've had enough. God knows why you have to make such an issue of it. God knows why you're so bloody proud of being a queer.'

Rory laughed. He shook his head and laughed. I thought it would be enough to make his father strike him, but looking at Hector, as I did, fearfully, I saw that he'd realised, amazingly, what I'd realised – that Rory might appear to be laughing, in a terribly false-sounding way, but he was near to crying. I went and put my arms round him and he put his round me, and we stood there like the two babes in the wood did before they lay down.

'Oh, God,' said Hector, and slumped back into his chair. All the rage had gone out of him. He sighed and closed his eyes and eventually said, 'We'd better all go to bed – this is no use. Things will look different in the morning.'

'I'll still be gay,' Rory said.

Hector didn't reply, just shuffled off, looking old and beaten. And, of course, he had to face Isabella.

The next morning I was up very early. A mini-cab was coming to take me to the station at seven, but I was up and ready by six, dying to be gone and hoping nobody would be awake, so that I could avoid any post-mortem. But Isabella came down just before the cab arrived. She made herself some tea without speaking and then, when I began to thank her for having me, she cut in and said, 'I hope you'll be discreet, Catherine. There's no need to repeat any of Rory's silliness.' It was so tempting to agree, especially as by then I could hear the cab coming up the lane and in a moment I'd be gone. But I managed to say that Rory wasn't silly, and that it had been hard for him to tell the truth and even that I admired him. 'Admire him?' Isabella said, disgust contorting her features. 'There's nothing to admire about what he thinks he is, young lady.'

So it wasn't surprising, was it, that I had no time after that for my dear aunt? I rushed back to Charlotte and told her everything and she said, 'Poor Rory.' I loved her more than ever. But when I told my father he said, 'Poor Isabella and Hector,' and I was outraged and asked him how dare he feel sorry for parents who were so cruel and behaved so brutally. My father said they hadn't, that he didn't see their reaction as cruel or their behaviour as brutal. 'So, if I'd come to you and Charlotte and said I was a lesbian you'd have left the room or yelled at me and told me not to be silly and all that?' I shouted at him. My father stood his ground, and said no, but he'd have been upset and shocked and it would have taken him a while to adapt; he wouldn't immediately have embraced me and said how lovely, I'm proud of you. I was so cross with him, and ready to work myself into a fine state of contemptuous rage, but he went on to say that no parent wants their child to have a life where belonging to a minority sets them apart and makes it more difficult than it already is to be happy. I said in that case it was up to society to change, not the minority, but he said I was missing his point, which was that parents want *easiness* above all for their children and they don't want to feel separated from them by something beyond their comprehension. We argued half the night but my father wouldn't budge. He maintained Hector and Isabella couldn't control their shock and that they would come round when they got over it and saw it wasn't as if their son had confessed to being a murderer.

But he was wrong: they never did. I was lying in a room Rory hadn't been in for years and years. There had been no *rapprochement*, either then or later. His parents didn't tell him never to darken their door again or anything similarly melodramatic, but it was as though they hadn't heard what he'd told them, just as he'd feared. He told me afterwards that when I'd gone nobody spoke the whole of the rest of that day. They ate separately, they went for walks – each of them alone – they sat and read in silence, and then they went to bed. He packed a bag and left in the middle of the night, walking the ten miles to the station, where he caught the first train back to Edinburgh, let himself into the house and cleared it of all the cash he could find. It was a quite substantial amount, though I forget how much exactly, and he used it to take himself off to Greece for a month, leaving a note behind saying this. That was the beginning of everything that followed, of what Hector called his 'waywardness'. After that, he hardly saw them again, except at our grandmother's funeral when to everyone's astonishment he turned up literally at the graveside. He communicated with them through us, through my parents and me, and nearly always it would be about money. He kept an eye on his elderly relatives on his father's side, knowing that Hector would never have told them he was gay and therefore he wouldn't have been cut out of their wills – and he was right. The announcement of a Cameron death, of the right family, would have Rory ringing us to get us to find out about the will. Once he knew the solicitors, he was in there like a flash claiming his whack. Again and again he'd be saved from penury, just in time.

For years now Rory had maintained he didn't care any more about the break with his parents. He claimed to have no feelings for them. The parental bond, especially the myth of the maternal bond, meant nothing to him. He thought of Hector and Isabella as weird strangers to whom he was connected by an accident of blood. He said he cared no more about them than I did about Susannah and that, like me, he denied he had anything of either of them in him. He was a freak, genetically independent. We were united, he said, in our repudiation of any link with our biological mothers. I'd struggled to protest that his case was different because Isabella had brought him up, as Charlotte had brought me up, and that this forged another and just as strong a bond, but he wouldn't have it. Isabella, he said, had not wanted any bond. She'd worked hard, on the contrary, to keep him at arm's length and had fought his own need for closeness. Hector he didn't feel so bitter about – he was a man, not so much had been expected of him. Isabella had carried him in her body and given birth to him and fed him and he saw it as terrible that she had no love for him long before he put her to the test. Mothers, Rory said, giving the lie to his own dismissal of the maternal instinct, should love their children. Nothing else mattered to a child.

I fell asleep finally still troubled, worrying about whether Rory had been right, and determined to talk to Isabella properly if she would allow me to. I wasn't, after all, here just to discover things about Susannah.

Chapter Eleven

ISABELLA, the night before, had seemed different, but I'd reminded myself I hadn't seen her in her own home since I was an adult. Maybe she'd always been hospitable and I'd just never appreciated it. She gave me a delicious dinner, cooked entirely by herself and very expertly, and was quite charming. Never in my life had I seen any vestige of charm in her before, but in her own home that night it was there and for the first time I saw Rory in her. She'd been to some committee meeting that day to do with her voluntary work for the aged, and she recounted to Hector and me with astonishing verve what had been said by the other members, imitating their various accents and intonations until she had us laughing out loud. I'd never known she was an excellent mimic — just like Rory. She had exactly his taste for spirited mockery and it was a shock. Even as I was listening to her, though, it had crossed my mind that Rory must surely know this, must have been aware of this other side of his mother.

The charm was not in evidence at breakfast. Isabella was back to being the curt, brisk woman I knew. She didn't ask how I had slept or betray any concern about me at all, but merely said she had a busy day ahead and I must look after myself because she had no time to run after me. I said, of course, that I didn't want her to bother about me and all I wanted was coffee and then I'd be on my way. We agreed we'd see each other in the evening and she issued an abrupt command to eat with her. 'Hector is dining out,' she said.

'We'll be cosy and have something on a tray.' I said that would be fine. I made my coffee – she jumped irritably when I dropped the bottom part of the espresso machine and told me to be more careful (though since it was metal and undamaged I don't know why) – and watched her getting ready to go. She sorted out her fearsomely large black handbag on the kitchen table and when she had it organised to her satisfaction and was holding her car keys at the ready she suddenly looked at me intently and said, 'Do you remember those dancing classes?' I said naturally I did, I'd adored them. 'I still have the kilts,' she said, 'yours the red, his the green. I came across them just the other day. I kept them for . . . well, I kept them, in case.' She did her jacket up, snapped her handbag shut, and said she'd be off. But still she stood there, looking at me, and I began to wonder if she had expected her remark about the kilts to call forth some other response from me, but what could that be? I'd said I recalled the dancing lessons and had loved them – what else was I meant to say? 'Good times,' she said at last, and then, turning away and walking to the door, 'What a waste it all was.'

A waste? Did she mean the cost of those lessons? Surely not. They were held in a dusty church hall without any kind of special facilities and the teacher was a very ordinary middle-aged woman, hardly a professional dance teacher. She taught only Highland dancing – reels, strathspey, sword dances, that kind of thing. There were about twenty of us and we all wore kilts and soft black shoes called pumps. I only attended these classes in the long school summer holidays when I stayed with Rory, between the ages of five and ten, and it was impressed upon me how privileged I was to be allowed to join in for such a limited period. A special case was being made for me – normally Miss Wallace required diligent weekly attendance all the year round. I was excited to be included and had no problem with being grateful and thanking Miss Wallace 'nicely' as instructed. The lessons were madly energetic and noisy and a lot of fun, with our teacher throwing herself around with an abandon which belied her years (not that I knew what they were). During the few weeks I took part there happened always to be the annual display and Rory and I were selected every year, for three or four years, to demonstrate one of the dances. We loved being the centre of attention, especially Rory, and, I expect, made an attractive couple with Rory so blond and me so dark. Isabella enjoyed getting us ready, putting us into frilly-fronted-and-cuffed white shirts as well as the kilts, and I was aware she was showing us off when she led us, one on each hand, on to the floor to perform. Rory always behaved beautifully on these occasions, quite excelling himself, because for once he was doing something he liked and at the same time pleasing his mother, a rare state of affairs. He was a much better dancer than I was, too. Watching him do a Highland fling was quite something. He was so quick and nimble, his feet flashing from position to position in half the time it took mine, his toes pointed in a way mine never would, and his head held high, whereas I tended to droop. If it had been any other kind of dancing, ballet, say, tremors of unease at his pleasure in it might have coursed through his dear mother's veins, but as it was Highland dancing she appeared to have no qualms – Highland dancing was manly.

Was that what she had been remembering, not anything as trivial as the cost, but her own pride in Rory's talent? And was 'the waste' the realisation that it had never come to anything, like all his other talents? I wasn't at all sure, but I suddenly saw how this subject she'd brought up herself could give me the opening I needed. I would tackle her that evening, when we were on our own, throwing back at her her own remark about 'the waste'. As I drove through the Edinburgh traffic I was planning in my head what exactly I would say to her, but I soon had to concentrate so hard that I forgot about it. The trouble was I didn't know where I was going. I'd told Isabella only that I was doing a job for the Tourist Board and wanted to find some remote moorland not too far away and she'd directed me to the Lammermuir hills – 'Plenty of moorland there for you.' I'd taken the road she told me to, but at some point I was going to have to trust to luck and turn off it on to a minor road to find what I hoped to find. I wasn't foolish enough to imagine I'd discover a hillside exactly corresponding to Susannah's painting, but considering that scene was pretty much of a nothingness I thought I stood a good chance of matching it well enough. But unfortunately it was raining, that light, misty rain so familiar in the Scottish hills, rain covering everything like the finest gauze, veils of it swathed across the hills. It made no sound on the car roof the windows, merely bestowing its endless damp caresses silently mile after mile, but I had the windscreen wipers going full pelt and still I was obliged to go slowly and peer anxiously ahead. I could hardly see at all, never mind decide which turning looked the most promising. I soon had no idea where I was. Isabella had told me I'd been to this area on picnics with Hector and Rory, when I was young, as well as with my grandmother, but I had no memory of the countryside though I thought I could remember the picnics. It wouldn't have much mattered anyway when visibility was so bad, nothing would have leapt out to trigger any deeply buried memories of being here before.

At least this time, this particular mad venture, would be justified by taking photographs, but I couldn't take any in those conditions. *Hidden Scotland*, indeed – everything would be hidden. But after another half-hour of trundling along the little road I'd blundered on to, the sky did begin to lighten and the rain became intermittent. I began to get my bearings and see that I was certainly in the middle of moorland. No heather, of course, but then it was the wrong season. The ground either side of the narrow road still had traces of snow wiped in strands across it and the burns were full of melted ice, but it was spring all the same. I was looking for a track, the sort we used to look for when Hector took us on picnics. If I didn't remember going with my grandmother, I recalled well enough going with Hector, but I suppose I was older. He liked to find a track so unused it took our sharp young eyes to spot it and then we'd drive up it, bumping along very slowly, and come to a halt when we could no longer see the road. Usually there'd be a stream, a burn, and Rory and I would be allowed to paddle, and Hector would be at his most indulgent, sitting in a collapsible chair he'd brought and nodding off behind a newspaper. Often we'd go off on our own, when we were sure he was asleep, and he'd wake up and panic because we'd vanished and then his roars would bellow out and we'd take our time answering, just to make him suffer more. When he took us home he'd complain to Isabella about our bad behaviour and say he wasn't taking us again.

All this mundane rambling was filling my head, not thoughts of Susannah, as I looked for a track and found one. I chose it because, although I couldn't see any cottage, I could see some large stones such as the ones in her painting, and the moorland rose up behind them as the hill did in it. It would do. It was a view as similar to the dull one she had chosen to paint as I was likely to find. Feeling glad that there was no one to see me, I parked the car and got out the bag with the paints and the painting in it. Then I filled a jar with water from the burn and, setting up a little camp stool I'd stuck in the boot, I self-consciously began to paint. I did more staring around than painting. It was all so bleak, so colourless. There was nothing to attract the eye and delight it. It seemed an event when a bird, one bird, flew languidly across the sky, barely flapping its wings. When it disappeared all was empty and still. I couldn't see any sheep, but on the air I could hear a scratchy-throated coughing that I knew belonged to some ancient ewe. I was soon cold crouching there, though I was warmly clad, and wished I'd brought a flask of coffee. Impatiently, I dipped my brush in the water again and mixed grey to start on the sky.

The correct grey was still difficult to capture even with the sky helpfully above me. The longer I gazed at it, the more delicate the grey seemed, paler, softer, more white than grey. The board grew damp as I washed over it again and again – all this, for a dreary grey sky. I knew that at any moment I would become so furious with my hopeless efforts that I'd tear the wretched picture up, so I moved on to the greens and browns of the hillside, of the moorland. This was easier. I matched Susannah's green quite satisfactorily, given that her paint was old and mine new, and it was fun stippling it with brown and occasionally a very small bit of dark yellow. There were all kinds of colours and tones in the grass, which gradually emerged the longer I looked, and I enjoyed adding minute touches of purple and dots of white. It took me a long time to achieve the effect I wanted – and not, perhaps, the effect Susannah had wanted – but I was pleased with the result, feeling I was improving her picture. It was beginning to look more interesting, its blandness livened up. Only the cottage, the croft, to do, and the stones. I hesitated. Without a croft in front of me to copy, I doubted if I could invent one, so I decided to paint over it, to obliterate her outline. I felt wicked, but it was quickly done because she'd only sketched it in and I only needed to paint over pencil and a very small attempt at shading. But I kept the stones since there were actual stones around to use as models. I grew bold, which was a mistake, and made the shapes too distinct, so that far from blending into the hillside, as they did, they stood out awkwardly in my painting.

But it was done, complete. I regarded my artistic effort critically. Not bad. A pretty little watercolour, not chocolate-box pretty, but now with what is called 'a certain charm', meaning pleasant, agreeable and maybe just a touch more than that, maybe a real suggestion of place. I felt the desolation of these hills had been evoked, the emptiness and loneliness yet the lack of grandeur or drama. I propped it up against the stool to dry properly and then went for a walk. I'd intended only to stretch my legs before getting back into the car, but I went on and on, even though the ground was sodden and my shoes soon soaked, and found myself climbing the hill I'd been trying to paint all this time. There was no actual point at which I felt I was at the top, no peak, but only a long, almost level plateau. The view ahead was of more moorland, miles of it, it seemed. But turning to go back, I was amazed to see the sea in the distance, the North Sea I supposed, off Cock-burns, where we had sometimes driven with Hector. If only Susannah had walked up here how much more interesting the view would have been to paint. If, of course, this was the area she had come to. If, of course, I wasn't stark raving mad to think it was.

I wandered slowly back and put my things in the car. I hadn't thought of Susannah once while painting – she had gone right out of my head. If the object of this exercise had been for me to commune with her through resuming the painting of a picture she had painted, it had failed spectacularly. It hadn't even seemed eerie any more, taking up where she had left off. I backed the car carefully down the track, feeling bemused. My mood deepened later as I drove back through Edinburgh's suburbs, and mixed with it was a dash of the usual resentment. What on earth had she been playing at, leaving me that sinister painting? Because I'd decided that was what it was after all, not bland but sinister. Suppose I'd been given the box when I was young, what would it have done to me, to come on this kind of trail in order to find the setting for the painting? I saw everything in black and white then. I'd have forced my father to help me decide on, and find, the location, if he didn't already know it, or bullied my grandmother, who almost certainly would have known it. And once there, wherever it was, I would have been wild with distress at the nothingness of it and frantic not to be able to make sense of its importance. Susannah should have thought of that. It shouldn't have been left for me to struggle and worry about meanings. If I took everything too seriously, as Rory alleged, whose fault was it?

When I arrived back at Isabella's, tired and dispirited, I dropped the painting on to the kitchen table and made myself some coffee. It was a relief that she wasn't back yet and I relished the peace and the lack of necessity to explain myself. But she came in before I'd finished and found me slumped at the table staring into space. She bustled about, reclaiming her territory as she liked to do, moving chairs a fraction of an inch, picking up the kettle and putting it down again, and in general fussing noisily until she was content. I hadn't time to hide the painting. Inevitably, her own tea made, she sat herself at the table and drew the painting towards her. I made a half-hearted attempt to prevent her, but she had it firmly in her hand and it was too late. 'Did you do this?' she said. 'I thought you were taking photographs, not painting.' I couldn't think what to say. 'Well,' I said, and then stopped. But one thing about Isabella, she could keep a conversation going all on her own, no bother. 'Quite pretty,' she said, holding it at arm's length. 'I didn't know you were artistic like your mother. She painted, you know. Not that I ever thought she was much good but I must say others did.' And out it came, the painting exhibited in the Summer Exhibition at the Royal Academy story. Telling this seemed to satisfy her, and she went off to get changed without asking any more questions. Like a lot of people of her type, she thought direct questions impertinent, both the asking and the being asked, so I counted myself lucky. If she was curious, she would consider it a loss of face to let me see she was – curiosity exhibited was vulgar. She was gone quite a while, long enough for me to wash and dry our cups and put the painting in my bag. When she came back, I hadn't expected her to refer to it again, but she did. 'Oh,' she said, looking at the bare table, 'where's that painting? I'm sure it reminds me of somewhere. I'd like to look at it again.'

I could hardly stop her. When I gestured to the bag, she took the picture out and scrutinised it. Then, without speaking, she left the kitchen with it and came back carrying a framed photograph. 'Look,' she said. I looked. It was an old photograph. I recognised the young woman in the middle of it, with a little girl either side cuddling up to her, as my grandmother and behind her was a man I presumed to be my grandfather, who died before I was born. They were sitting on some rocks on a hillside and just visible in the background was a stone croft. 'Jock took it,' Isabella said, 'that's his croft, we were out to see him. Now, if the croft was there wouldn't you say it was the place you've painted?' I shrugged, and said it could be, but it could be scores of other similar places, and Isabella asked me where the place I'd painted was anyway, and I tried to tell her. 'You weren't too far off,' she said. 'Jock's croft was south of Gifford. We used to visit him often. He was your grandmother's cousin – she was fond of him. He was a gamekeeper. We used to go out there to see him, spend the day with him. We'd take our own food and he'd make us tea. We had grand times. Look, there's me, and there's your mother.' She compared the photograph and painting once more, then said, 'Maybe it isn't so like. But your mother once tried to paint Jock's croft, to please him. She was going to give it to him as a present. A great fuss she made about doing it. She'd just got the paints as a birthday present and was showing off. It ended in disaster.'

It seemed an open invitation to ask how, so I risked asking. Isabella said I should go into the sitting-room, where she'd lit a log fire, and 'get comfortable' while she heated some of her home-made soup and warmed some rolls and brought them through. It was the cosiness I'd been threatened with. But the room was attractive, in a faded chintzy sort of way, and the armchairs deep, and the fire blazed away and warmed me in more ways than the obvious. I felt quite content to sit there and wait for my aunt and didn't dread the thought of the intimacy she was evidently aiming for. It struck me that perhaps she wanted the chance to talk to me every bit as much as I wanted to talk to her. She came in with a tray of food and I leapt up to take it from her and there was a bit of bustle as we settled ourselves with the soup. 'Did you eat today, Catherine?' she said. I shook my head, and she tutted. 'You should eat. You're too thin, way too thin. Now, tell me about your day and what you've been doing.'

I'd already mentioned the memory box to Isabella, when we had dinner at the Savoy, but she hadn't said if she'd known about it. I asked her now, before I got on to the painting, and she said her mother had told her of it and she'd thought it 'just like Susannah'. Precisely what she meant by that I wasn't sure and didn't pause to enquire. I said the painting, half-finished, had been in it, with the paintbox, but no explanation, but I didn't say what else had been there. She knew already about the address book, so I said that had been in it too, without listing the other things. Somehow I couldn't bear to involve Isabella any more than I needed to and I felt her expression of irritation at her sister's eccentricity would only deepen if I did. I hated being in the position of asking directly for her help and was careful not to do that, but that was what I was in effect doing and should have done already. Isabella, after all, was the only one alive, as I had long ago realised, who had known Susannah and was likely to be able to throw at least some light on some of the things in the box. But it was humiliating to expose my own confusion and reveal how hard I was straining to interpret my curious legacy – I didn't like her knowing.

Her expression had changed while I talked, the annoyance disappearing from her features to be replaced by a look almost of guilt. Carefully, she set her soup bowl aside and, looking not at me but into the fire, she said she was glad I'd come to her about the painting (though of course I'd done no such thing; it had all been an accident) to ask for her help because she knew about it. She reminded me, in a self-congratulatory manner, that the moment she'd seen it she'd felt she recognised the place and hadn't she gone and got the photograph and wasn't she now proved right? She gave a little purr of satisfaction. But now she knew it was Susannah's painting originally she could tell me much more. She said this was the painting she thought had been destroyed, because of what happened while it was being painted; and, in fact, she could hardly credit it had survived all this time, more than forty-five years. Susannah had started it on one of those outings to visit cousin Jock, one of those days when she and Susannah and their parents had driven to his lonely croft up among the heather and spent the afternoon with him. It was, as she'd described, the first time her sister had used her paints, given to her the week before for her fifteenth birthday. Susannah had settled herself on a little stool and announced she was going to paint Jock's croft from there and their father had said she was too far away and also that if she did the croft from the other side the view would be much more interesting with maybe a glint of the sea. But no, Susannah wouldn't listen – 'She was always stubborn,' Isabella said – and remained where she was while the others went up to the croft, and Jock came out to greet them.

'I don't know how long went by,' Isabella went on, 'an hour perhaps. It wasn't such a good day, there was no sun by then, it had clouded over after we left home and it was a wee bit chilly for September. It must have been September because Susannah's birthday was the end of August; yes, September, the first week, I think. But it was quite cool up there and Jock had a fire going and he made tea and Mother had brought scones and we sat there and chatted and drank the tea, and then Mother said that Susannah would be frozen and I should go and tell her to come and get warm, she'd been painting long enough.' Isabella paused, and stroked the arm of her chair as though it were a cat she was calming down. 'They were always fretting about her health. If I had a cold, it was "Take an aspirin and go to bed with a hot-water bottle," but if *she* had one, it was a big fuss. She was delicate, or so they said. I couldn't see it, of course. I couldn't see anything delicate about her. She seemed tough to me.'

She'd gone to bring her sister up to the croft and found her lying on the ground, paintbrush in hand, and she'd thought she was dead. She'd shouted for her father and ran panting back to the croft and everyone came rushing out and down the hill to the stricken Susannah. It had been 'panic stations' after that, with no possibility of calling an ambulance – Jock had no telephone and the nearest house was miles away – and yet the terrible fear that moving the girl would be harmful. 'Father and Jock lifted her into the back seat of the car and covered her with a blanket. I crouched down in the gap between the back seat and the front, wedged in I was, and Mother squashed in beside Susannah and held her head, and Father drove with Jock beside him to direct the way to the hospital. I thought she was dead. Her lips were bluish, and around her nose, and I couldn't hear her breathing. I don't know which hospital we raced to. I stayed in the car. Mother said, "Stay here and don't move," and that's what I did. I remember there were some sweets in the glove compartment and I ate them and then worried I'd be scolded because I ate the whole packet. They were wine-gums. I still thought she was dead but I couldn't think what she'd died of.' She paused and looked suddenly apologetic, and I wondered if she had been remembering that she'd wished this sister who didn't like her was indeed dead, but that this was too awful a confession to make to me even now. 'Well,' she said, 'Father came out of the hospital eventually and said Susannah was going to be fine, but they were keeping her in for a while and Mother was going to stay the night. We took Jock home and then we went home ourselves. I remember it was almost dark and Father could hardly see to gather up all the stuff we'd just left scattered around, Susannah's stool and easel and her paints. I suppose he picked the painting up and put that in with the rest. We went home and I went to bed and when I woke up I could hear him on the telephone and I thought, "She's died in the night." But she hadn't, she was recovered and we went and got her and Mother. And then they had to tell me about her heart.'

It was the time for me to ask for a proper explanation of what was actually wrong with her heart, something I'd never done. I forced myself to do this and Isabella tried her best to give me the medical details, as they had been explained to her.

Susannah had been born, it appeared, with a genetic heart defect which went undetected until the collapse when she was visiting Jock with the rest of the family. She had a condition known as cardiomyopathy – Isabella spelled it out for me – which classically presents itself as a rhythm disturbance of the heart, but without a test like an electrocardiogram, which of course Susannah had never had, there are no easily recognised symptoms except for acute breathlessness, possible chest pains, and fainting. It was true Susannah did get very breathless, but this was put down to the way she was always so excitable as a child and was constantly over-exerting and pushing herself. She never fainted, until that day at Jock's, and if she had chest pains she never complained of them. Once she had had an ECG and her condition was diagnosed, she was told to take great care, but at that time the drugs and pacemakers which today would have stabilised her heart rhythm were not available. 'Mother would have wrapped her in cotton wool at once,' Isabella said, 'but she wouldn't have it, she said she didn't want to live as an invalid. She was given the only drug then available to regulate her heart and though it wasn't nearly as efficient as drugs developed later, just a few years later, it had some effect. She went on living normally and she seemed to manage. But she started taking risks once she left home for university.

'She said she didn't want to think about her heart and she wasn't going to,' Isabella said. 'And she seemed so strong to me, I never saw her collapse again, though I know from Mother and from your father that she did. She just pretended she was fine and did everything everyone else did, more than they did, just to show them. She should never have gone in for sailing. She weakened herself, Mother was sure – she was demented with worry every time Susannah went sailing or anything like that. And then she chose to have you, a baby . . . a death warrant.'

Isabella loved saying that. She looked at me directly then and I felt accused of matricide and all the old resentment surged up. 'Wasn't my fault,' I said, childishly, and she said of course not and she hadn't meant to imply this. I was feeling so upset, hearing everything she'd told me, but instinctively wanted to hide my distress, not wanting my aunt to know how affected I was by the sudden realisation of how *brave* my mother had been. She said we needed a drink after 'all that'

196

and went off to get the whisky. She poured out a minute amount each into large cut-glass crystal tumblers and seemed to imagine a great rapport had been established between us, whereas I felt more distant from her and more uncomfortable than I had felt since entering her house the day before. I was faintly repelled by her dislike of her dead sister, which seemed to me to poison everything she told me about her. Why had she hated Susannah so much? Surely most women would feel sympathy for a sister suffering from a heart disease which couldn't, in their day, be cured. Why the antagonism? Why her air of having been wronged? But I couldn't bear to launch into all that with Isabella. It would, I was sure, take such patience and skill to unravel the tangled skein of their relationship and I hadn't enough of either. Another puzzle Susannah could doubtless have solved for me, if she had lived, if we had sat beside a fire like this, being 'cosy', mother and daughter being intimate . . . On cue, Isabella said, 'It's so nice having you here, Catherine. It's like having my own daughter.'

I put my glass down carefully. Never mind about the history of a painting, left to me, it would now seem, as a pathetic admission of a frightening illness first realised, *this* was what I should be exploring and trying to understand. 'You've got a son, Aunt Isabella,' I said, 'just as good as a daughter.' She frowned and said sons were not the same, no matter what they were like (said with emphasis), they couldn't be as close, they couldn't be woman-to-woman with all that this meant. I wasn't sure what it did mean to her, but I knew it didn't mean anything special to me. 'I'd rather talk to Rory than any woman friend,' I dared to say. 'He's better than any woman.' I saw immediately how this had been interpreted and hurried to add that I'd meant Rory was interested in everything and so close to me, and that there had never been any barriers between us. 'Is he happy?' Isabella interrupted me as I launched into another paean of praise. 'Do you think he's happy, living the life he leads, running away from his family, causing such trouble and distress? Has it made him happy, doing what he wanted, thinking only of himself, selfish as ever?' She spoke abruptly, but it was obvious she was suppressing strong emotions of some sort, anger mostly, I thought. I should know, I should be able to recognise it and see behind it and feel sympathy for someone as plagued as I am by this emotion. I'd always resisted the horrible idea that I am like Isabella in this respect, in how hard we both find it to control our anger, but there was plenty of evidence, over the years, to prove that it was true. I could never understand what my aunt had to be angry about, but then, until the death of my parents, I had had no cause either. We were both just made that way, given to sudden, unjustified feelings of rage out of all proportion to what had provoked them. It made me sad to see myself as others must see me when I witnessed Isabella's struggle to keep a tight hold on her fury – and her failure to do so.

There was no point in inflaming her further, so I said that no, I didn't think Rory was happy (and she gave a small smile of what I presumed was gratification), but I didn't agree he was either entirely selfish or that he'd wilfully run away from her and Hector. 'Oh?' she said, sharply, sitting up very straight. 'And what do you think he did, then? I can't think of any other description to give it. He ran away. He stole money, then he ran away. And in all these years, *all* these many years, we've seen him precisely twice. Twice. At funerals. He has telephoned only when he wants something. He has not, and does not, behave like a son to whom parents have been devoted. There. That's your Rory, Miss.'

Her fury was not so much frightening (though I did feel, ridiculously, slightly afraid) as inhibiting. It's so hard to talk rationally with someone almost unhinged with anger, and I felt I had to wait a few moments and then be very, very gentle. None of the things I'd been going to say seemed possible while she was so agitated – I'd only make her more aggressive and nothing would be achieved. I began, finally, by suggesting, timidly, that perhaps just as she thought Rory hadn't behaved like a son maybe he could be forgiven, just possibly, for thinking she'd let him down as a mother when he most needed her? I let myself sound in doubt, when of course I was not, but my careful tone didn't pacify her much.

'Let him down?' she said. '*He* let us down, you forget that, you forget how he behaved – he was *always* letting us down, making us ashamed of him.'

'He couldn't help being gay,' I murmured.

She winced at the word 'gay', but shook her head and said vehemently, 'It was nothing to do with that, his constant bad behaviour, nothing to do with what he says he is – '

'Don't you believe him? Don't you believe he is gay?'

'I don't know anything about that and I don't want to know. My point is – '

'Aunt Isabella,' I said, 'that *is* the point. It's why Rory acted as he did, why he was so unhappy; he couldn't be himself and it got worse and worse having to hide what he was from you and – '

'Oh, for heaven's sake! It's only *sex*, all this *fuss*, it's got nothing to do with anything. Why on earth he wants to shout it from the rooftops, as though it makes any difference – '

'But it *does* make a difference. It isn't just sex, it's about all his life, it influences all of it, it's what he *is*.'

'Nonsense! You think you know everything, and you don't. We gave Rory all our time and attention and he – '

'But what about love?'

'Love? Love? What would you know about that, Madam? You're cheeky, you've got above yourself, just like your mother after all – you think you know everything about everyone and you do not. Have you had children? No. Well then, be more careful what you say.'

'But I've been a child,' I said. 'I know what it feels like to *be* loved. Charlotte loved me in a way Rory never felt you loved him, even if he was wrong. And that matters, doesn't it, what he felt?'

'Feelings!' Isabella sneered. 'He was as loved as any other child.'

'If you say so.'

'I do say so.'

'But you walked out of the room, that night he told you and Hector he was – '

'Oh, we're not back to that, are we?' She stood up, pulled down her sweater and said briskly, 'Right, time for bed, I think, Catherine. I don't know what got into you, but you seem to have spoiled our evening to your satisfaction. You seem to have a talent for spoiling things. I don't want to quarrel, but I think I've had enough, so if we're going to part friends tomorrow I'll be off to my bed now. Put the lights out when you leave this room. Thank you. Goodnight.'

And off she went, or so I thought. I was sitting there feeling slightly stunned, trying to recollect exactly where I'd fouled things up, when suddenly I heard the door open again and her voice saying, 'You're making too much of that silly box. Susannah wasn't in her right mind, that's all.' I got up and turned to look at her, but she hadn't come right into the room. She was standing in shadow behind the opened door. 'Do you mean she was mad?' I said, hating not being able to challenge her, to look her in the eye. 'Not at all, not at all,' the reply came, 'not mad, just not in her right mind, Mother said. That box was a bad thing. Mother thought it should have been destroyed, that's all. Susannah didn't know what she was doing. All I mean is you have to remember that.' The door closed. I went on sitting there, feeling numb. 'Susannah didn't know what she was doing . . .' Was it true? And why was Isabella always so bitter and resentful speaking of her sister, even now, all these years later, when death should have wiped out all memory of trivial feuds? But was it trivial, whatever had happened? It was so stupid for these kind of family secrets to be kept.

I heard Hector come in and wished I'd gone to bed. I prayed he would not look in the room where I was still sitting and quickly put out both lamps to encourage him to think it was empty, but I was too late.

'Ah, Catherine,' he said, 'enjoying the fire, eh? Looks cosy. Where's Isabella? Gone to bed? Age, y'know, gets us all . . .' He waffled on, and to my dismay joined me by the fire, a glass of whisky already in his hand. 'Nightcap,' he said, waving it about. 'Want one?' I said no, I'd had a glass. 'Good stuff,' he said, 'good for sweet dreams.' I smiled politely. 'But you're young,' he droned on, 'you don't need any help with sleeping, eh?' I said that was right. 'Not like your mother,' he said. 'She was an insomniac even when she was young. Drove my Bella crazy. Bella likes her sleep, always did.'

I felt the first stirrings of interest. 'Were they very unalike, Susannah and Isabella?' I said.

'Oh yes, goodness me, chalk and cheese, those two. Never got on. Drove their mother mad with all their bickering and worse.'

'Worse?'

'Screaming matches sometimes, and Susannah wasn't supposed to get worked up: bad for her.'

'What did they scream about, what kind of things?'

'Boys, sometimes, usual stuff, jealousy and so on.'

'They had the same boyfriends?'

'Don't know about that. One, they had a spat over one.'

'Who?'

'Before my time. Only heard about it from Bella before she

took me home to meet her mother. Said her sister would be there and I wasn't to speak to her because *she* wasn't speaking to her. They'd had a God almighty row and weren't speaking.' He laughed. 'Ridiculous, eh?'

'Was it, though?' I asked. 'I mean, if Isabella's never really forgiven her even though she's been dead so long?'

'No, no, no,' Hector said, 'of course she's forgiven her, 'course she has. They just didn't get on. Then there was the baby.'

'What baby?'

'Said enough,' Hector said – 'off to bed now,' and he hauled himself out of his chair. 'All water under the bridge.'

I almost pushed him back down. 'Uncle Hector,' I said, 'what baby? What's this about a baby? Whose? I want to know.'

'Bella doesn't like to talk about it.'

'She isn't here. I promise never to let her know you've told me a thing. What baby?'

'Bella's. Cot death. Terrible thing.'

'Bella had another baby? Before Rory?' He nodded, and I realised I'd get more out of him if I asked questions to which he could respond with a shake or nod of his head. 'Was it a girl?' Nod. 'Was she very young?' Nod. 'Months old?' Shake. 'Weeks?' Nod. But then a nod or shake wasn't going to do. 'How does Susannah come into this?' He sighed, and rubbed his red old face with both hands and spoke from behind them. 'Looking after the baby. Didn't have one of her own, you see. Bella was sorry for her. Left her with the baby for the afternoon so she could play mother. Came back . . . Wasn't to blame, of course. Doctor said these things happen, they happen. Both of them like mad women, screaming and crying . . . demented, both of them, ill, both of them. Bella blamed Susannah, said she'd kill her, Susannah said she'd kill herself . . . my God, it was terrible, terrible. Thought neither of them would ever get over it.'

'Why did nobody ever *tell* me this!' I shouted, and he jumped and looked agonised and then listened at the door, clearly afraid Isabella would appear and he would have to explain himself. 'All these secrets!' I wailed, 'they poison everything. I should have been told long ago.'

'Does no good, knowing,' Hector said, wearily, and repeated his refrain of 'water under the bridge'. 'Off to bed now, Catherine, enough said.'

I lay awake most of the night. Nothing in the memory box about this, oh no. It was surely the most traumatic incident in Susannah's life, but she hadn't wanted to give me her version. I tried to think of this reticence as a good thing – she was sparing me, she only wanted to call to mind, my mind as well as hers, happy things – but I couldn't. I wanted there to have been some token in her box of her suffering over the death of her sister's baby daughter. It would have made her real to me in a way none of the objects she'd left had. And suddenly, in the small hours of the morning, Isabella did not seem cold and curt and unloving. I wondered if Rory knew any of this – but of course he didn't. Why not? Why hadn't his parents told him? Why, and how, had they kept this tragic secret to themselves? Because it was too painful to share?

I was in a state of absolute confusion before I fell asleep.

Chapter Twelve

I HAD set my travelling alarm clock for five in the morning, anxious to leave without seeing either my aunt or uncle. I was sure Hector would not have told Isabella about his confession to me – he would be terrified she would find out about his indiscretion – and I did not trust myself to be able to hide what I now knew. It would show in my face, all the distress and compassion I felt for her, and she would be suspicious. One day, some other evening by a fire, I would try to get her to tell me herself what Hector had told me. If I had the courage. I saw how courage comes into it, how terrible things always need courage to be remembered and described. How could I blame all the adults in my family for not having this courage when I myself already doubted if I had sufficient? 'Water under the bridge,' Hector mumbled, and it was so tempting to agree and let it flow on uninterrupted.

I left Susannah's painting on the kitchen table, with a note saying I didn't want it and that if Isabella didn't either (and I was sure she wouldn't) she was to destroy it. And I wrote down Rory's latest telephone number, only just recorded on my answer phone before I'd left London. Then I drove out of Edinburgh quickly, choosing to head for the motorway coming from Glasgow by going through the Pentland Hills via Abington. I was in a daze at first, going over and over the implications of what Hector had told me and the implications it had for my understanding of Susannah, but the road was narrow and twisting and forced me to clear my head and concentrate on it. Once I'd joined the motorway, I began to feel tired and knew I could never manage to drive all the way home without regular stops. I'd eaten and drunk nothing, not wanting to risk disturbing my aunt and uncle by even the smallest sound, and I felt light-headed. I chose to stop for breakfast in Carlisle, remembering how I'd regretted, when I picked up my rented car there, to go to Whitehaven, that I hadn't had time to look at the cathedral and castle. My father had been fond of Carlisle and had described both ancient buildings to me.

I found a large car park just below the old west wall of the city where I could safely leave the car with my valuable photographic equipment locked in the boot (though I took my Pentax 42, never wanting to be entirely without a camera). Groping around the little compartment where I kept change to use for the ticket machine, my hand touched Susannah's address book – God knows how it had got there: I'd no memory at all of what I'd done with it after Bequia. But it seemed a colossal hint, real hand-of-fate stuff again, and I couldn't resist slipping it into my pocket. I knew perfectly well that there was a Carlisle address in it as well as one for Whitehaven and I thought I'd sit in a café after I'd bought a street map somewhere and look it up, for fun. It would almost certainly be an hotel, maybe somewhere Susannah had stayed on her way to Whitehaven when she visited her future mother-in-law.

The tourist office was in the pretty, old Town Hall, which was painted terracotta and looking almost Italian, and I got a street map there. Then I wandered around the area in front of it for a while, thinking how surprisingly attractive it was, this spacious pedestrian centre with its sandstone bricks and great tubs of spring flowers. I could see the cathedral down a street just off it and, choosing to walk a roundabout way to it, down a narrow street, I came to a café in a sort of arcade beside some shops, and went in. The coffee was delicious and so was the toasted scone and I felt remarkably content sitting there, a stranger in a city I did not know. It had come over me before, travelling around on jobs, eating or drinking in a city that was completely new to me, that odd sort of thrill which derives from being anonymous and unconnected. It panics some people, but I love it. It makes me look at the world in an entirely different way and some of my best work has come from plunging myself into new environments like that, especially towns and cities.

Nobody had the slightest interest in me, or if they did they didn't betray it. I felt furtive in a way, as though I were on the run, and of course I was, from Isabella, from the job I'd said I'd do, from the painting. It was silly not to have carried on up the coast to the Highlands, but I had just wanted to go home in a hurry and I was used to acting on such irrational whims. Maybe I wouldn't do this *Hidden Scotland* project after all, maybe I'd keep out of Scotland. I hadn't definitely promised I would, only said I was interested. In this mood of rumination I drank the coffee and took the address book from my bag. Nobody knew what I was looking at. It could be my own address book and I could be consulting the street map spread on the table in front of me to find the house of an old relative or to discover the location of some public building or office. Nobody was going to be in the least curious and this somehow generated excitement in me. My heart beat just a trifle quicker as I flipped over the pages to 'C'. There were two addresses there for Carlisle and one for Calais. The Crown & Mitre was easy enough – I'd walked past it only minutes ago, the large hotel looking out on to the Town Hall. The other said Glebe House, Ashburner Close. I found Ashburner Close on the map at once, listed above Ashley Street and Ashness Drive. It didn't look too far away. I decided to walk there. The route was simple enough and it would do me good, give me some welcome exercise before the five-hour drag back to London. It was only just after nine in the morning still; I had plenty of time.

I strode down Scotch Street, which took me to a bridge crossing the River Eden, and then up a steep hill, past the College of Art, where my father had done a foundation course before deciding he really would rather be an architect, and so going on to Edinburgh. The river, I saw as I crossed the bridge, was almost at the point of overflowing its banks and ran swiftly, in a series of loops, carrying broken branches on its surface. There was a park on the north side of it and the road I walked along at the top of the hill was shaded with trees, so that although I was still within the city it felt like the country, it was so pleasantly rural. My father, I thought, could easily have settled here instead of Oxford and I wondered if he had ever considered it. Ashburner Close was off Tarraby Lane, which I came to after a mile or so. It surprised me by being an untarmacked road, indeed more of a lane, with grass growing down the middle of two ruts which were bedded with gravel. There was only one house in this close and that was Glebe House, the name painted on a white Victorian gate.

It had begun to rain soon after I'd crossed the river and since I had neither umbrella nor raincoat with me I was quite wet by the time I found the house. The rain fell so softly (it was what Charlotte used to call 'good-for-the-complexion rain') and was so light that I hadn't realised the damage it was doing to my appearance until I hesitated at the gate. Glebe House was a very respectable house, one where the inhabitants would, I was sure, be suspicious of strange callers looking like drowned rats. It was not a large mansion, but in its own way imposing, a Jane Austen sort of house, two storeys, double-fronted and painted white, with a pretty porch at the front door. I could see pots of hyacinths, blue and white, standing on the shelves either side of it. The gate was set in a thick hedge of holly, which appeared to go right round the garden of the house and was high enough to obscure most of it, unless one was looking, as I was looking, through the gap where the gate was. I felt hesitant about opening the gate and going up to the porch. My hair was plastered to my head, my shoes squelched, and my sweater was wet enough to be clinging to me. I looked a sight, I knew, and it would not help anyone believe the preposterous tale I had to tell about a dead mother and an old address book.

But as I stood there, trying to force myself through the gate (because I am not a door-stepping person like Rory; I don't have the nerve for it), the front door of the house, which I could just see through the glass door of the porch, opened. A man came out and stood for a moment putting something on his feet and then stepped out into the rain before putting up an umbrella, a large, blue golf-type umbrella which then obscured his face as he came down the path. He was tall, as tall as my father had been, and I had had time to see, before the umbrella went over his white hair, he was fairly elderly. For some reason, I'd been convinced a woman lived alone in this house and I was surprised enough still to be standing quite still as this man advanced towards me. I knew he hadn't seen me and would be startled, so I coughed to give him warning, an absurd little bark of a cough, but he heard it and stopped and peered out from under his enormous, unwieldy umbrella. He wasn't, in fact, at all alarmed. He smiled at me quite cheerfully and nodded, and I returned the smile and nod, and he gestured to show he'd like me to open the gate for him, which I did.

I hadn't spoken but he didn't seem to expect me to and went off walking down the lane with a half-wave of thanks. It struck me that he might have a wife in the house and that he'd imagined I was calling on her and he didn't need to ask

208

who I was, or what I wanted. But a similar thought must have struck him, and caused him some hesitation or concern, because he turned and walked back to me. 'Have you come to see Mary?' he asked. 'Does she expect you?'

'No,' I said. 'I'm a stranger. I don't know her, or you, of course. It's the house I'm interested in.'

'Oh, it's not for sale, my dear, goodness me, no.'

'I wasn't thinking that,' I said. 'It's just that I think my mother once stayed here and I wanted to see it. Have you lived here long?'

'All my life,' he said, smiling. 'I was born here, and so were my brothers, and Mary.' Then he peered at me and said, 'But you're wet, soaked, and no coat or umbrella,' and he extended the shelter of his own umbrella to me. We stood there, quite close together, and I was aware of being scrutinised. I met his eyes steadily and we stared at each other. He had dark brown eyes, like my father, so dark the pupils hardly stood out. 'You said?' he murmured encouragingly.

'My mother,' I said, 'I think she stayed here once, a long time ago. You may have known her. It's complicated . . .'

'I've known a lot of people,' he said. 'Good gracious me, yes, I've known a lot of people in my life. You mustn't be surprised if I don't remember your mother's name. What was it?'

Two minutes later we were in Glebe House. I've heard so often of people turning pale with shock, looking stunned, seeming struck dumb, but I've never heard of anyone doing the opposite, becoming animated and *laughing*. This man laughed when I told him Susannah's name. He closed his eyes and laughed and said, of course, he remembered her and that I must come at once and meet Mary. I protested that he had been going out and that I didn't want to delay him, but he said he was only going to post a letter and it could wait. Then he led the way back down the garden path to the porch.

'Come in, come in,' he said. 'Don't worry about being wet – we have a dog and she makes far more mess than you could.' And as soon as he opened the front door I could hear a dog barking and a woman's voice telling it to stop. 'It's all right, Mary,' the man shouted. 'It's me. I've got a young visitor with me.' He walked ahead of me down a narrow passage with a stone-flagged floor and into a kitchen, where a woman of about his own age, I thought, was sitting at the table peeling potatoes, and a springer spaniel was racing round and round excitedly.

The woman, Mary, didn't seem too pleased to see me, though she was polite enough and immediately offered me some tea. The man urged me to sit down, pointing out the chairs were plain wood and couldn't be damaged by my wet clothes. It was he who put the kettle on and made the tea, Mary watching him all the time as though she didn't trust him and saying, 'The red mug, John,' and, 'Milk in the door of the fridge, John,' as if directing someone quite unfamiliar with his surroundings. The tea made and in front of me, the man, whose name I'd now learned was John, settled himself opposite me and said, 'You'll never guess who this is, Mary.'

'Of course I won't,' she snapped, 'so you'd better stop playing games and tell me.'

'It's Susannah Cameron's daughter!' he said, laughing again, and spreading his arms wide as though he'd just won a prize. 'Imagine! After all these years!'

I noted Mary's hands stopped peeling the potatoes for a moment, and that her eyebrows went up, but there was no incomprehensible laughter from her, and she said nothing at all. I felt it was time to offer the explanation John hadn't asked for, or shown any sign of wanting, and began to explain myself, reducing the story to as few words as possible, but obliged to mention how I'd come by the address book. I produced it when I got to this point and said, 'On the "C" page it has your address, but no name. I couldn't resist coming here, on the off chance.'

'Now isn't that extraordinary?' John said. 'Our address and no name. I wonder why.'

'You wonder too much,' Mary said, grim-faced. 'That's always been your trouble.'

John ignored her and turned to me. 'You're not a bit like her,' he said. 'She was blonde, you know – lovely long blonde hair and blue, blue eyes, heavenly eyes – '

Mary made a dismissive sound, which she covered up with splashing a peeled potato into a pan of water beside her.

' – heavenly, lovely girl, slight, not very tall. I'd never have guessed you were her daughter.'

'Tactless!' said Mary.

'I don't mind,' I said. 'I'm used to it. It's always been commented on, ever since I was a child, how unlike my mother I look. I'm like my father, like his side of the family, all tall and dark-haired and brown-eyed. But I am Susannah's daughter all the same.'

'But you never knew her,' John said. 'Very sad, very sad.'

'Don't be sentimental, John,' Mary said, 'the girl was only a baby. It wasn't sad at all for her.'

'Oh, I'm sure it was,' John protested. 'Losing a mother is always desperately sad. Look how sad we were when we lost Mother – '

'For heaven's sake,' Mary said, clearly exasperated, 'our mother was eighty-two when she died. It isn't the same at all, you fool.'

'Anyway,' I said hurriedly, seeing this degenerate into a squabble between brother and sister when I had so much I wanted to find out, 'this address is in the book, with no name. None of the addresses in it have names and most, but not all, are hotels or similar.'

'How curious,' John said. 'Well, my name is very boring, it's John Graham – '

'John Charles Henry Graham,' said Mary.

' – and there are scores round here called that, couldn't be more ordinary or commonplace. And Mary's name is just as common, Mary Graham, hundreds of them.' I waited for Mary to contest this and reveal the middle names I was sure she must have, but she visibly tightened her lips and kept quiet. 'Our parents were John and Mary too, and our branch of the Graham clan have been here for centuries. Our great-great-great grandfather – '

'Really, John,' said Mary, slicing a potato in half viciously, 'she doesn't want to hear all this.'

'I think it's jolly interesting,' he said, 'families and their houses, and us being born in here. I like to tell people about it.'

'You like to tell people far too much,' Mary said, 'and half the time they don't like to tell you you're a bore.'

'I'm not bored,' I said. 'I love houses and their histories. I like to hear who's lived in them. I always liked knowing about our house in Oxford, though it wasn't old like this one and hadn't always belonged to one family.'

'Were you born there?' John asked,

'No. I was born in Edinburgh. Then after my mother died my father married again and we moved to Oxford when I was about eighteen months.'

'Poor Susannah,' John said, 'she was lovely – '

'He was in love with her,' Mary said, and another potato was tossed noisily into the pan.

'Yes, I was, oh dear me yes, I was,' said John, smiling even more broadly, without a trace of embarrassment. His love for my mother had certainly not left any lingering residue of bitterness. He seemed perfectly happy, even proud, to recall his passion.

'What happened?' I asked, made bold by his cheerfulness and the absence of any sign that he had suffered.

'Your father happened,' he said. 'We were all very young, you know, things changed, relationships, as they do.'

'So it was just an affair?' I pressed.

Mary tutted and was about to say something, but her brother got in first.

'An *affair*?' He was incredulous. 'My dear girl! No, not an affair, if you mean what I take it you mean, what it means today, the full thing. It was the Fifties, we wouldn't have dared, not in our part of the world. But we were in love, it didn't mean we weren't.'

'*You* were,' Mary said, '*she* wasn't.'

John stopped laughing and looked hurt for the first time. 'Oh, I think she was. I think Susannah was in love with me too, Mary. I certainly believed she was.'

'You believed anything,' Mary said. 'You still do.' She'd finished peeling the potatoes at last and got up from the table to take the pan to the sink, where she began emptying it and filling it with fresh water. I saw that she'd walked the few necessary paces with difficulty and must suffer from arthritis or some such complaint. Maybe her brusqueness could be explained by this, if she was in pain all the time. She had her back to me, but I badly wanted to ask her about Susannah, feeling her memory was sharper and less clouded by emotion, as John's was bound to be if he had been so in love.

'Did you know my mother too, Miss Graham?' I asked, careful to address her respectfully and sure that no rings on her left hand would mean she had never married.

'I met her,' Mary said, without turning round, 'but I wouldn't say I knew her. She stayed here. She came home from some sailing holiday with John and we all met her, naturally. All the men were mad about her, even Father, a bit. George doted on her, and Frank too, though he was only fourteen. The whole lot of them eating out of her hand. It was ridiculous.'

'You didn't like her?' I suggested, but Mary was immediately indignant, turning at last to stare at me.

'Didn't like her? I didn't say that. You're twisting my words. I wasn't in love with her like my brothers, how could I be? But it doesn't mean I disliked the girl. She seemed nice enough but a bit wild. She didn't ignore me, like some of John's other flames used to, but she wasn't going to waste much time on me. I didn't expect her to, why should she? I knew she wouldn't last, and she didn't.'

'How did you know?' I said, watching Mary carefully. Whatever she said, I deduced she had not liked Susannah and I wanted to know why.

'Oh, I can't remember, I just knew. She was clever, ambitious, I felt. John wasn't her sort.'

'I was clever,' John objected.

'But you weren't ambitious, that's the point,' Mary said, returning to sit at the table, but seeming lost without the potatoes to fiddle with.

'I jolly well was.'

'No, you weren't. You wouldn't still be here if you'd been ambitious. It's proof enough.'

'I like it here.'

'Quite.'

Once again, they were side-tracking me, enjoying their own bickering, and it was wasting time. 'Did your mother like her?' I asked Mary, to get her back on the subject of Susannah.

'Yes, she did. She thought she was interesting, not empty-headed like most of John's girls. She made her welcome.'

'How did she come to stay, anyway?'

'I invited her, of course,' John said.

'But where did you meet her? Did you study architecture too? Were you on the same course?'

'Heavens, no. I was older. I read law at Durham, a few years before. No, I met her on a boat, up beyond Ullapool. Do you know it, north-west coast of Scotland? A friend's boat, twelve of us invited. I knew him from school, he was at St Bees too, and Susannah met him through another friend. It was a class II ocean yacht, the boat – '

I tried to interrupt, 'Which friend – ?' but he was off for the next five minutes describing every detail of the boat his friend had had. There was no stopping him, and I had to wait as patiently as I could, longing now for his sister to shut him up, but she seemed to enjoy all the irrelevant (to me) detail. I thought how very relaxed he looked, sitting as my father used to like to sit, sideways on to the table, his right leg crossed over his left and his hands clasped behind his head. He was wearing beautifully polished brown brogue shoes and a tweed jacket and fawn-coloured cords – every inch the small-town solicitor I'd by now deduced he'd been. It was somehow disconcerting to see him so very undisturbed by my surely fairly dramatic visit – he was almost too benign, too untroubled. I wasn't, after all, uncovering the tale of smouldering passion I half wanted, but something more banal, and he was part of the banality.

'There were eight of us men and four girls and your mother was one of them. I'd been at school with George Senhouse and so had two of the others, but the rest were all students he'd met at Edinburgh. His father owned the boat . . . now what was her name – '

'John, the name doesn't matter,' snapped Mary; 'she doesn't care about it.'

' – *Carita*! Yes, she was called *Carita*. Lovely old boat. A bit heavy, but dependable. We sailed her right round the Scottish islands and up to the top of the mainland coast. And afterwards I asked Susannah if she'd like to come and stay and she accepted. I was jolly flattered, I can tell you.'

'I can't think why,' Mary muttered. 'Nothing to be flattered about.'

'I don't think her family knew,' I said. 'Her sister, my Aunt Isabella, says she didn't know about a trip – '

'Oh, her mother knew,' Mary said. 'It was all very proper. Mother wrote to her mother and had a nice note back. People had manners in those days, believe me.'

'How long did you say she stayed?'

'A week,' John said at the same time as Mary said, 'Ten days. Came on the Friday, left a week on the Monday.'

'What did you do together?' I asked John, wanting Mary to stop interrupting now, but he turned to her and said, 'What did we do, Mary?'

'Played tennis a lot,' said Mary. 'We had a grass court in those days. But she got tired easily, it was odd.'

'We went for walks,' John said, 'in the park, along the river. And I borrowed Father's car and took her out to Wetheral, and that sort of thing.'

'I think she was bored,' Mary said. 'I used to think she looked bored when she came in.'

'She was not bored in the least,' John said, indignant, his perpetual smile fading for once. 'We got on so well, we never stopped talking – we had lots in common. I missed her like anything when she left.'

'You moped,' Mary said.

'I wrote to her and she wrote back, sweet letters. She said staying here was the nicest holiday she'd ever had.'

'Nicest!' said Mary.

'Yes, nicest. I wonder if I kept those letters . . .'

'If you did, you'll have lost them. You lose everything.'

'I invited her to come again, in the next long vac, but the next thing I knew I had a postcard from somewhere abroad, I forget where. She'd gone off with young Senhouse again, in another party. 'I wasn't asked to join it, I'm afraid.'

I wanted to pick up on this Senhouse character, but now Mary was in full spate. And perhaps he meant nothing.

'He was jealous.' Mary said, 'George Senhouse was always jealous of you, right through school.'

'I never heard from her after that.'

'Yes, you did,' Mary said. 'You got a Christmas card and you were so upset you tore it up.'

'Did I?' said John, and I wasn't sure whether or not he was pretending he couldn't remember. If he was, he was quickly reminded, because his sharp sister could remember every detail.

'You flung the torn card down and stamped out of the room in a paddy, and Mother and I put it together, so we would know what had upset you so much, and it said she wished you a happy Christmas and that she was going to have a very happy Christmas herself, because she had just got engaged to be married to a man who was from your part of the world, from Whitehaven, an architect like her, or hoping to qualify as one, and they'd marry when they had both finished their degrees. And she said she hoped to see you again one day. Mother and I reckoned that was what had made you specially furious. Well, you got over it. Silly boy, getting so upset.'

Mary said 'silly boy' not at all contemptuously, which was how she seemed to say most things to her brother, but affectionately. It was obvious that she cared deeply for him and probably hadn't disliked Susannah at all, but only what her defection had done to John.

'My heart was broken,' John said.

'Rubbish. You hardly knew the girl. Three weeks on a boat, ten days here, a couple of letters and a postcard – how could your heart be broken? You don't know how silly you sound.'

'I know what I felt,' John said. 'You can't know how I felt.'

'Maybe. But I know you got over it and had another crush soon after – that red-haired girl, Beatrice – '

'Oh, *Beatrice*. That was nothing. She – '

'So "nothing" you got engaged to her. Correct me if I'm wrong, do.'

I couldn't hold back any longer. When John looked as if he would indeed correct her I blurted out, 'George Senhouse, was he Susannah's boyfriend too?'

'He was a *friend*,' John said. 'Must have been, to ask her to sail with him, don't you think?'

'But was he . . .?' and I suddenly stopped, feeling awkward in front of this pair, too embarrassed to ask if a man I'd never heard of until now was my dead mother's lover. 'Was he more than that?' I said, lamely.

'Haven't the foggiest,' said John, rather stiffly.

That was it. I could see I wasn't going to get anything more about Susannah or Senhouse out of either of them. This would be one of the addresses Susannah would have thought I would never arrive at. I'd been there nearly forty-five minutes and there was no point in lingering, but when I thanked them for talking to me, and for the tea, and got up to leave, John said he'd walk to the road with me and post that letter. I thought how strange it was that neither he nor Mary had asked me about myself – they were obviously of the same breed as Isabella, believing the asking of direct questions to be impertinent – but as I walked along with John I couldn't resist asking some myself. I wanted to know if he had ever been married – no, never. And neither had Mary. The other two brothers had married and had families, but they had stayed together in their family home and been 'quite happy'. I couldn't help speculating in my head as to what 'quite happy' meant. Happy, but missing something? Happy, and not feeling the lack of anything? John wasn't the man to discuss such things with. He must have bored Susannah to death: Mary had been right.

The rain had stopped and a weak, watery sun was struggling to force its way through the greyness as we strolled slowly down Ashburner Grove to the road. John said he was turning left, to the postbox, and I was turning right, to go back into town. We stood for a minute on the corner. John shook my hand and said it had been interesting meeting me and I thanked him again for listening to me. Still he stood there, clearly wanting to say something but apparently unable to find the words he wanted. 'She went back to Edinburgh by train,' he said, at last. 'We walked the way you're going to walk. She didn't want me to call for a taxi and Father was out in the car.' I nodded, saying nothing, though badly wanting to say 'So?' His smile had gone and he was frowning hard and suddenly looked much older than he had done before. 'She died giving birth to you, you said?'

'No,' I corrected him, 'she died when I was six months old, of heart disease. She'd had something wrong with her for a long time.'

'That's sad', he said, 'for you never to have known your mother, very, very sad.' I almost wished Mary was there to tell him again not to be so silly. But he still hadn't finished. At last, a small hint of curiosity was betrayed. 'Your father,' he said, 'did she meet him on that long trip abroad, the one she went on with Senhouse? Was he one of the party then?'

'No, I don't think so. She didn't meet him until afterwards. My father said they met in a lecture. They'd been going to the same lectures all year but he'd never seen her before. That was his story, anyway.'

'Ah.' He coughed, and fidgeted a bit. 'I think Senhouse was smitten with her, I think he had designs on her. He might have been her – er – boyfriend. There's no knowing now, is there? He was always boasting about that trip, you know.

Every time I met him afterwards he'd go on about it. It took them three months. Sailed off somewhere right across the Atlantic, then sold the boat and flew back. I wish I had that postcard, I wish I could remember where they went.'

'What was Senhouse like?'

'Oh, sporty. He wasn't clever. He was rich, though, very. Good-looking, I suppose.'

I kept my voice casual: 'Do you know where he lives?'

'Good heavens, no. Lost touch centuries ago . . .'

Eventually, he shook hands with me yet again and we parted. I walked away, thinking of this George Senhouse character, rich and sporty, good-looking, smitten with Susannah, enticing her away on an exciting trip to the other side of the world, and then losing her all the same to my father. But why hadn't she told her mother and sister about this thrilling voyage? How could she have just vanished for three whole months? Some kind of deception must have gone on to account for her absence, but why deceive her mother, to whom she was devoted? I decided, as I walked on, that the answer to that was that she wanted to shield her mother from worrying. As I'd shielded Charlotte from knowing about my abortion, she'd shielded her mother from worrying not just about the dangers of the sailing but about her fragile health. And maybe she did have a fling with George Senhouse. She'd have wanted to shield my morally rigid grandmother from that.

I was halfway along Tarraby Lane when I realised I'd left behind my car keys. I remembered that I'd taken them out of the pocket of my trousers when I sat down at the Grahams' kitchen table – they were tight-fitting trousers and the keys made an uncomfortable bump. Stupidly, I'd put them not on the table in front of me but on top of my camera case on the floor and they must have slipped off, or the dog knocked them off. It was embarrassing to have to go back, but obviously

I did have to. I ran. I wanted to collect the keys before John got back from posting his letter. I was panting as I turned in at the gate of Glebe House, hoping Mary herself hadn't gone out, but as I ran up the path she was standing at the front door, dangling the keys. 'Silly girl,' she said. I gasped my thanks and reached for the keys, but she held on to them. I thought maybe I hadn't apologised enough and began to say sorry for disturbing her again, but she stared at me and said, 'George Senhouse?'

I didn't understand. 'Yes?' I said.

'He came here looking for your mother once. Didn't like to remind John. Actually had the cheek to come asking if John knew her address. Said he had something he wanted to give her. Of course, John had had the heave-ho and didn't know her whereabouts. *He* had always thought Senhouse had stolen her from *him*. Daft, both of them. Well, take your keys. Just thought I'd tell you, don't know why.' And she handed over the keys and turned to go back into the house.

'Miss Graham!' I called, and she stopped.

'Miss Graham, is George Senhouse dead?'

'Dead? Good heavens, no. But he is in a nursing home, I believe, somewhere outside London. Not a well man, but not dead. His sister still lives in Whitehaven, no, in Maryport. I shouldn't go bothering her, though, she's a bit of a tartar. It's going to rain again. You should get back to your car.'

I felt that strange excitement again, that weird sense of elation, as though I was going to discover something crucial to my understanding of Susannah, and I tried hard to caution myself to be sensible and to remember the many disappointments already. But I knew, as I walked rapidly back towards the city centre, that of course I had to try to track down George Senhouse. Maryport was not far away, nearer than Whitehaven, but I didn't necessarily need to go there at all. I could get the number from directory enquiries, and telephone.

Almost back in the city, I stopped and leaned on the stone bridge and watched the water. The traffic on the road behind me was so heavy and noisy it wasn't exactly the place to stand and stare, but I wanted to pause and calm myself down, and I liked the river. Luckily, I saw a man taking his dog down some hidden steps and I followed him and walked a little way along the bank in the opposite direction to him. It was too wet to sit on the grass, but I came to a big log and perched there for a moment, just leaning against it. Susannah had been a mere visitor in Glebe House. There had been nothing of her there permeating the atmosphere. She'd been in and out of it all those years ago and left nothing of herself in it, only a lingering wisp of memory in the minds of two elderly people.

I took the address book out of my bag and fingered it. Such a little item, full of half-promises. I ran my finger down the torn alphabet and stopped at M. An hotel in Manchester, another in Malvern. And an address, of course, in Maryport. How simple puzzles are if you know the solution first. I tore the page out and put it carefully in my wallet. I wouldn't try fitting the name Senhouse to this address and getting a phone number until I was home. Meanwhile, I had something to do. I looked around and found some small stones, and tearing a piece off the street map I made a parcel out of it all, tying it securely with an elastic band I'd used to pull back my hair. Then I threw the package into the river, where it sank immediately and was pulled away underneath by the force of the current. I felt relieved – more than relieved, pleased. Except for this last discovery, the address book had been perhaps the most frustrating of the things in the memory box. If I had been completely mad, instead of only half crazy, I might have set myself to trail round checking every wretched address in it and that would have got me nowhere: it wouldn't even, on its own, have led me to George Senhouse. The suggestion of mystery about it – that lack of names – had been a cruel trick. I felt, by throwing it away, I was calling Susannah's bluff, saying: Here's your poxy book, keep it. It was childish, petulant, but saying this to myself helped me to feel better.

I decided, as I left Carlisle and rejoined the M6, that I would never come back here either. I wouldn't revisit Edinburgh, or Carlisle, ever again through choice.

Chapter Thirteen

THE moment I got home I sat down with the sheet I'd torn from Susannah's address book and rang directory enquiries. I didn't even make myself a cup of coffee or anything to eat, though I was thirsty and hungry, and also exhausted after my long drive. I had to find out at once if anything was going to come of the Maryport address. It all proved so straightforward I felt almost disbelieving – I had the telephone number for a Miss Pamela Senhouse in Maryport in two minutes flat. And I didn't hesitate. I rang her immediately, before I could remember Mary Graham warning me that she, this Miss Senhouse, was 'a tartar'.

A voice with a strong Cumbrian accent answered, a youngish female voice, and I knew it couldn't be the person I wanted. I asked for Miss Pamela Senhouse and instead of asking me who I was or what I wanted, this woman said, 'She's took badly. She isn't here, she's in Hensingham.'

'Hensingham?'

'The hospital. They took her in last night.'

'Are you . . .?' I let it trail off, hoping she'd fill in the information I wanted.

'Edna,' she said. 'I'm Edna.'

'Oh well, Edna, I'm sorry to hear Miss Senhouse is ill, but what I actually wanted was to ask her for the address of her brother George.'

'It's pinned here,' Edna said. 'She keeps it near the phone. She's always forgetting the number and worrying about it, so she pinned it here.' And obligingly she read out not the address but a telephone number that I recognised as near Brighton, or at least it was a Brighton exchange. I thanked Edna effusively and she said, 'Who shall I tell her rang up?'

'A family friend, an old friend of her brother George. She wouldn't know my name, but it's Musgrave, Catherine Musgrave.'

'Wait till I write it down. I'll forget.'

I repeated my name, hoping Miss Senhouse would find my surname comfortingly familiar since it was as local as her own. I wanted to ask Edna whether she was the housekeeper or the cleaner or a neighbour, but I thought I shouldn't ask too many questions and I could hear what I took to be a doorbell ringing in the background, so I just said thank you and goodbye.

Dry-mouthed by then but determined to take the last step, I rang the Brighton number. Despite Mary Graham's warning, I was a little puzzled to find it was a nursing home. Nursing homes, surely, were for *very* old people, and he couldn't be that old. I asked for the matron. I was told the Home Manager had gone home, she didn't live on the premises. I was asked quite sharply who I was and to state my business. I lied and said I was a niece of George Senhouse and could I visit him the day after tomorrow. Permission was given, I could visit any time, but early afternoons were preferred, and since Mr Senhouse was usually asleep soon after six the evening was not a good idea. I put the telephone down, feeling shattered but also thrilled: – the idea of at last seeing this mysterious man who had taken Susannah off to Bequia was just that – thrilling.

After I'd had a bath and eaten something, I turned to my mail, which lay in quite a pile behind the front door. There were stacks of letters from estate agents and I looked forward to going through the enclosed lists of houses for sale when I was not so tired. I had almost decided to choose Chelsea but was still tempted by thoughts of settling higher up the river and getting more for my money. I watered the plants, opened the windows and felt happy to be back, but then I always did – pity the returning traveller whose heart sinks on coming home. Mine always lifted, however good the holiday or expedition. Everything was as I had left it, everything was how I liked it to be. I'd only been away four days but it felt more like four weeks of strain and I was glad to be rid of it. I lay on my bed opening the rest of the post – two cheques from magazines, a letter commissioning me to take photographs for a travel piece on Normandy, and a postcard from a friend in Sri Lanka. Then I attended to my answerphone. It wiped out, for the moment, my excitement about George Senhouse.

The first recorded message was unexpected. I didn't recognise the voice at all. It was a hesitant, middle-aged female voice, calling me *Miss* Catherine Musgrave, and though I'm quick on the uptake – too quick, my father used to say disapprovingly – it wasn't until the message was over that I realised who the speaker had been. It was Tony's mother. She was calling because she felt I would want to know that her son Anthony – that confused me, too – was very ill. He'd asked for me and she felt it was only right to let me know this 'in case you want to do anything about it'. Her voice was shaky, but I wasn't quite sure whether with distress or nervousness. Not an easy thing to do, call your son's ex-girlfriend, the woman who you knew had hurt him so much, who had sent him packing. I bet she hated me, I bet she had me down as an absolute bitch. I'd be even more of a bitch if I didn't rush at once to University College Hospital, where she'd said Tony was in intensive care after a car accident. She hadn't left the time or date when she rang, but the next caller, my dentist's receptionist, cancelling an appointment, had, so I knew Tony's mother had rung three days ago. All this time, she would have been waiting to see if I was going to respond, but then surely she would have realised, knowing my job, that I might be away.

I rang the hospital immediately, not giving myself time to think. I shouldn't need time to think anyway – such a thing should be automatic in those circumstances. Eventually, I got a sister who was prepared to tell me only that Tony was off the critical list and holding his own, but still very ill. She wouldn't tell me exactly what was wrong with him, so I still didn't know how he'd injured himself. He was a careful driver, so I felt it must have been somebody else's fault. But I didn't really want to know what had happened. It's odd how most people when they've told this kind of news go straight for the details. I didn't want to know, but did I want to see Tony? No. Did I want him to think I didn't care that he'd been badly injured? No. And what about his mother, shouldn't I ring her? Probably.

This is how I deal with things these days. People who live on their own do this. I ask myself the questions a partner, or a parent, would ask and then I reply as though I am someone else. Backwards and forwards I go, trying to be sensible and logical, and yet I know that if I had someone to discuss a problem with this would not be how it would go – the discussion wouldn't be so simple and tidy, and the other person would think of arguments for and against which, left to myself, I did not. I do my best, but it is all a kind of cheating. And another kind is prevarication. I put decisions off and there is no one to tell me I shouldn't. It was to delay making my mind up about visiting Tony, and/or ringing his mother, that I went back to my answerphone. I'd switched it off without listening to the end of the tape, even though I knew it was full. Now I went back to it, hoping to be distracted by further messages and through distraction come to some conclusion as to what I felt about poor Tony.

Rory's voice said, 'So who's been playing at the good little niece, then? Ring me – you have a lot to answer for, petal.' Well, that was distracting. His mother must have rung him. I hadn't thought I needed his permission to give her his latest number – she was his mother, for heaven's sake, whatever the situation between them. I'd once asked him, when it emerged he hadn't even spoken to either of his parents for something like three years, whether he wouldn't want to know if one of them was desperately ill. I'd pressed him to imagine this, and suggested his response would surely be to want to rush to their side, but he laughed and said I was a drama queen and that I had lurid visions of deathbed reconciliations which were absurd. 'But you'd go, wouldn't you?' I'd pleaded, and he'd shrugged and said if he was asked he supposed he would have to, but it wouldn't upset him if he couldn't be found and he missed the chance. He didn't think the sight of his mother or father on their deathbeds would change anything. The trouble with Rory is that he doesn't know the first thing about deathbeds. I do. I knew that if he was ever called upon to witness Isabella or Hector dying it *would* change everything. The vigil, the kind I kept with Charlotte, would alter his feelings. I told him so. He said he very much doubted it but hoped not to be put to the test. He hoped that when the time came his parents would have the decency to die as my father had done, suddenly, with no warning at all, excusing him entirely from being involved.

At least I knew Isabella was in good health and Rory's flippant tone showed that whatever she'd rung him for was not serious. Had she offered him some kind of olive branch? If so, I intended to claim the credit for any *rapprochement* between them, though I knew Rory wouldn't think credit was due. He always maintained the rift between them was an excellent thing – it meant he could lead his own life without constantly being called to account by disapproving parents. All he hoped was that they hadn't cut him out of their wills, but he was pretty confident they wouldn't have gone that far, what with their strong belief in family. The money and property they had came mainly from Hector's family and had been passed down to him rather than earned by the sweat of his brow, so he would see it as his duty to go on passing it down, whatever then happened to it. Or so Rory hoped. Wickedly, I'd pointed out that both his parents, but particularly Isabella, were heavily committed to the various charities they supported and could quite easily leave their pile to them. And Hector, pillar of the Tory party, could choose to fill its coffers with his loot. Rory had no guarantee that he'd inherit a penny and nor did he deserve to. He said that was rich, coming from me, coming from someone who'd inherited a thumping amount without deserving it either, but I said at least I'd loved my parents and never deserted them. Rory said he didn't know I could be so smug.

Anyway, it was interesting, as well as distracting, to wonder what had passed between Rory and Isabella, so I rang him back there and then. 'About time,' he said when he heard me and, before I could stop him, said he was coming round, then put the phone down. I rang him again, wanting to shriek that he mustn't even think about it, I was exhausted and worried about what I should do over Tony and it was nearly midnight, but there was no reply, not even an answering machine clicking on. I lay on my bed furious with myself. How stupid I'd been, calling him at all. He'd keep me up half the night and never stop talking and bore me rigid. But he only did two of those things. He didn't bore me; on the contrary, he wiped Tony and my own tiredness out of my mind so entirely that when he'd finished I felt quite calm and knew what I was going to do.

He arrived determined to act out the whole telephone conversation with his mother, fuelled by the bottle of wine he got for himself from my kitchen the moment he came in. We lay on my bed together and he did both their voices, imitating Isabella's to such perfection it was as though she were in the room. 'She said, "I would like to speak to Mr Rory Cameron," in that impossibly prim way she has – you know how she likes to sound all official and curt and always clears her throat first – and I asked who was calling in a really stupid, over-the-top and not even remotely accurate cockney accent, and she said, "I may have the wrong number. Would you kindly inform me if this is the number for Mr Rory Cameron?" I thought about keeping it up and pretending I was some kind of thug and had never heard of this *Mister* Cameron, but it was too tiring. It all came back how maddening she is . . . no sense of humour – she's a sad cow – but anyway I gave up and said, "Mother dear, it is I," and she went into one of her how-can-you-be-so-silly-and-rude routines and said she had almost hung up. I longed to say why didn't you, I couldn't give a fuck, but I said, "That would have been such a shame," only mildly sarcastically, and she said, "Rory, are you being impertinent?" Oh God, it was so tedious. I had to work really hard not to scream. I asked how Dad was, just for something innocuous to say, and she said he worried about me which didn't do his ulcers any good or his blood pressure, and I thought, Oh my God, now I'm blamed for giving him ulcers, when really he's got them because he's a pig and eats and drinks too bloody much. I was so pissed off I decided to ask her why she was ringing and she said, "Does a mother have to have a reason?" I thought, This one does, darling, but I was very good and said not a word, and she said she'd thought we had an understanding that I would at the very least keep her informed of my whereabouts. I said, I couldn't resist it, "What are you, my probation officer?" and oh, Christ, that set her off again and I had to jump in before I went completely mad and say I'd thought she and Dad wanted nothing to do with me, that I'd offended them so deeply by being proud to be gay. Well of course I said that deliberately, hamming it up, and she burst out, "Don't say that!" and I said, all innocent, "What? That I'm proud? Or gay? Or both?" and she said I knew what she meant and was determined to torment her – *me* torment *her*. I was buggered if I was going to put up with that, so there we were, bitching away at each other and any moment one of us was going to hang up and the betting was on *moi*, when suddenly she said, "Catherine came to stay." Then she said you and she had had "a little talk", and it had made her think – and I thought, Well, that's a breakthrough – and she felt that we should see each other and try to put things right. I took a deep breath and said that I wasn't clear what she thought could be "put right" and that I was as I was and so far as I was concerned everything was "right" already, and she said, "Rory, you *are* our son." I said, "How true," and waited. I could hear her sort of choking with effort and I waited and waited but she said nothing else and for one horrible moment I thought the old bag was going to cry – oh, dear me. I'd answered the phone in the kitchen and I had to lean backwards and open the fridge and grab a bottle of wine and take a slug to steady my nerves. She obviously mistook the glugging sounds as I poured it down the old throat for some kind of distress signal and she said, "Now, it's no good both of us getting upset, Rory," and I managed not to laugh – in fact I managed to say in a *most* convincingly caring voice that no, it was not. What a panto-mime, and all your fault, Catherine.'

'I didn't do anything. Don't blame me.'

'You had "a little talk" with her, Madam.'

'So.'

'So that started all this, and whatever you said brought on this fit of conscience.'

'I can't remember saying anything that could have.'

'She said you'd made her think about what being a mother meant – '

'Oh, that . . .'

'Yes, that. It was embarrassing listening to her, frankly. Why did you go to stay with her anyway? She never got round to telling me.'

'I was on a job. It was convenient.'

'Liar.'

'Oh well, no, I *was* supposed to be on a job, sort of, but I was trying to trace that stupid painting in the box, the unfinished thing – '

'Did you?'

'What do you think? Anyway, your mother saw it and she remembered a lot about it, but I'm not going to tell you, because I don't want to talk about it. I left it with her, it's over – '

'And so you had a girly heart-to-heart about me?'

'No. We just got talking – '

'Just? Pray, just me no just – what do you mean, *just*?'

'I can't remember how it came about, honestly I can't. You just came up. She and you. Talking about the wretched painting and Susannah, the whole mother thing, that kind of stuff. She seemed so nice suddenly, and she'd asked earlier if I remembered those dancing classes we went to – '

'Spare me the nostalgia.'

'Fine. But that's what happened. She *does* love you, Rory, I'm sure she does. Think what it must have cost her to ring you up and ask for your forgiveness – '

'Heh! She did no such thing. There was *no* "asking for forgiveness". Good God, she – '

'OK, OK, exaggeration, but she did ring up and I think you should respond. I think you should go and see her, and Hector, pay a flying visit and see how it goes.'

It was so tempting to choose that moment to tell him what

232

Hector had told me, and yet I hesitated. Rory's reactions were never dependable. He would not necessarily dissolve with sympathy for his mother just because she'd had a baby only a few weeks old who died of a cot death. He would be more likely to home in on Susannah's involvement and to relish, in a way I would hate, the drama of the confrontation between the sisters. And he would want to know more details and might harass his mother to give them to him. He'd want to know the baby's name and whether she had a grave and poor Isabella might loathe his open curiosity. He'd touch something she had buried deeply and perhaps cause her great pain. And once told, Rory would ignore all my pleas to be tactful and careful – I would have no control over him. He might even be angry that I imagined this revelation excused or at least offered some sort of explanation for his mother's attitude to him. There was just no knowing. So all I felt I could do was urge him to go and see Isabella and try to be friends. It was cowardly, but it seemed safest. 'Pay a flying visit to them,' I repeated. 'Please, Rory, I think you should.'

'I've said I will.'

'Brilliant.'

'But only if you come with me.'

'No.'

'You have to. I can't go on my own. You have to help.'

'No. I promised myself I'm not going back to Edinburgh ever. It's all in the past and I'm finished with the past – it does my head in.'

'But you love the past, you dote on it ... those blue-remembered hills, tra la ...'

'Shut up, Rory.'

He did, and then he fell asleep. He turned towards me, as I lay on my back listening to him, murmured, 'Goodnight,' and fell asleep. I knew that would happen, I knew I'd get stuck with him for the night. I could have prodded him awake and forced him out, but he looked so sweet asleep, like a child and not a thirty-something man. No other man I'd slept with had ever looked like Rory. Those other male faces which had slept next to mine had always seemed emphatically masculine, the beginnings of a beard bristling round the chin and mouth, skin coarsened in frowns and grimaces, but Rory's face was smooth and blond and bland in repose. He was still a pretty boy and I found myself wishing his mother could see him.

I didn't sleep. I lay and thought about Tony and knew I would have to go to see him. I practised in my head how it would be: the still ward, the sight of him bandaged and hooked up to drips, the pity it would arouse in me. Would he be able to speak? He would see me at his side and probably say my name and hold out a hand, if he had a hand free to hold out, and I, what would I say and do? I was not going to kiss him, nor would I cry or murmur endearments. I'd touch him, if I could, if there was an arm I could safely stroke, but I would not embrace him even if it were possible – not give him hope that all would go on to be well between us. I only wanted to show him I was not heartless and that I cared about his injuries. But as I went over this scenario, I was obliged to contemplate another. Suppose the sight of Tony stirred more than pity in me? Suppose common-or-garden compassion gave way to tenderness and a desire to be with him again? I didn't want that. I didn't want to succumb to that sort of emotion with all that might result. I wanted to keep myself apart and yet not be heartless.

Rory woke up about an hour later, just as I was on the verge of at last dropping off myself. He moaned, said he had a terrible headache, and I got up and brought him some aspirin. While he was making a production out of taking it, I rang the hospital again. He listened, face lighting up with the realisation something dramatic was going on. All he heard me say was Tony's name and how was he, but it was enough.

'Tony?' he said, when I put the receiver down. 'In hospital?'

'An accident. Don't ask me, I don't know. His mother left a message. He's in intensive care but stable.' Rory leaned on one elbow and studied my expression without saying anything. 'Don't look at me like that.'

'I always thought you made a mistake there,' he said.

'Did you now?'

'Chucking him out, for no reason, lovely, lovely Tony. If I'd been so lucky . . .'

'If you're awake you could go now.'

'Oh, come on, Catherine, it's half past four.'

'So? You've often been out till half past four.'

'Tube hasn't started yet.'

'It will have done by the time you've walked all the way to Highgate to get it. You can make yourself some coffee first, if you like, and have a shower.'

'You know what, you've been too long living alone.'

'And you haven't?'

'I'm hardly ever on my own even if I live on my own. But you, you're growing weirder every day on your own. I bet you talk to yourself. It's that bloody box – '

'Don't call it that. I won't have it cursed.'

'It wasn't a curse, but it's put a curse on you.'

'Don't be so stupid, so ridiculous. It's had no effect on me at all.'

'Ha! It's made you twice as irritable as you usually are, and three times as moody.'

'Well, I've given up now. Not that it's any of your business.'

'Finding mother time is over?'

'Charlotte was my mother.'

'Oh, not that again. You're like a cracked record when you

get on to that – ' and he mimicked me saying that Charlotte was my mother.

'You've always exaggerated how wonderful Charlotte was and how you adored her. It never convinced me . . .'

'Shut up, Rory. I hate you when – '

'Of course you hate me *when*. You're full of hate. The minute anyone disagrees with you, it's hate, hate, hate – ' and he spat the word out again and again. 'Well, I'll tell you what *I* hate. I hate people who work so bloody hard at creating illusions, like you've done, with boring old Charlotte, as if you were terrified to admit you knew she was dull and boring and not what you wanted your mother to be any more than my mother is what I want a mother to be.'

I left the room, slamming the door, and ran into the bathroom, where I turned both taps on to drown the sound of Rory still yelling at me. He came and banged on the door and shouted through it that he was going; then he went, banging every door he could, viciously. I sat on the edge of the bath, trembling. As ever, Rory knew how to wound. Even when I knew that what he'd said was not true his stabbing accusations hurt. And always, there was the merest, most fleeting fear in the back of my mind that he had identified something in me I had never allowed myself to think. He was wrong to say I had not loved and adored and been happy with Charlotte, but maybe it was true that I had never admitted she was not, in every respect, *the mother I wanted*.

It took me ages to calm down. I knew I should go to see Tony, but I couldn't, not in the state Rory had left me in.

I slept a couple of hours and woke feeling so dreadful I knew it would have been better not to have slept at all. Not even a stingingly cold shower made me feel more alive and I couldn't face coffee. I dressed all in black, which was probably tactless in the circumstances, but I couldn't be bothered to choose different clothes and just pulled on the trousers and sweater and jacket that were to hand. There was no point in driving because I'd never be able to park anywhere near the UCH, so I took a bus and was glad it got stuck in traffic and didn't reach Gower Street for an hour. I sat listlessly, staring out of the window on to the crowded streets and pavements, but seeing nothing, thinking only of the Radcliffe Hospital in Oxford where Charlotte had died. Day after day I went to that place, dreading it, the atmosphere, the smells. Often when I came out I had to lean against the wall and steady myself, I was so dizzy with the tension of escaping. Once, I fainted in a lavatory there. A safe place to pass out, a hospital lavatory: plenty of nurses around to see to me, you would have thought, but the joke – joke? – was that nobody was there and I came round from my faint on my own and saw to myself.

It's fear, of course. It must be. Fear that I will come to this, lying ill, and dying perhaps, in such a place, trapped, with no hope. I think of the pain and the horror of missing limbs and of terrible sores that will not heal and of the cruelties and indignities of suffering. And I even feel faint if I don't get out quickly enough. Charlotte knew and said I must not put myself through this ordeal and I said I despised myself and that it was she who was enduring the ordeal and nothing would keep me away. 'Just going to the loo,' I'd say about twice every half-hour towards the end, and then I'd dash to the lavatory and splash my face with cold water, or sit with my head between my knees till the dizziness passed. It did poor Charlotte no good at all. And now here I was, about to go into another hospital to see another very ill person, and I was behaving as badly as ever.

So why was I doing it? I am not a good person. I don't do things because it is the *right thing* to do them. I shirk what others see as my duty all the time, just like Rory. I'd brave a hospital for him, too, of course, for Rory. For my parents and for Rory I could always force myself to do anything, but for

Tony? It wasn't moral blackmail: his mother hadn't pushed me with her phone call. It was more a need to face up to something, but I hadn't a clue what it was. Settle something, be sure of something about myself which had only emerged lately. The noise as I got off the bus in Euston Road and walked round to Gower Street and the hospital was for once welcome – because of it I couldn't think at all. I went in at the main door numb with apprehension, my jacket collar turned up against imaginary draughts and my hands folded across my chest as though holding myself together. I didn't know the way, but I didn't trust myself to speak at all and relied on the many notices and signs to direct me to the ward I'd been told Tony was in. On and on I walked, down dreary corridors, up flights of stairs, past the stretchers and trolleys and all the impedimenta of hospitals, sucked further and further into this world I loathed. I felt, long before I found the right ward, that I'd lost any identity I had ever had.

I couldn't just walk in to see him and walk out again. The intensive care part of the ward he was in was more of a large cubicle than anything else, cut off from the main ward but visible from it through glass panels. There were four beds in it, all occupied. I had to give my name to a nurse sitting at a table at the far end of the ordinary ward and she referred to a list. I thought how lucky it would be if my name was not on it – I hadn't, after all, said I would visit, nobody knew I would come – but it was. Only family and close friends who had the family's permission were allowed to visit, and then only one at a time for no more than ten minutes and not more than four visitors in any one day. The nurse told me all this while she held out a white gown thing and a gauze mask to put on, explaining there was a risk of taking infection into the unit and these were a precaution. My hands trembled as I tried to tie the strings of the mask, and she did it for me, smiling sympathetically. Tony should fall in love with this nurse, who was what a nurse should be, and marry her.

He was in the far corner of the unit. She took me in, past the other still beds. The silence was not complete – there were various hissings from machines and odd rhythmic clickings – but it was intense behind these superficial sounds. Tony was stripped to the waist, half propped up with a tube coming out of his right armpit and another from his side. I hadn't asked what his injuries were and the nurse had presumed I'd know. But I could see that though his head and chest were bandaged his face was unmarked, and that he had both arms and legs. The nurse checked something to do with one of the tubes and then indicated she would leave. She pointed at her watch and held up all ten fingers and mouthed she would return. I held up five of my own and mouthed, 'Enough, thank you,' and she nodded.

His eyes were closed. He needed a shave. His skin, usually olive-coloured and easily tanned, was yellow. There were dark, dark shadows under his eyes. I could easily take either of his hands. They were not bandaged. They lay by his side, inert, the palms upwards. He was always so fit and strong and his body now, whatever damage had been done internally, still looked whole and healthy, the muscles in his shoulders clearly defined. It wasn't like looking at Charlotte, all wasted as she was, a skeleton by the end. I could look at Tony and not flinch. There was nowhere to sit – there wasn't much space at all – so I stood motionless, looking at him. Then he opened his eyes, slowly, as though the lids weighed a ton, and through the slits he saw me. His eyes were dark brown, like mine, and with so little of the eyelids lifted only a black glint showed. I held my breath, praying he was so doped up he would not be able to recognise me, but slowly the eyelids closed again and instead of feeling relief I felt dismayed.

Now I did take his hand, timidly, placing mine over his,

lightly, covering it rather than holding it. He was hot, the skin on the back of his hand burning. I exerted the slightest of pressures and his eyes opened fractionally again. 'Tony?' I murmured. His lips parted a little and his eyes opened a little further, but he frowned and looked in pain and I was afraid to repeat his name. I felt strangely breathless and kept trying to swallow, over and over again, as though I were practising to say something. But there was nothing I could say even if any words were capable of reaching him. I could lean over and whisper in his ear that it was me, Catherine, and that I loved him. Except I wasn't sure that I did, or even that I ever truly had – not as he wished me to, not enough to link myself with him for ever and let myself be absorbed into his life. All I wanted him to know was that I had come because I was sorry for what had happened to him, sorry to see him in this state, and I cared about him, and had always wanted to remain friends. It wouldn't be enough.

The nurse came back and I lifted my hand from his and turned and left the unit with her. I thought myself completely composed, but she must have thought otherwise because she urged me to take a seat for a moment in the corridor and brought me a glass of water. 'He's improving,' she said. 'He's stable now, doing well. He'll probably be moved into the ward tomorrow and be more alert.' I nodded and thanked her, and asked if I could leave a note. She brought me a Biro and a piece of paper and then tactfully left me to write whatever I wanted.

I sat for ages, wondering what I did want to write. All I wanted was for him and his mother to know that I'd been, but for neither of them to get the wrong idea. Finally, I wrote only a couple of lines, saying I'd come to say how sorry I was to see him so ill but that I'd been told he was stable and improving and I hoped he would soon be better. I said I would come again, when he was feeling better. And I signed it 'Love, Catherine'. Anything less would have sounded too cold, too harsh in the circumstances – even for me. There wasn't an envelope available, so I folded the paper over and made a little packet of it, and printed Tony's name on the front. I didn't care if anyone else read it; it wasn't private.

My definition of happiness is coming out of a hospital. The moment I leave one, no matter what I have left behind, I feel giddy not only with the release of tension but with joy that I am alive and well and able to walk away unhindered. God knows, Gower Street is a noisy, ugly street and walking round to Tottenham Court Road nothing improves, but I felt exhilarated, thrilled to be striding out and breathing air which, though heavy with petrol fumes, did not carry the smells of disease and disinfectant upon it. I'd done what I needed to do, I'd gone to see Tony, and I'd been lucky in more ways than one. If he'd been fully conscious, if we'd had to have any dialogue, things might have disintegrated into some sort of distressing scene and I'd have been trapped by my own emotions, forced perhaps to agree that I cared about him more than I found I did. But none of that had happened. I'd been, I'd left evidence that I'd been, and I'd signalled that I would come again, without saying when.

As I travelled home it occurred to me that, when he came to, Tony might even be angry that his mother had called me, and she would have to defend herself by telling him he'd asked for me himself. He might deny that he had, it would amount to such loss of face to him, or say she ought to have realised he was in agony, or drugged, and didn't know what he was saying. I thought how lucky I'd been in a trivial way, too, choosing to visit the hospital so early in the morning. The nurse had told me Tony's parents had rarely left his side until the day before and that they would be back very soon. I didn't like to think of an encounter with his mother, who would have been blaming me for months for his unhappiness and who would have found it impossible to credit that any woman could resist her son.

Mothers are like that. Charlotte was like that – she stood up for me whatever I did and would never believe I wasn't as wonderful as she thought I was. Isabellas were rare, I thought as I travelled home. And Susannah? There she was, forcing herself into my head again. Impossible to tell how Susannah would have been. Devoted to me, I suppose, but perhaps not uncritical. I'd learned enough about her since I'd opened her box to question and challenge the image I'd been given of her as a sweet, gentle, sunny-natured idol. She was reckless, always doing things dangerous to her health. And she was capable of inspiring some degree of alarm, if not fear, in her sister, to whom she had been less than kind. She was ambitious, fiercely so, and this implied, I thought, an element of aggression completely lacking in my father. Even without learning any more from George Senhouse, I knew she'd had her secrets, maybe even her regrets: she was much more complicated than I'd ever been given reason to imagine. I wondered how different things might have been if I'd been old enough to see her dead. I'd seen Charlotte dying and dead. Susannah had always been just an idea, vague, lacking any substance. But if I'd visited her as I'd visited Charlotte, or even as I'd just visited Tony, if I'd seen her ill and in pain and then dead, would I have struggled so hard to deny her any place in my life? She had needed to be real before I could acknowledge any loss.

I let myself into my flat and thought I should give my lie some substance. After I'd paid my visit to George Senhouse, I should go away again, on my own, not with Rory. There was still the *Hidden Scotland* job to do, but going to Scotland was not what I needed. I'd cancel it. I'd go to France this time and wander about for a while. But first I felt the time had come to dispose of the memory box itself, to have some sort of symbolic burning or tearing apart. It lurked in my darkroom, a constant reminder of someone I could never really find. Before I went away I would get rid of it. I went straight to it and pulled it out into my sitting-room. It looked very unthreatening – bright, cheerful and anodyne. I couldn't believe I'd regarded it with such dread a mere six months or so ago. It seemed years since I'd unpacked it, excited in spite of myself. I stared at it now, and wondered how I could for one moment have believed this box had such power. The list of contents, neatly numbered, was inside it. I picked up a pen and carefully ticked them off, in a done that/been there mood. At number 11, I paused. I'd done no more than glance at number 11. It alone of all the contents was still in the box. I'd not so much forgotten about it as considered it not worthy of my attention. I'd put the cardboard tube back in the box after I'd taken it out of its other resting place, to show Rory, and never thought of it since.

Number 11, two pictures, rolled up and put into a cardboard tube. Slowly, I unfurled them.

Chapter Fourteen

Two pictures, both of a mother and a baby. I'd taken one look, back in September, and never looked at them again. Now, re-rolling them to flatten them, I put them side by side on the table in front of me. Feeling the paper, I deduced that my original guess had been right – these were pages cut from an art book, or an expensively produced catalogue, an act of what my father would have called vandalism. The paper was thick and smooth, the colour reproduction excellent. These pages had been cut out very neatly. I could make out the faintest trace of pencil along the left-hand edge of one and the right-hand side of the other. Susannah had ruled a line before she did her cutting, either with scissors, or possibly a knife, even a razor. Still, the book or catalogue would have been ruined.

My father had only let me look at his art and architectural volumes under his supervision until I was quite old. It was treated as a great privilege. I had to wash my hands thoroughly first, scrubbing them in hot water with a nail brush, and then I had to sit at a table. (I wasn't allowed to hold these books on my knees.) I was even shown the way in which I must turn the pages, by holding the top corner of each page, using as little pressure as possible, and flipping it, not dragging it, over. My father said these books of his were not like other books. They were, literally, works of art and precious, and must be treated as special and valuable. When I was very young, five or six, being given permission to look at what he referred to as his 'treasures' had been thrilling. I had hurried to fill all the conditions and been only too eager to obey his command to sit up straight and not lean on the bigger volumes. But later, in early adolescence, I'd resented what I thought of then as the unnecessarily fussy strictures he'd imposed and I'd tried to flout them without his knowing. I'd go into the downstairs cloakroom next to his study and run the water, leaving the door open, and then say I'd washed my hands, when I hadn't at all. For heaven's sake, I'd think, I haven't been down a coal mine, my hands are clean anyway, and I'd get a guilty but pleasurable *frisson* out of cheating. If my father left the room, I'd deliberately turn pages roughly and slouch over the books, not quite daring to inflict even minimal damage, but getting as close as I could to risk doing so. Later, I stopped wanting to look at them at all, if it was going to be such a performance. I went for cheaper offerings which were more user-friendly, though he pointed out their inferiority in every respect. Those 'treasures' were worth their exorbitant price and I knew it, really – any fool could see the difference.

How had Susannah, the obedient wife, brought herself to violate an art book of the calibre these plates had obviously come from? But then I remembered that she had had her own collection of books, not very large, nothing like as extensive or impressive as my father's, but her own. There had been a bookshelf in my father's study which had held Susannah's books as well as some of his. They were on the top three shelves, too high for me to reach without standing on something, and I was never interested enough to do that. But I knew they were her books and had some special significance or my father would not have kept them. When I was doing 'A' Level history of art, he mentioned them to me and suggested I have a look at them because they might be useful. Grudgingly, making a feature as I always did of not wanting anything to do with what had belonged to Susannah, I had a cursory look. The books were all concerned with women artists (so no wonder the collection was small). There was stuff there not only about the famous women – Gwen John, Rosa Bonheur – but much less well-known ones, and some I had never heard of like Emily Carr Osborn and Cecilia Beaux. I began secretly to use these books although I'd told my father, at my most offhand, that they weren't much good. In fact, I did whole essays based on what I found in some of them and got very good marks.

I suspected these pictures had come from a book in her own collection – well, it was fairly obvious – but I couldn't search for it because I'd sold it, the entire collection. I'd been in such a hurry to get rid of anything to do with Susannah that I hadn't even examined her books carefully. I think I regretted my haste very soon afterwards, but at the same time I was glad to have had them removed. It was a sort of betrayal to get rid of them like that, but then I'd spent a lifetime cutting all connection with her and it was just part of the same sort of rejection. But, confronted now with these plates cut from somewhere, I was ashamed to think I had had the means to identify them and had lost the opportunity through my own impetuous act. And my knowledge of women artists, assuming it was a woman I was looking for, was not sufficient for me to guess who had painted these portraits. It was a long time since that 'A' Level course and I hadn't gone on to enlarge or consolidate the knowledge I'd absorbed. But it struck me, looking so hard at those two pieces of glossy paper, that the point might not be the artist who had made these prints (I had just enough knowledge to recognise them as prints rather than paintings). The point might just be what she had chosen to represent. The artist might be irrelevant. As usual, I was being *too* clever, imagining Susannah as devious when simplicity was the clue to tell me what had been meant.

So, I tried to think simply. What was I looking at? In the first picture, a woman in a pretty, pale blue, flowered dress, a long full-skirted dress, was sitting on a chair, the padded back glimpsed behind her right shoulder, holding a naked baby on her lap and kissing it. She had dark hair, tidily pinned into a roll on top of her head. Her right hand cupped the baby's bare bottom and her left, rather large and out of proportion, pulled the baby to her. If I'd drawn a line from the top left-hand corner to the bottom right the whole of the top triangle would have been virtually empty. The colours were pale blue and grey except for the flesh tone of the baby's skin. The second picture showed another dark-haired woman, possibly the same one, but a different baby (fair-haired instead of dark). This one was wearing a cream-coloured gown, with faint patches of darker cream all over it. The chair she was sitting on was upholstered in a cream and apricot pattern and behind it there was what looked like a wooden bed made up with white linen. The woman was full face, the baby in profile. Again, she was holding the child tightly.

Still trying to react simply, I noted how pretty the compositions were, after all, mother and baby in both cases carefully arranged. The colours were soft and seductive, the notion that everything in the pictures had been melded into a harmonious whole very strong. These were not complicated pictures – they were indeed perfectly simple and made a clear appeal to be taken at face value: a mother loving her baby. That was all. Yet as I went on looking I couldn't help but look deeper and reject the superficial conclusion which had been so tempting. These were not just about a mother loving her baby, nor were they simply pretty-pattern effects. The baby in the first picture was surely struggling. It was resisting its mother's kiss. The mother had her eyes closed in ecstasy over the kiss she was bestowing, but the baby's eyes were open and its mouth pulling back. In the second picture, the opposite was true. There, the baby was doing the clinging, pressing its face eagerly into its mother's cheek, and the mother, looking weary and forlorn, as though the baby weighed heavily in her arms and she longed to put it down, was merely enduring the kiss. Interesting. Two pictures, perhaps two points of view, or two sides of the same coin. I couldn't be sure the two women were the same. Both had dark hair, worn in the same style, but the body language was different enough to suggest they were not. The first woman was confident and at ease, the second tense. It wasn't possible to tell the sex of the baby, but I felt they were both girls, for no good reason. I couldn't tell, either, how old they were. I see so few babies I had nothing to guide me, but remembering photographs of myself at that age I thought these two might be six months or so. The message was becoming, if anything, too simple after all. This was Susannah, this was me. She'd wanted to show me not only how she had loved me but *how I had loved her.* The second picture was particularly poignant, showing her weakness and distress as she tried to hold me, wriggling and lively in her tired arms. These were not to be dismissed as chocolate-box fodder. They were touching and painful and full of maternal feeling.

But did the artist matter? I still didn't think so, but not knowing who had made these prints nagged away at me and I knew I had to investigate properly, just to be sure I was missing nothing. It was easy enough to visit the Courtauld Library, to find out who had: there was nothing difficult about identifying the artist, who turned out to be well known, if not to me. It was the American artist Mary Cassatt. There was plenty of information about her. Cassatt used the children, often babies, of relatives and friends as models and she had become famous as 'the painter par excellence of mother and child scenes'. I discovered that in 1891 Mary Cassatt worked on a set of ten large colour prints, which included *Mother's*

Kiss and *Maternal Caress* – and there they were in reproduction. She'd gone from painting to print-making and become expert at it. The text I skimmed didn't say why or how. It was surprisingly more concerned with her life. It startled me to learn that this woman, famous for painting mothers and babies, never had a child of her own. She had given no maternal caress. She was born in 1855, settled in Paris, remained single. Her portraits of maternity, whether paintings or prints, had been lauded for their feeling, but the emotion they captured had never been felt by her. All she had done was observe. She hadn't painted from any personal experience at all. This struck me as extraordinary, proof that true art does not need to come from the personal, but as soon as I thought that I checked myself – this *was* personal. Mary Cassatt might not have had children, but her work spoke not of possession but of yearning. She could have yearned for the babies she didn't have and this yearning, this ache, was what went into her pictures. A woman yearning for something she couldn't have, something she was going to miss. The library was closing as I handed in the book.

Back home, I took what I promised myself should be a last look, for the time being, at the prints. I wondered what they would say to the casual observer who walked past them as they hung on a wall somewhere, or flicked through the book they had come from. Take away their significance for me, and what was there? Only, surely, what I'd originally thought: pretty pictures. If I chose to load them with grief and loss it must be because something had changed in the last few months. I'd been forced into admitting there *had* been loss, and with it pain. Susannah's pain, the thing I hadn't wanted to know about. And now my own, the pain of appreciating her agony of mind. I had mocked those who had tried to suggest, with such a solemn desire to be profound, that I had been cruelly robbed by the death of my 'real' mother before I could know her. Where had it sprung from, this determination to mock? Why had I fought so hard to keep this dead woman out of my life? Why be so violently opposed to being like her in any way?

At any rate, I was done with all that by the time I packed the prints away again. Susannah had finally become my mother, Charlotte my stepmother. It was possible that nobody except myself would know. To whom, after all, did I ever speak of either mother these days? Only to Rory, perhaps. And in the future to anyone who came into my life to whom I might be close. Tony maybe. It will, I suppose, become a kind of litmus test — if I love him, or anyone, enough to speak of my mother and mean Susannah, then I will be sure of him. I had made sense of it. I knew that the contents of the memory box, however much I had derided them, however much they had infuriated me, had revealed my mother to me in unexpected guises which had not been visible either in photographs or in the little snatches of oral history I had allowed to penetrate my defences. I'd be able to tell someone in the future that the astonishing thing is that I think she may have been quite like me. No, that *I* am quite like *her*. I'd be able to venture the opinion, diffidently, that we would probably have got on quite well. I would have to admit, if pushed, that, yes, it was sad that I had never known her and that, yes, there was a yearning in me now to have done so. I wanted her after all.

Well, I couldn't and can't have her. Even if I had felt and admitted this yearning years before, I would never have been able to have her. Think how bitter I might have become, pining for a dead mother, how wretched I could have made myself, how I could have convinced myself my life was completely blighted. It would have been hell for Charlotte. She could have spent her life trying to make up for what I claimed so desperately to miss. She'd always marvelled at how I gave her all my love and devotion, and that she had never been put in the unfortunate position of so many stepmothers, and this happy relationship had in turn bound me to my father, who never had to feel I was bereft of maternal love.

It struck me, as I packed the prints away, how odd it was that I had never enquired closely into how my father himself coped with my mother's death. I knew the facts, what he'd actually done, how he'd managed, and all that, until my step-mother came along, but I didn't know anything about his feelings during that time. We'd never talked about it. I hadn't asked and he hadn't volunteered the information. He wasn't that sort of man. It had been hard enough for him to tell me my mother was not Charlotte but a woman who was dead. I was not quite five when he had to make a point of telling me – it was probably just before I was due to start school and, I suppose, he felt some duty to make sure I had the relationships straight. I have a feeling that he may have been bullied into it by Isabella because I remember she and Rory were staying with us the week before. Perhaps she had resented my open adoration of my stepmother, my arms forever round her neck, the kisses between us frequent and warm. Did Isabella want to spoil things? She certainly can't have acted out of loyalty to the memory of a sister she had reason to hate.

But when my father started talking about 'your real mother', wanting to tell me something to make Susannah alive in my imagination, I leapt off his knee and ran screaming, 'Mummy, Mummy, Mummy!' through the house until I found Charlotte. I wouldn't let her out of my sight for the rest of the day. My father didn't come after me. He let Charlotte deal with my distress (which of course she did, very well). He never mentioned Susannah to me again for years and years and he never, ever, referred to her again as my 'real' mother. I aided and abetted his wish to bury her completely by never asking questions about her and, if she came into the conversation, as she inevitably did when my grandmother was staying with us, walking out of the room.

How much had he loved her? I had only seen him happy with Charlotte and had no idea what he had felt about my mother. I had inhibited him, with my fierce repudiation of the very notion that Susannah had been my mother, but even so I think he should have, at some point, when I was grown up, tried to talk to me about her, about the two of them, their relationship. He couldn't, by the time I was in my twenties, possibly have thought that any confession of his would affect my own love for Charlotte. But he never said a word. I only knew from her family how they met and when they married and where they lived and what they did. It was as though, like me, he wanted to obliterate her memory. But unlike me, he had known her and loved her and had some obligation, I would have thought, to treasure the memory of what they had been to each other. Did my mother know she couldn't trust him to do that? Did she know very well that he was the sort of man who can only survive by blocking out tragedy, eliminating from his memory all things acutely painful?

I think now that perhaps my father forgot Susannah. I suspect he became embarrassed, even ashamed, as the years went by that he could hardly remember her. It may have alarmed him, this blank where once she had been, in which case it would have been wonderfully convenient that I never required him to tell me about her. Can you bring yourself, if you are a kind man like my father, to confess to your daughter that you can't recall much about her mother? Difficult. But it occurs to me that there is a situation even more difficult: letting a daughter realise that her mother's death might have been, from your point of view, a blessing in disguise, because it opened the way to finding another woman with whom you were far happier. But my father would never, of course, have let me realise any such thing, even if it had been true. There are plenty of reasons why he never unburdened himself to me, quite apart from the discouragement I gave him. He would be mindful all the time of how I might interpret anything he told me, and feel it was dangerous to try to describe his state of feeling so long ago. I doubt even if he were alive now that I could get him to do so. My mother, through her box, had made herself real to me, but she would have remained lost for ever to him.

At least I think so. It is all hypothesis, the sort of stuff it would have been good to discuss with Charlotte. She, for sure, would have been able to tell me more about how my father thought of my mother than he could himself. I regret so bitterly that she is not here for me to turn to – she would have been so glad, since she was the one never comfortable with the suppression of everything to do with my mother. Often, she'd tried to bring Susannah into the present, asking her own questions of my grandmother and of Isabella in my hearing, and it was she who kept her photographs around, finding and replacing them when I hid them. But how much had my father actually told her? She'd told me often enough that what first struck her about him was his lost look, his distracted air, which in a young and handsome man made him look so vulnerable. Yes, she'd wanted to mother him, that was her first instinct. When she'd learned that he was a widower with a baby daughter she'd felt so sorry for him and had assumed his bereavement was too recent for him to want to make new friends. She'd felt he stumbled through each day and that it was her duty (she was secretary to the senior partner in the firm for whom he worked) to help him in all the small ways she could. She would never have dreamed of asking him out after office hours nor did she think for one moment that he would ask her. She reckoned it would take him years to get over such a tragedy and when he did, if he did, he would not be interested in her. She had seen the photograph of his dead wife on his desk and knew that she could not compare – she was too ordinary, too plump, too plain to measure up against Susannah.

It was her boss who brought them together, a mere three months after my father had lost his wife. He had two tickets for a concert which he and his wife could no longer attend. My father was in his office showing him some drawings when this man said to both Charlotte, sitting there typing, and my father, 'Why don't you two use these tickets?' Charlotte had blushed crimson and had been about to decline as quickly as possible to save my father from embarrassment, when he had said he would love to if Miss Fraser was willing. 'It was as if he'd been waiting for an opportunity,' she'd told me, and when, loving this story, I had teased my father, he had smiled and said it was exactly right, he'd been longing to ask Charlotte out but hadn't had the courage. They went to the concert and that was more or less it. They were rarely apart afterwards and only delayed marrying out of a sense of decency. He fell in love with a woman already in love with him and was happy ever after.

Happier than he ever was with my mother, though? Maybe. I wondered whether I would discover, when I finally visited him next day, if George Senhouse had found someone else to be happy with too. At any rate, my father may have felt something for Charlotte he had never felt for my mother, whatever he had felt for her. And what would be wrong about that? Nothing. Isabella had once expressed disapproval (her forte) in my hearing as to how quickly my father had 'got over' my mother's death. 'She was barely dead before he took up with Charlotte,' she'd said to my grandmother many years later, when an anniversary was coming up of their wedding and she was rambling on about her memories of it. My grandmother didn't hesitate for a moment. 'Good,' she said,

'I was glad. He needed someone. No point spending his life mourning.' I wish she was still alive too, my grandmother. I could have talked to her. It would have made her so happy that I wanted, at last, to hear every detail about my mother. There was only Isabella left, and I had tried her. She was the wrong person to ask anything of. Long before the tragedy of her baby's death, she was hostile to her dead sister for reasons I'd never fathomed, and which maybe had no real basis, but were only the sort of chemical reaction one sibling can have towards another. And she was never close to my father. Everything Isabella had to say was prejudiced. She could tell me anything she wanted about my parents and nothing could be disproved by me.

I recalled the words I had had carved on my stepmother's gravestone, 'Beloved mother of Catherine'. Maybe I shouldn't have done that. Maybe it not only took something away from my mother but gave my stepmother something she had no need of. Maybe it was an insult to them both. Could the two exist together, on equal terms? I had never thought so, but knew it was the final thing I had to decide before letting the power of the memory box fade.

Chapter Fifteen

I FELT nervous setting off to visit George Senhouse in his nursing home and unsure that I should be going to see him at all. It might be embarrassing, for him, for me. I don't like to embarrass people, whereas Rory loves to: he does it deliberately. I tried, on the train to Brighton – I'd had enough of driving after that long journey back from Scotland – to think of what I was going to say to Mr Senhouse, but I couldn't seem to frame questions properly. I'd done the same, I remembered, on my way to meet Gracie Monroe in Bequia and then, when I'd got there, I had forgotten what I'd decided to ask. But this was different – this encounter called for specific enquiries. I always knew Gracie would be most unlikely to be able to tell me much, that the chances of her knowing who Susannah was were minimal and the whole idea was a bit ridiculous. This time I knew for a fact that the person I was going to see had not only known Susannah but had been close to her, for a short time at least. It made the starting point easier but the questions somehow harder.

Looking out of the train window, I wondered idly why George was in a Brighton nursing home (though actually it was five miles from Brighton). He was a Cumbrian and his sister still lived in Maryport – but then I knew nothing about him. Perhaps he'd moved south long ago and settled in Brighton. But I thought of John Graham, who must be about George's own age, and how fit and lively he had been, both physically and mentally, and I thought again how strange it was that George appeared to live permanently in a nursing home. Something must have happened to him, and realising that I began to worry that he might not be in any state to tell me anything at all. I could be going to see a man wrecked by illness, whose memory and speech were both affected.

I got a taxi at Brighton station and enjoyed the ride along the coastal road to the nursing home. The sea was rough, great grey waves smashing on the shingle sending up sheets of spray which reached over the esplanade, drenching pedestrians. I thought of the Caribbean and its beautiful blues and greens and the tenderness of the creamy lines of foam at its edges. I wondered if George's home looked over this sullen sea and if he, too, watched it and thought of that other ocean where he had sailed with Susannah. But when we reached Downside House I saw it had no windows facing the sea. It was a couple of miles inland and in a dip, surrounded by trees. The views would be of the downs. I'd imagined an old building, perhaps a converted manor house, but it was new and looked more like a modern hotel, which was a surprise. My head, I realised, had been full of Dickensian notions of nursing homes, which had made me think of them as workhouses.

Nothing could have been further from the truth. The entrance hall was light and airy, circular in shape, with a floor tiled in pretty green-and-white patterned tiles. There was a round pine table in the centre on which there was a large jug full of yellow tulips. As soon as I walked in a woman came out of a room to the right, smiling pleasantly and asking if she could help. I'd feared a dragon – more mistaken notions, though this one had been encouraged by the curtness of the woman who'd answered the phone when I made that first call. I said I'd come to visit George Senhouse and had checked that I could two days ago. She nodded and said he might not be back in his own room yet, he might still be finishing lunch in the dining-room, but she would take me along. I felt desperate to be forewarned of his condition, so as I accompanied her down a corridor leading off the hall, I asked how he was. 'Just the same,' she said. There seemed no point in pretending I knew what that meant, so I confessed I had no idea and asked point-blank, 'Why is he in here?'

She knew it was odd, of course, that any visitor should have to ask what was wrong with the patient they were visiting, but she expressed no surprise and didn't seem in the least suspicious of me. She told me George had had a serious accident several years ago in which he'd damaged his right arm so badly it was useless. The accident had been at sea, but she didn't know the details. The reason he was living here, though, wasn't because of what the accident had done to him but because soon after it he had had a stroke which left him paralysed on his right side. The paralysis had lifted partially, but his speech was still very indistinct and he was too incapacitated to live on his own. His wife had died long before all this happened and though he had two sons, both married, they lived abroad. 'He gets very depressed,' she finished. 'He doesn't get many visitors, so he'll be delighted to see you.'

By this time she'd reached George's room and led me into it. As she'd predicted, he wasn't there, but she said he'd be back from lunch soon and I should make myself at home. I was glad when she left me, needing time to adjust to everything she'd told me. Clearly, this man wasn't going to be anything like the healthy John Graham, and if his speech was impaired the chances of any kind of fruitful conversation were poor. This was all going to be a waste of time and I chided myself for not having checked up on George's condition before ever I came. I stood hesitantly in the middle of the room, wishing I could run away without being seen, but I felt I was trapped. George would by now have been told of my arrival and common decency demanded I should stay for at least a few minutes. Uneasily, I paced about the room, noting how comfortably it was furnished. I thought probably the furniture was his own – it didn't look institutional. There were a couple of armchairs covered in a rose-strewn chintz and a footstool with an embroidered top, and a small walnut desk, all of which looked somehow personal items. The room was L-shaped and in the smaller part there was a bed with a table beside it. I looked at the framed photographs on it, and on the window ledge. There was George, I presumed, on his wedding day. His bride looked haughty and stared defiantly at the camera with an air of refusing to smile. George wasn't smiling either. He was very handsome, tall and athletic-looking. I thought of Susannah and felt a funny sort of flutter in my stomach.

There were no more photographs of his wife, but there were several of children I took to be his sons. They were all taken on boats and in these George was smiling and looking supremely contented with a son on either side. The last frame I peered at was the most recent of these photographs. It was of one of the sons' wedding. George had aged well, very well. This event had obviously been before the accident and stroke because he looked so fit, still quite the sporting hero John Graham had described. His hair was white but there was lots of it and his face was more attractively weather-beaten than wrinkled. I'd picked the photograph up to study it more closely when I heard voices and the sound of what I guessed was a wheelchair being pushed, its wheels squeaking slightly on the floor. I put the photograph down hurriedly and turned to face the door. It was a shock to confront the man being wheeled in. I would never have recognised him from the photographs I'd just been scrutinising. Anyone, sitting in a wheelchair and recovering from a stroke would look different, of course, but the contrast was violent. Here was a once tall, powerful-looking man now so shrunken and thin that he appeared lost in his clothes and the skin of his face too loose for its size – it literally hung over the prominent cheekbones.

Only his hair was the same, thick and plentiful, but even that told against him, because it was now much too luxuriant for the wasted face.

'There we are, George,' the young woman, who'd wheeled him in, said. 'Here's the visitor we heard about. Isn't that nice? Now, are you going to get yourself into your armchair or do you want help?'

George ignored her. He was staring at me and frowning. I felt myself blushing, the heat rushing through me together with an obscure sense of guilt. Remembering that George was said to have difficulty speaking, and not wanting him to struggle to ask who on earth I was and what did I want, I said quickly, 'Mr Senhouse, you don't know me, but my name is Catherine Musgrave and I'm the daughter of someone you knew a long time ago. I'm Susannah Cameron's daughter — maybe you remember her?' Instantly, his expression changed. The frown lifted and he gave a little grunt. The nurse, who was still patiently waiting, said again, 'Do you want a hand, George, then?' and he shook his head and gestured, rather rudely I thought, for her to go. Then he put the brake on the wheelchair and began slowly to lever himself up, using his left hand only. It was painful to watch as he strained first to stand up, then to walk to an armchair, but finally he managed the two or three steps and sat down. 'Sit down,' he said to me, nodding at the other chair. To my relief the two words were enunciated perfectly.

We faced each other at a distance of a mere foot or so. I tried to smile and keep very still, realising he wanted time to inspect me. I knew he was checking off my features one by one and comparing them with Susannah's, the way people who'd known her always did before delivering the inevitable verdict that I was not a bit like her. I waited for this, but George surprised me. He nodded and seemed to relax a little, or maybe he was simply making himself more comfortable in his chair. He took a deep breath, paused as though exerting some kind of control, or following an exercise he'd been taught and had to struggle to master, and then he said, 'A look of her,' and nodded again. I felt absurdly pleased and relieved.

'People don't usually tell me that,' I said, smiling and realising that for the first time in my life I was happy to be told I had anything of Susannah about me. 'They all say how *un*like her I am – '

'Not *like*,' he interrupted, 'look of her. Different.'

'Sorry.'

'Strong face,' he said. 'Same express – '

But he couldn't manage the whole word 'expression' and it frustrated him. He tried again and I jumped in to say it for him, though worried that this was the wrong and tactless thing to do, but he accepted it. He looked so tired, with the effort of speaking, that I thought I should talk and answer those questions I felt he was bound to have but which he wasn't able to ask without exhausting difficulty.

'Mr Senhouse,' I said, 'you'll want to know why I've come to see you like this, so suddenly, out of the blue.' He nodded. 'Well, my mother died when I was six months old . . .'

'Heart?' he asked.

I said yes, registering that this meant he had known about Susannah's condition. He'd known and still taken her on that daring sailing trip all the way to the Caribbean. 'You knew about her heart, then?' I asked, and again he nodded. 'And yet you took her with you to Bequia, sailing all the way to the West Indies?' I tried not to sound critical but instead to suggest admiration.

'She was – ' and the word sounded like 'trimmed'. I guessed 'determined' quickly, and that was right. This was awful, I was subjecting him to such an ordeal, and I hurried on explaining the reason for my visit, passing over the memory box without listing its other contents and merely focusing on the address book and how curious I'd been about the addresses in it, which had led me first to Bequia and then to the Grahams and finally to him. 'So really', I finished, 'I just wanted it confirmed that Susannah actually did sail to Bequia and that it was with you.'

He smiled and lifting his head up and stretching his neck back he said, 'Wonderful, it was wonderful!' Every word came out perfectly and he was so delighted he repeated 'wonderful' several times. I saw, as he went on beaming at me, that the right-hand side of his face didn't smile like the left but was frozen, yet it was possible to glimpse what a great, generous smile he had once had. I was about to ask him about the cabin which I'd never been able to find, when he pointed to a chest of drawers in the corner of the room. 'In top drawer,' he said, slurring the words badly after his triumph with the previous ones, but I was still able to understand first time. 'You want me to get something in the top drawer?' He nodded, looking eager and even excited. I opened the drawer. It was full of photograph albums, a dozen or so of them arranged in two layers in the wide, deep drawer. 'Dates,' he said. I saw each album had a label with a year's date on it. He had terrible trouble trying to tell me the date he wanted but finally I identified 1956.

I brought the correct album over to him and put it on his knee. It was a large, oblong album and on its cover was a small photograph of a boat under which the date was printed. Slowly, after gesturing that I was to stand and look over his shoulder, he turned the pages. There was no need for any commentary. Susannah and he were in every photograph, sometimes in a group, sometimes just the two of them. They always had their arms round each other and they were almost always laughing. Or kissing. They were both tanned and their hair bleached with the sun. They wore shorts or bathing costumes, Susannah's a bright pink. I didn't need to ask if they had been lovers – it was all so obvious. There were no photographs that I knew of which showed my father and Susannah looking as this couple in Bequia did. George came to the end of his album and stopped at the last photograph. I recognised where it had been taken – it was high up on the hill where Gracie Monroe lived. George and Susannah were facing each other, arms entwined round each other's waists, her face slightly uplifted, his slightly lowered, so that they were looking into each other's eyes. We both stared at this photograph for a long time, as though paying it our respects.

Finally, George closed the album. I sat down facing him again. His expression was odd. I couldn't decide whether I should understand by it that he felt he had made some sort of statement by showing me the album and was waiting for a response, or whether it was telling me there was nothing more to say. I settled for feeling he wanted me to react. 'So you and Susannah were lovers?' I asked. He laughed and raised both his hands in what looked like exasperation at my idiocy – of course they were lovers. 'So what happened?' I said. 'Why did she marry my father? Why were you kept a secret?' He stopped laughing and sighed and picked up a notepad and pencil lying on the table beside him. He wrote something with his left hand, laboriously, and showed it to me. It said, *'Is your father dead too?'* I said yes. This seemed to relieve him, and he began to write some more. I watched as he covered three sheets of paper, writing excruciatingly slowly, wishing so desperately that he could talk easily to me and tell me in minute detail all about his relationship with Susannah. He'd obviously been right-handed and writing with his left was almost as hard for him as trying to speak coherently. I felt I was asking far too much of him and that my very presence and my questions were a cruel intrusion on his memories. I really wasn't entitled to put him through this.

But he looked calm enough after he'd read through what he'd written and handed it to me. I read it myself, twice, and said, 'Thank you,' and folded the sheets of paper carefully and put them in my bag. I stayed another half-hour, telling him everything I could think of about Susannah's subsequent life after she married my father. I wasn't sure how much he would know – it wasn't clear from what he'd written if they'd severed all contact and completely dropped out of sight of each other, or whether perhaps mutual acquaintances might have kept them informed of each other's lives. I told him properly about the memory box now, saying I was sure its purpose was to tell me things no one else would or could, and that I felt some sort of written explanation was probably intended but never got made and so I was left with a puzzle and he was a part of it. I said I was sure he had been of vital importance to her, and the trip to Bequia the most exciting thing that had ever happened to her. It had been her great adventure, he had been her great romance. And I said that what I had just learned from him, from what he had written down, linked me to Susannah more securely than anything could ever have done.

Before I left, as tea was brought in, I said I would come again. I meant it. I had no intention of getting what I wanted out of George Senhouse then abandoning him. We shook hands and, on impulse, I bent down and kissed him, and he gripped my hand tightly and seemed touched. On the way out, I walked down the corridor with the woman who had first shown me in and took the opportunity to ask some more about George. She'd said he didn't get many visitors and I wondered why he hadn't moved to be near his sister. She said he'd been living in America before his accident, for years and years, she thought, and when it happened he was taken to hospital in Brighton. He'd only been in this country on holiday and had no residence here except for a cottage somewhere on this coast. Once the accident was followed by the stroke he was in no fit state to return to America and it was his sons who had made the decision about this nursing home. She didn't know if he would have preferred to be in the north or not.

It seemed such a sad way to end his days. All the way back on the train I was thinking about George and wondering how I could fill in the gaps in his story. I thought it would be easy enough to get his sons' addresses and write to them, or even to go and see his sister in Maryport, who would have all the history, but somehow I doubted if I ever would. That part of his history which concerned me most I now knew. I took out what he had written and smoothed the sheets out. Already I almost knew the words by heart. If only Susannah had told this tale in her words how much more they would have meant than poor George's stumbling sentences all these years later. And yet he'd managed to give me the essential facts from which I could construe the rest, or fancied I could. It was an ordinary enough story after all, and it was quite easy to fill in the detail for myself. When they returned from Bequia by air, after selling the boat, Susannah believed herself to be pregnant. She was distraught at how her career would be ruined before it had begun – she would have to drop out of university – and at the thought of her mother's distress, but never for one moment did she think of trying to get rid of the baby. He wanted to marry her anyway and was secretly glad that her pregnancy would force her to marry him then and not make him wait three years until she'd finished her degree. They agreed to marry at a register office and tell no one until it was over. And then, the morning of the day they were to be married, Susannah found she wasn't pregnant after all. She refused to marry him, saying marriage was no longer necessary. He was furious. He hadn't thought theirs was to be a marriage of mere convenience. They quarrelled. He was so upset and disappointed he said things he later regretted and he thought maybe she did too. At any rate, there was a lot of shouting and she left his room saying she never wanted to see him again. He never for one moment believed she really meant it, but was too proud and angry to go after her and she never phoned or wrote to him. He kept expecting to hear from her but never did. He knew he should go to her but he was hurt and felt humiliated, and he didn't. Then he left to go to America to do a business course. She'd known he was going and he kept expecting that, as the date for his departure drew near, they would somehow make it up. But they didn't. He left and was away a year. He did write then, but got no reply and wasn't even sure she'd got his letter. When he came back she wasn't at her home but on holiday 'with friends', her mother said. He thought John Graham might be one of these friends and contacted him, but he didn't know where she was or who with. George went back to America to start a job and met and married Celia.

All this was written down in short, choppy sentences, betraying little emotion except for the last line. 'We threw it away,' he'd written. 'My fault. Regretted it ever since.' I supposed 'it' meant true love, or something similar. Clearly, George didn't feel he'd found it again with Celia. Susannah had been luckier. She'd found my father and he was perfect for her, or so everyone had said: they were love's young dream. Well, my grandmother had said so, but then what, after all, had she known? She hadn't known about George Senhouse for a start, nor where her daughter really was when she'd said she would be working in America at a camp during the vacation. (George had told me about this subterfuge when I'd asked him how on earth Susannah had managed to conceal the Bequia jaunt from her mother.) Susannah, it turned out, had been incredibly devious and cunning and I'd reached the stage of beginning to question every single thing I'd been told about her. But, as I'd said to George, I'd also reached the stage of seeing myself in her more truly than I had ever done. She made mistakes. She loved George but she wasn't prepared to marry him just to prove she did. She expected him to think as she did and when he didn't she was sure he would in the end. All she had to do was leave and he would follow. He was in the wrong and she was not.

But did she love my father, in time, later, just as much? Was the bust-up with George a blessing in disguise? Back to questions again, of the maddening variety that no one could answer. Maybe Susannah had been luckier than George, but even if my father had still been alive, I doubt if he could have completely convinced me on that score. He wouldn't know how he compared with a former lover she may never have mentioned to him. But of course he *did* make her pregnant and gave her me and made her happy in a way George had not, so she was luckier in the end. Except George had had children too – oh, it was too confusing, and too pointless, trying to sort out what I thought, how Susannah came out of all this. I longed to talk about it with someone clear-headed who would be able to assess all this in a way I could not and point out the real significance of what George had told me. Tony could do it. He'd enjoy the challenge. But he was ill and ought not to be bothered with my problems. His own were far more serious and pressing – how could he be expected to care about a muddle that had happened so far in the past? I shouldn't even mention any of this to such a sick man.

But I did. The next time I went to see him Tony was out of intensive care and in a side room of his own. He was awake, his eyes were fully open, and he was propped up on his pillows. The tubes had gone, but not the bandages, and though he looked awful he was alert. He didn't smile when he recognised me but instead made a grimace I remembered so well, a mock-mournful pulling down of the lips and a raising of the eyebrows which was meant to convey everything being too much for him. I couldn't help but smile myself and kiss him, lightly, gently, on the side of his face. 'Well,' he said, his voice croaky and not like his at all, 'surprise.' I said I didn't know why he was surprised, I'd left a note saying I'd come again, hadn't I? Then I asked not how he was feeling but where it hurt, and he groaned and said everywhere, but that the damage wasn't as bad as first thought. He'd had his spleen removed, and some of his ribs were broken, others cracked, but the main worry was his head. He'd had an operation 'to clean something up', as they'd put it, and now he was supposed to be all right, his brain wasn't after all injured, 'or not much'. But every bloody movement was agony and he had no energy. And the worst part was not the pain but lying thinking all the time of how the accident had been all his own stupid fault.

I'd thought that the last thing he would want to do would be to tell me what had happened, and I'd certainly had no plans to ask, but it seemed he desperately needed to go over it all. He insisted he'd been entirely responsible for the collision with the lorry. He'd misjudged the distance when turning from a side road into a main road and failed to estimate the speed of this approaching lorry. It was so unlike him – he was such a good and careful driver, as I knew – and he couldn't credit he'd made such an error of judgement. The only consolation was that no one else was hurt.

'Don't think about it,' I said. 'It won't help, brooding about what's over. I know, I know, it's stating the obvious, but that's because it's true.'

'Can't help it,' he said. 'My head's full of it. I've nothing else to think about.'

So that was why I told him about my visit to George Senhouse and then, of course, to make sense of this had to work backwards to the finding of the memory box. I was afraid of tiring him, but he seemed to love the distraction and it was only towards the end of my little account that his eyes began to close. He struggled to stay awake but I squeezed his hand and said I must go, and when he said, 'But you'll come again?' I said yes; it was impossible to refuse. I visited him three times that week and saw him get just a little stronger each day. He was able to concentrate more and though our conversation was full of pauses, when he drifted off occasionally, it became increasingly personal. I knew how dangerous the situation was becoming. Tony was growing more and more convinced, I could see, that my visits and concern for him meant we might get together again. There was an edge to his voice when he talked about Susannah and George, going over what I'd told him about what had gone wrong between them. 'Poor George,' he said. 'I can imagine how he felt.'

'He should have gone after her,' I said. 'He was to blame too.' I knew what was coming as soon as the words were out of my mouth. But Tony didn't say what I'd thought he would say, not then. He was silent, and we passed on to trivialities, as we very often did.

The next week, I arrived one day to find him out of bed, sitting beside it looking exhausted and frail but pleased with himself. He said he'd been told that in another couple of weeks, if he maintained this progress, he could go home. I didn't ask if 'home' would mean his parents' home. I didn't want to think about his discharge at all. How could I say that when he was better I'd stop seeing him? I couldn't, and anyway I didn't know that I wanted to. I didn't know any more how I felt about him. What I'd been feeling since I heard of his accident was, I reasoned, just common-or-garden sympathy, the sort anyone would feel for someone they'd once been close to. Sympathy, pure and simple. But it wasn't either pure or simple. It wasn't only sympathy I felt now but some of the old attraction that had once drawn me to him. Not physical attraction but some sort of emotional tie. I realised I had missed him and that my misery over my parents' deaths had obscured how much. I'd missed his company. All the things that had grown to irritate me about him seemed suddenly of no importance. We might clash in personality, but that very clashing had fired something in me and without it I'd become deadened.

'Remind me,' he said one day, the day he actually walked to the end of the corridor with me, 'remind me what happened. I've forgotten, honestly. Why did we split up? Remind me.' I said nothing. We were at the lift and I prayed for it to come quickly. All my normal sharpness deserted me. 'Come on,' he urged. 'What did I do, or not do? What happened to us? All I can remember is the shock of it.'

'Nothing happened,' I said. 'It was me. I didn't want anyone near me. I was in a state.'

'And I couldn't help.'

'Nobody could. I just wanted to be by myself, to be miserable on my own, sort myself out.'

'So are you sorted?'

'A bit.'

'And you're happier on your own? Happy?'

'Not exactly happy, but better. I'm not so messed up.'

'No, that's me now, the messed-up one.'

'But that's because of the accident. You'll soon be back to normal and . . .'

'Will I? Well, I don't seem to want to be. What's the point?'

The lift came. I kissed him and got into it, so relieved. He'd looked as though he might start to cry and I couldn't bear it. The only way to cure his distress would be to suggest that we might live together again and I didn't want to say that, not yet, not while he was still far from well. I wanted to wait and see how things went once he was out of hospital and back at work. I knew that by thinking this I was admitting I *would* see him once he was discharged, but that had become inevitable. He was the one who had refused just to be friends. If he thought that by constantly visiting him I was saying I wanted to be more than friends again I couldn't help it. I would have to make him accept that friendship must come first and there could be no guarantees about the future beyond that. I did want him back in my life, that was all.

It was odd how comforting it was to acknowledge that and how happy it made me feel, whatever the problems ahead.

Chapter Sixteen

So, it was all over. I'd finished with the memory box. Discussing the whole business with Tony soon after he was back in his own flat (not a very nice flat, but he said it was only temporary), I think I came at last to understand the effect my mother's death had had on me. I never consciously thought anything as extreme as 'If I have a baby I will die', but there may have been something of that fear in my attitude.

I still believe I don't want a child even if, against the odds, I could conceive, but I'm not scared of the thought any more. I don't think I was ever meant to be a mother and it doesn't disturb or distress me. I've heard, and read, often enough about the bliss of maternal love, but I've never been convinced. I've always doubted that it transcends all other kinds of love. Even Charlotte, to whom motherhood was all-important, would never have said, if put to the test, that her love for me was greater than her love for my father (ah, but she was not really a mother . . .). What I've always rejected is the notion that if I had had, or ever do have, a baby, I would succumb at once to being a slave to it. But does that merely show my lack of understanding? Maybe I do have to experience motherhood to appreciate what my own mother tried to tell me through her memory box.

I think of both my mothers, and what their passionate love for me, their baby, their child, gave them, and it all becomes so impenetrable. I may have precipitated my mother's death, but from everything I have learned the price was never too high. And my stepmother, unable to have a child herself, said her life was made complete by me. So, if I remain childless, am I an incomplete woman? Is there, buried deep inside me, so deep I am not aware of it, a capacity to love as my mothers loved which I am cruelly stifling? Impossible to know, but I doubt it, and I don't want to know. I will not allow myself to think such a monstrous suggestion could be true. It is not. I am certainly not incomplete. The memory box has shown me that, if nothing else. What Tony calls the missing link has been found. I am now connected to my mother and complete.

I think my mother chose the wrong things to leave in her box but there was nothing wrong with her motivation. She was not, as I've thought often enough during the last months, trying to control me from beyond the grave (as I liked, dramatically, to think of it, relishing the cliché). She did not resent the fact that I had a future which she did not. What she could hardly bear was the realisation that she would have no part in it and that she might be obliterated in my memory. She knew that I would have no memory except what others gave me and she preferred to try to ignite a spark herself. She couldn't simply say goodbye to a baby who could not understand her words and then go. It was too hard, too painful. If she thought about my life after her death the agony and fear were so great she became bitter. It was far less cruel to allow herself to think that through the memory box she would be able to speak to me in her own voice and that, in time, because I was hers, I might learn to hear and understand.

I burned the box itself in the end. I burned it in the garden of the house I bought before I went to France. Tony helped me. I had a proper bonfire, before the builders moved in. The box itself was never worth anything and I felt no sense of betrayal burning it. I am not so clear about what its contents, its funny jumble of objects, were worth. Sometimes I think the little discoveries I made through them are significant, sometimes I think they were worthless. Sometimes, thinking about what was in that box, I am flooded with emotion, sometimes I feel blank. I find I can think of the box as deadly serious, on the one hand, and as unimportant on the other. It gave me a hard time, whichever way I look at it, and I *don't think* my mother really intended this. She had no energy for games. She always had to conserve her energy for important things. Only her brain was wildly energetic in those last weeks as she grew weaker and weaker, concentrating ferociously on me.

It has all been returned, this intense concentration. I concentrated on her over last winter to the virtual exclusion of everything else. Except for Rory, and briefly Isabella and Hector, I kept myself to myself and associated with no one. My work brought me only minimal contact with anyone else and never interfered with constant thoughts of my mother. It has not been a particularly healthy state of affairs. I haven't slept well, I haven't eaten well. I've become quite thin and drawn. Tony says we are both convalescents. I've neglected the friendships I have (few enough) and given up most activities. I didn't go to a theatre or a cinema all winter, I have a small heap of invitations to which I have not replied and my answerphone has mostly had its messages wiped off without being attended to. I haven't wanted to be reached. All that is so negative, it sounds pathetic, but out of it has come something much more positive. I have moved on, bought my house, finally emerged from the numbness which afflicted me after my parents died – I can feel again. It is as though a point of crisis has been passed, a point brought about and then negotiated through the memory box. The past, my mother's past, about which I knew virtually nothing (nor wanted to), instead of being put behind me, has been put in front of me and dealt with. It feels right.

I was telling Rory this the other day. He is still in London

– there was no miraculous reunion with his parents but he has grudgingly agreed to keep in touch – and naturally has his eye on my lovely new home with what he meaningfully calls 'plenty of spare rooms'. I told him I'd burned the box and with it my resentment and suspicion of my dead mother. I told him I want to have some memorial to her. My step-mother has a gravestone (and I will let the inscription stand), but my mother hasn't. I went back recently to the crematorium where she was cremated. I deliberately went on the day she had died because I'd been told a Book of Remembrance was always open, listing all the people who had been cremated, day by day. Her name was not among the twenty-three names (evidently a popular time to die). I enquired about this and was informed there was no record of Susannah Musgrave, or Cameron, because none had been requested and paid for. My father obviously hadn't wanted it. I agree with him. But still, I craved some sort of appropriate memorial.

I thought, and still think, of planting a tree in her memory and having a plaque put in front of it, but where? I intend always to live in this house, but who knows – I may move and then the tree in this garden would be left behind, perhaps uprooted, or chopped down by strangers. I even thought of a seat, a wooden bench, inscribed with her name. That would be movable, but it seemed like an old man's memorial. And yesterday I thought of it – a box. I could have a box specially made, hand-crafted out of silver, not too big, so that it would be easy to take with me wherever I go, not too small so that it might get lost. About the size of a jewellery box, say, eight inches by three; and on the lid, no inscription. I'd have it lined with emerald velvet, the softest I can find, and keep her necklace in it. When people admired it I would say, 'Mm, my mother left the box.' No one need know it wasn't this box. There would be a slight mystery about it; but if pressed, and few I thought would press me, I would be able to talk about her as I have always talked about Charlotte.

Romantic? Perhaps. Sentimental? Probably. Comforting? Certainly. And that is all that matters to me, as it mattered to my mother, the comfort of it. Her box served its purpose. For her. Mine will serve mine. For me. And neither of us will have ever been quite sure what that purpose was, beyond soothing pain and striving to communicate.

Is there a better one?